Praise for the *New*
Cat in the St

OUT OF C

"Humor and plenty of Southern charm . . . Cozy fans will hope James . . . keep[s] Charlie and Diesel in action for years to come." —*Publishers Weekly*

"The old Southern charm recollects Rita Mae Brown's Sneaky Pie series (without the talking animals), while Charlie's investigative techniques may bring some of Agatha Christie's characters to mind." —*Library Journal*

"Like its predecessors, *Out of Circulation* offers a pleasing blend of crime and charm, filled with familiar and cherished characters, biped and quadruped."
—*Richmond Times-Dispatch*

"Even if you don't like cats, there's plenty to enjoy in this traditional cozy." —*RT Book Reviews*

"This fourth installment of the Cat in the Stacks series keeps you involved until the last page."
—*Cozy Mystery Book Reviews*

FILE M FOR MURDER

"Readers who have come to love Charlie and Diesel and the small-town ambience of Athena will find *File M for Murder* another pleasant diversion, complete with an intriguing plot in which the silence of the library threatens to become the silence of the grave." —*Richmond Times-Dispatch*

continued . . .

"This charming, classic cozy features full-on Southern charm. Well plotted and evenly paced, with fairly laid out clues for those who like to solve along with the sleuth. Charlie and Diesel are a delightful detective team, and the idea of a male amateur sleuth/librarian with a cat is a refreshing twist on an old trope." —*RT Book Reviews*

"Will make you a cat lover if you are not already one." —*Once Upon a Romance*

"This cozy mystery makes for a leisurely and enjoyable read. It is well plotted, and the protagonist and the secondary characters are multidimensional and likable. And of course, there's Diesel . . . a thoroughly lovable cat who is an integral part of the story." —*The Conscious Cat*

"James has [a] winner with this one, readers won't want to miss it." —*Debbie's Book Bag*

CLASSIFIED AS MURDER

"Bringing local color to life, this second entry in the series . . . is a gentle, closed-room drama set in Mississippi. Ideal for Christie fans who enjoy a good puzzle." —*Library Journal*

"Readers will enjoy this entertaining regional whodunit as the librarian and the cat work the case." —*Genre Go Round Reviews*

"A hit with bibliophiles and animal lovers, not to mention anyone who likes a well-plotted mystery. The characters are unique and often eccentric. Having a male amateur sleuth with a subplot that explores his relationship with his adult son brings a fresh twist to the genre." —*RT Book Reviews*

MURDER PAST DUE

"Combines a kindhearted librarian hero, family secrets in a sleepy Southern town, and a gentle giant of a cat that will steal your heart. A great beginning to a promising new cozy series." —Lorna Barrett, *New York Times* bestselling author

"Courtly librarian Charlie Harris and his Maine coon cat, Diesel, are an endearing detective duo. Warm, charming, and Southern as the tastiest grits."

—Carolyn Hart, national bestselling author of the Bailey Ruth Mysteries

"Brings cozy lovers an intriguing mystery, a wonderful cat, and a librarian hero who will warm your heart. Filled with Southern charm, the first in the Cat in the Stacks Mysteries will keep readers guessing until the end. Miranda James should soon be on everyone's list of favorite authors."

—Leann Sweeney, author of the Cats in Trouble Mysteries

"*Murder Past Due* has an excellent plot, great execution, and a surprising ending. This book is a must read!"

—*The Romance Readers Connection*

"Miranda James begins the Cat in the Stacks Mysteries with a bang . . . [An] absolute breath of fresh air."

—*Fresh Fiction*

"Readers will adore Charlie and Diesel."

—*Socrates' Book Reviews Blog*

"Read *Murder Past Due* for the mystery and an enjoyable amateur sleuth . . . You'll find yourself wishing for the next book to catch up with Diesel." —*Lesa's Book Critiques*

Please visit Diesel the cat at facebook.com/DieselHarriscat.

Berkley Prime Crime titles by Miranda James

Cat in the Stacks Mysteries

MURDER PAST DUE
CLASSIFIED AS MURDER
FILE M FOR MURDER
OUT OF CIRCULATION
THE SILENCE OF THE LIBRARY
ARSENIC AND OLD BOOKS
NO CATS ALLOWED
TWELVE ANGRY LIBRARIANS
CLAWS FOR CONCERN
SIX CATS A SLAYIN'
THE PAWFUL TRUTH
CARELESS WHISKERS
CAT ME IF YOU CAN
WHAT THE CAT DRAGGED IN

Southern Ladies Mysteries

BLESS HER DEAD LITTLE HEART
DEAD WITH THE WIND
DIGGING UP THE DIRT
FIXING TO DIE

BLESS HER DEAD LITTLE HEART

Miranda James

BERKLEY PRIME CRIME
New York

BERKLEY PRIME CRIME
Published by Berkley
An imprint of Penguin Random House LLC
penguinrandomhouse.com

ISBN: 9780425273043

First Edition: October 2014

Printed in the United States of America

Cover illustration by Dan Craig
Cover design by Lesley Worrel
Book design by Kelly Lipovich

This book is dedicated with love and thanks to the two amazing women who inspired their fictional (and much older) counterparts: An'gel Ducote Molpus and Dickce Ducote Little. Blessings in life come in different guises; if you're lucky, they sometimes have sassy mouths and big hearts. Thank you for your friendship and your inspiration.

ACKNOWLEDGMENTS

Were it not for my good friend Carolyn Haines and one of her many fascinating brainstorms, I would never have met the real An'gel and Dickce at the wonderful and wacky thing that is Daddy's Girls Weekend. Thank you, Carolyn, for being such a fascinating influence in my life.

Special thanks also to Terri Dunn, Cheryl Carlson, Carole Sauer, Katie Ruffin, Kelly Robinson, Gail Bonneau, and Betty Milton. These ladies keep me entertained on Facebook on the days when I need it most.

Michelle Vega is awesome (I seldom use that word, and when I do, I really mean it) as my editor and friend. She has more patience than that guy in the proverb, and I would never finish a book without it. My agent, Nancy Yost, and her associates, Sarah Younger, Adrienne Rosado, and Natanya Wheeler, are awesome as well. I cannot thank them enough for what they do to help me earn enough to buy cat food for Pippa and Toby and other good things as well.

My friends in the Wednesday night critique group hold my feet to the fire and help make everything I write so much better: Bob, Julie, Kay F., Kay K., Laura, and Millie. Curry, Susie, Isabella, and Charlie open their home to us every week and give us space to hone our craft, and that is such a generous gift.

At a difficult time, my friends at Murder by the Book came through. A special thanks to McKenna Jordan, the owner, along with John Kwiatkowski, Sally Woods, and Brenda Jordan for their friendship and support.

Finally, as always, loving thanks to the two bedrocks of my writing life, my friends Patricia Orr and Terry Farmer. *Sine qua non.*

AUTHOR'S NOTE

Readers might be wondering how to pronounce the rather unusual names of the Ducote Sisters. Here's a quick guide:

Miss An'gel's name is pronounced "ahn-JELL."

Miss Dickce's name is pronounced just like "Dixie."

Their family name, Ducote, is pronounced "dew-COH-tee."

CHAPTER 1

Miss An'gel Ducote fixed her houseguest with a gimlet eye. "I expect you to behave like a proper gentleman while you're here."

Diesel Harris regarded his hostess unblinkingly for a moment before he meowed.

Miss Dickce Ducote snorted with laughter. "Good gracious, Sister, you don't need to lecture him on how to conduct himself. Diesel has better manners than some of the two-legged fools who've set foot in Riverhill."

"True." Miss An'gel pursed her lips as she continued to regard the large Maine Coon cat. "He is in unfamiliar surroundings, though, and I've heard that cats don't like change. He might be upset because Charlie and the rest of the family have gone off and left him." She pointed to the frayed Aubusson carpet that covered a third of their front parlor. "I'm not sure this can withstand accidents, if you know what I mean."

"Really, An'gel. That rug has been on the floor for a hundred and twenty years at least and has withstood far worse." Dickce shook her head. "Diesel is a smart kitty. He already knows where we put his litter box. He's not going to make a mess on one of our priceless antiques."

"That's all well and good." An'gel glared at her sister, at eighty the younger by almost four years. "Even if his bathroom habits are impeccable, what shall we do if he starts clawing the furniture?"

"If you were this worried about the contents of the house, why did you ever agree to keep Diesel? Most of the furniture survived the Civil War and troops of Union and Confederate soldiers at various times. How much damage could one cat do?" Dickce glared right back. "Frankly, I seem to recall that you *volunteered* to cat-sit. Charlie never once opened his mouth to ask you. In fact, he looked mighty startled when you said we'd be *delighted*, though he's such a gentleman, he hid it immediately." She sat back, arms folded over her chest, and waited.

There was no arguing with Dickce when she was in one of her contrary moods. An'gel suppressed a sigh as she threw up her hands in mock surrender. Before she could speak, Diesel warbled loudly and placed his large right front paw on her knee. An'gel stared down into the cat's eyes, and she would have sworn he was trying to reassure her.

Dickce pointed at the Maine Coon. "See? He's telling you he's going to be extra-special good."

The triumphant note in Dickce's voice irritated An'gel, but she pretended it didn't. Instead she stroked the cat's head and told him twice she knew he was a good boy.

"Come sit with me, Diesel." Dickce patted the sofa cushion beside her. "You can stretch out and nap with your aunt Dickce."

Diesel pawed at An'gel's knee again and meowed. He gazed up at her, and she had the oddest feeling that he was asking her permission. At least the cat was smart enough to know who was really in charge here. "Go ahead, it's fine with me."

The cat blinked at her before he turned to amble over to the sofa. He jumped up beside Dickce and settled himself with his head and front legs in her lap. Dickce stroked him and grinned at her sister when Diesel started to purr loudly.

An'gel picked up her glass of sweet tea and sipped at it. There was nothing better during the dog days of summer. Their housekeeper, Clementine, made the best sweet tea in Athena County, if not in the whole state of Mississippi. "The only reason I'm glad to see August come around every year is the fact that we don't have any committee meetings to attend, any garden club functions to arrange, or any other social commitments. It's nice to have a vacation."

"It sure is." Dickce nodded. "I keep thinking we ought to retire and live a quieter life, but I know we'd both be bored and ready to strangle each other in a month or two." She laughed. "This is a big house, but probably not big enough to keep us from getting on each other's nerves every other minute."

An'gel chose to ignore that leading remark. "Besides, you know as well as I do that no one else will keep things organized and running the way we do." She shook her head. "If the community had to pay someone to do what we do, the town couldn't afford it." She felt a cool breeze across her neck as the air-conditioner kicked in. How had earlier generations of Ducotes survived the hot summers without it? She took another sip of tea.

Dickce frowned. "Did you hear that? Just before the air went on. Sounded like a car drove up."

"I heard it." An'gel stood. "We weren't expecting visitors this afternoon. I'm not in the mood to entertain."

"Tell whoever it is to go away." Dickce yawned. "I think I'd like to go upstairs for a nap."

An'gel strode to the front window and pulled the heavy red damask drapes aside to peer out at the driveway. "I don't recognize the car, and I can't see who's driving. Clementine is probably taking her break now. I'll go."

The bell sounded before An'gel reached the door. She opened it to find a woman about her own age standing there, finger on the bell, poised to ring it again. Her hair was an unnatural shade of red, and her wrinkled face was devoid of makeup. She didn't look like a salesperson, but she did seem vaguely familiar.

"Good afternoon. What can I do for you?"

Startled, the woman took a step back. "My goodness. An'gel, it's you, isn't it? I never expected *you* to answer the door. Surely you have a servant to do that." She smiled. "Aren't you going to ask me in?"

An'gel peered at the woman's face as she tried to recall who she was. Recognition dawned, along with the first stirring of dismay. What on earth was Rosabelle Sultan doing here? The last time Rosabelle had visited, about fifteen years ago, she had stayed three weeks—two-and-a-half more than she was welcome—and had departed with a substantial, and not-yet-repaid, loan.

An'gel stepped back and waved the visitor in. "Of course I am, Rosabelle. This is a surprise. Weren't you living in California?"

Rosabelle opened her mouth to speak. Her eyes widened, and she dropped her purse. She pointed to a spot behind An'gel. "What on earth is *that*?"

An'gel turned and saw the cat. "That's Diesel. Dickce

and I are cat-sitting for a friend." She stooped to retrieve the visitor's purse and handed it back. "I know he's large, but he's a pet. He's friendly and gentle. You don't have to be afraid of him." *And if the cat has any sense, he'll stay away from you anyway*, she added silently.

Rosabelle clasped the purse to her side. "If you say so, but I've never seen a house cat that big before. Does he have some kind of glandular condition?"

Diesel moved closer and stood by An'gel. He stared at the visitor but did not approach her. An'gel had never seen him act like that, but she couldn't fault his intelligence. Rosabelle never brought good tidings. Besides, An'gel realized, Rosabelle smelled funny, like a sweaty bouquet of roses.

"No, he's a Maine Coon. They are large cats, and he is larger than usual, about thirty-six pounds. Nothing unnatural, though." An'gel turned and gestured for her guest to follow. "Dickce's in the parlor. Come along and say hello."

"I'm so happy to find you both home," Rosabelle said, sounding tired. "I've been driving for such a long time. I'm just glad I remembered the way."

"Wasn't that lucky?" An'gel murmured. She raised her voice at the parlor door. "Dickce, you'll never guess who it is. Rosabelle Sultan."

Dickce's gaze locked with her sister's, and her mouth twisted in a brief grimace. An'gel gazed stonily back. They would find out soon enough what their former sorority sister wanted. Then, with a smile, Dickce stood to greet the visitor. "My goodness, Rosabelle, what a surprise this is."

"Dickce, I declare, you are just as darling as ever. I never did know how you and An'gel managed to keep your figures." She dropped her purse on the floor and plopped down beside Dickce. "I always felt like such a lump around you two."

An'gel could have told her how, but good manners precluded her telling a guest that she always ate like a pig at a trough. She eyed their visitor critically. Perhaps Rosabelle had reformed her habits, or had been seriously ill. She was thinner than An'gel ever remembered seeing her. Her dress was at least two sizes too large, and it had surely come off a bargain-store rack. The hem of the skirt was unraveling on the right side, and the material had the threadbare look of a long-used garment. Rosabelle must have fallen on hard times. An'gel took a deep breath. She and Dickce were going to be hit up for money—money that would never be paid back, if the past *loans* were anything to go by.

"Would you like some sweet tea?" An'gel recalled her duties as a hostess. "Or something else?" *Like leech repellent*, she added silently.

"Sweet tea would be fine." Rosabelle leaned back and closed her eyes. "That might revive me."

"I'll go," Dickce said. "You rest there, and I'll be back in a minute." She frowned at An'gel as she headed toward the door. "Where is Diesel?"

Startled, An'gel glanced around. "He was with me in the hall. He didn't go outside. Maybe he went to see Clementine."

Dickce glanced at their visitor, who still had her eyes closed. She pointed at Rosabelle and pinched her nose before she left the room.

"What brings you all the way to Mississippi from California?" An'gel resumed her seat. "I can't believe you drove all that way by yourself."

Rosabelle's eyelids fluttered open, and she blinked at An'gel. "Oh, dear, I fell asleep for a minute there. I am plumb worn down to the bone from all that driving." She covered her mouth as she yawned. "It took me several days to get here, but I had to come."

"Do you have business here? I didn't know you still had family in the state."

"Nobody in Corinth anymore," Rosabelle said, her eyes tearing up. "Everyone left years ago. No, I came because I had to get away from California."

An'gel waited a moment but Rosabelle did not continue. "We haven't had a word from you in many, many years, I reckon. Last we heard, though, you had remarried."

"That was my second husband." Rosabelle nodded. "Tom Thurmond. He was a dear man, but he died seven years ago. I married again a while after Tom passed." She sighed. "Antonio Mingione. Handsome as the devil, but a rat. A complete and utter rat."

"A rat? Where?" Dickce sounded alarmed as she arrived with a silver tray bearing a glass of tea and a pitcher. "Maybe Diesel will catch it for us."

"Not that kind of rat," An'gel said. "A two-legged one. Rosabelle's current husband."

"No, not current." Rosabelle sniffled. "He died a year ago."

"My goodness, how awful." Dickce handed their visitor the glass and took her place on the sofa.

Rosabelle sipped at the tea. "I can't tell you how wonderful it is to be back here, where people know how to make sweet tea." She drained the glass, and Dickce refilled it for her. "Thank you, so kind, like you always were. I could always rely on the Ducote sisters for their kindness."

The sisters exchanged wary glances.

"We've always done our best." Dickce patted the woman's arm. "Sounds like you sure are in need of some kindness."

"Kindness and sanctuary," Rosabelle said. She burst into tears.

An'gel had seen this act before. No doubt the *rat* of a husband had run through her funds and left her destitute. The only way to deal with her was to be firm. "Buck up, now, and tell us what's wrong."

Rosabelle stared at her two hostesses in turn through streaming eyes. She looked so intentionally tragic, An'gel wanted to smack her.

"Come on, now," Dickce said gently. "Whatever it is can't be that bad."

Rosabelle sniffed loudly and groped in the pocket of her dress for a tissue. "Oh, yes, it is. It's murder."

"Murder? What on *earth* are you talking about?" An'gel said.

Dickce spoke at the same time. "Who's been murdered?"

Rosabelle glanced at each of them in turn. She drew a deep breath. "Me. *I'm* going to be murdered."

CHAPTER 2

Dickce suppressed a laugh. Rosabelle had a habit of uttering outrageous things in an attempt to garner sympathy, but claiming someone was trying to murder her was over the top, even for her. Dickce glanced at her sister. An'gel didn't appear any more impressed than Dickce herself felt. The delicate but brief flare of An'gel's nostrils demonstrated only irritation, not concern.

When she spoke, Dickce worked hard to keep her tone nonchalant. "Rosabelle, dear, why would anyone want to kill *you*, of all people?" *Unless they were tired of you always begging for money and never repaying it*, she thought.

"Dickce's right," An'gel said. "Someone would have to hate you tremendously to want to kill you. Surely no one hates you that much."

Rosabelle whimpered and rubbed a hand across her face. "That's just it. Someone *does* hate me that much."

She paused for a sobbing breath. "The trouble is, I don't know *which* member of my family is behind it all."

Dickce rolled her eyes at her sister. An'gel frowned. Dickce found it difficult to take their visitor seriously, but she knew An'gel would feel honor bound to listen to Rosabelle's histrionics and try to make her see sense.

"Come now, pull yourself together." An'gel's brisk tone did not seem to affect Rosabelle's soft sounds of distress. "What happened to make you think you're the target of a murder plot?"

Rosabelle sighed and leaned back against the sofa cushion. "Little things. Little accidents." She closed her eyes and whimpered yet again.

"What kind of accidents?" Dickce wondered if one of Rosabelle's family members had tried to push her down the stairs. The temptation might be more than one of them could stand.

Rosabelle opened her eyes and stared at Dickce. "Oh, I know you both think I'm making this up, but I promise you these things happened." She paused for a breath and glanced toward An'gel before she focused again on the younger sister. "Water on the stairs, for one thing. It happened three times, but luckily I spotted it each time and managed not to fall and break my neck."

"Maybe your maid is sloppy," Dickce suggested.

"I don't have a maid. I can't afford one." Rosabelle sounded aggrieved. "Someone deliberately spilled water on the stairs—the marble stairs, mind you—so I would slip and tumble down."

"That does sound odd." An'gel frowned. "Were there other incidents?"

"There most certainly were." Rosabelle sounded heated. "Food poisoning, not once, but twice."

"You poor thing," Dickce said, her sympathies aroused

despite her previous skepticism. Perhaps there was more to this after all than simply Rosabelle's constant need for attention. "Were you terribly ill?"

"I like to have died." Rosabelle shuddered. "The first time, that is. The second time, I thought my coffee tasted too bitter, so I poured it down the drain. Even so, I drank enough of whatever the poison was to be sick for the rest of that day and part of the next."

An'gel grimaced. "Oh, dear! Just how sick were you the first time? And do you have any idea what the poison was, or how you got it?"

"I was in bed for nearly a week," Rosabelle said. "I have no idea what was in my food. All I know is, I woke up during the night after dining with my family, having convulsions and being horribly sick. Luckily my granddaughter Juanita, who was staying with me at the time, heard me and came to my rescue."

Dickce asked, "Did anyone else get sick? Surely it was something you had for dinner."

"That was why I knew it was a deliberate attempt to kill me," Rosabelle replied, sounding a bit smug. "No one else was affected. I was fine before dinner, so one of my family must have slipped the poison into my food."

"I would certainly be suspicious under those circumstances," An'gel said. "Which members of your family had an opportunity to put poison in the food you ate?"

"My daughter-in-law, Marla, cooked the dinner. She could have done it for sure. She knows I think Wade married beneath him, and she takes every opportunity to be unpleasant to me when Wade's not around." Rosabelle tossed her head. "If I weren't in polite company, I could tell you what I think of her with a single word, and I'm sure you can imagine the word I mean—it rhymes with *witch*."

"Might she do a thing like that simply out of spite, just to make you a little sick for a few days?" Dickce asked. "What motive would she have to kill you?"

"She hates me, I tell you. She's just nasty." Rosabelle shuddered. "The kind of family she comes from, they'd stick a knife in your back without even thinking twice."

An'gel said, "Could she have another motive besides spitefulness?"

Rosabelle stared at her hands in her lap. "My house. She knows I've left it to Wade in my will. It's valuable property, though I might have to sell it because I'm so strapped for cash."

Dickce wanted to ask how much the house was worth, but she knew An'gel would have a hissy fit with her later for doing such a vulgar thing. The house might be worth millions, she reckoned, depending on where the property was in California. Real estate out there was crazy expensive, according to what she heard on the news.

"Did anyone else have the opportunity to doctor your food?" An'gel asked.

Rosabelle nodded. "Oh, any one of them could, I suppose. Marla fancies herself a gourmet chef, so she plates everything instead of us serving ourselves at the table. Then she puts the plates on the table, and of course I always sit in the same spot, at the head. Anyone could have slipped in there and added the poison just before Marla called us all in to eat."

"That does make identifying the potential culprit difficult," An'gel said. "Though it sounds to me that Marla is the most likely party. She had more opportunity."

"Did you end up in the hospital?" Dickce asked.

"No, Juanita is a registered nurse, and she took care of me." Rosabelle gave a brief smile. "She's a sweet girl, and she knows how I detest hospitals. She stayed with me night and day, my ministering angel."

"Did this happen before or after the incidents on the stairs?" Dickce asked.

"Before," Rosabelle replied. "If it had happened after those attempts, I would have been immediately suspicious. Looking back, of course, I realize it was the first salvo in the campaign."

"I suppose that means you didn't report the alleged poisoning to anyone or try to have anything analyzed." An'gel picked up her tea glass, eyed it for a moment, then set it down again.

Dickce didn't blame her. She felt a bit unsettled herself at the thought of food or drink right now. She also felt guilty for not taking Rosabelle seriously. For once, their guest's right to sympathy appeared legitimate.

"How long ago did all this happen?" An'gel asked.

"Just the past couple of weeks," Rosabelle said. "I decided the best thing to do was to disappear and take myself out of harm's way while I try to figure out what my next steps should be." She smiled weakly at each sister in turn. "Naturally I thought of you two as my haven from danger. You've always been such good friends, but I doubt my family would ever think of looking for me here."

The sisters exchanged a wry glance. After a testimonial like that, how could they not respond graciously? Dickce nodded at An'gel to indicate she was okay with having Rosabelle as a guest.

"Of course you may stay with us," An'gel said. "You ought to be safe here, and Dickce and I will put our heads together and help you figure out what is behind these nasty little incidents." She stood. "I will talk to Clementine, and we'll have a guest room ready for you right away."

"Oh, thank you." Rosabelle smiled. "I knew I could count on my old sorority sisters. You'll never know how much this means to me."

"You're welcome," Dickce said as An'gel left the room in search of their housekeeper. "Would you like more tea?" She gestured toward the pitcher.

"That would be lovely, thanks. I am a bit parched." Rosabelle passed her glass to her hostess, and Dickce refilled it. Rosabelle sipped at the tea with her eyes closed. "I know I'm home when I'm drinking sweet tea like this."

Dickce refilled her own glass and drank from it. "Yes, I know what you mean. It surely is a comfort."

An'gel returned with Clementine. She introduced the housekeeper to Rosabelle.

"You just come with me, Miss Sultan," Clementine said, her voice husky from decades of smoking. "We'll get you settled in the best guest room upstairs, and you'll soon be feeling right at home."

"Thank you," Rosabelle said as she stood. "I would love to have a nap, if y'all don't mind. I'm bone weary from all that driving." She followed Clementine toward the door but paused before they stepped into the hall. "I forgot about my bags." She looked back and forth between the sisters.

Dickce suppressed a sigh. "Let me have your keys, and An'gel and I will get the bags in. Then I'll move your car to the garage. We have space enough for it."

Rosabelle rummaged in her bag and extracted the keys after a brief search. By that time Dickce had reached her, and Rosabelle handed the keys over without a word.

Dickce waited until Rosabelle and Clementine disappeared upstairs before she turned to her sister. "Do you really think a member of her family is trying to kill her?"

An'gel shrugged. "What she told us sounds serious, but

a little part of me is still skeptical. We both know how prone she is to exaggerate to get attention."

"That's all she ever wanted to be," Dickce said. "The center of attention." She sighed and rattled Rosabelle's keys. "Let's unload the car."

Twenty minutes later An'gel and Dickce were back downstairs in the parlor. Diesel had rejoined them the minute Rosabelle had gone upstairs. He had even followed them back and forth while they brought in the seven suitcases they had found in the car. Then he had ridden with Dickce to the back of house, where she had put Rosabelle's dusty sedan in the garage. Now he lay on the floor beside An'gel's chair, dozing.

Clementine stepped into the parlor to report that Rosabelle was sound asleep in her room. "Her head done barely lay down on that pillow, and she went right out."

"Thank you, Clementine," An'gel said. "I'm afraid our guest is going to mean extra work for you, but Dickce and I will try to see that she isn't too demanding."

"You never mind about that, Miss An'gel," Clementine said. "I'll manage. Now I best be getting back to the kitchen and seeing about your supper." She turned and disappeared into the hall.

"If Rosabelle causes too much of a mess," Dickce said, "we're going to have to insist on getting some help."

An'gel nodded. "We'll fight that battle when we get to it." She reached for her tea, the ice now melted, but her hand stilled at the sound of a vehicle approaching the house. She turned her head in the direction of the front window.

"Now what?" Dickce asked, exasperated at the thought of more company. She stood. "I'll go this time."

An'gel nodded. "Fine by me." She picked up her tea and drained the glass.

Dickce reached the door before whoever it was could

knock or ring the bell. She opened the door and stepped onto the veranda. The car, a Mercedes sedan, did not look familiar. Nor did the man who emerged from the driver's side. Dickce could see another person in the car, perhaps a woman, though the hair was cut rather short.

The man, tall and thin, with a slight stoop, shut the door and approached the house. "Afternoon, ma'am," he said when he reached the veranda. "Are you one of the Misses Ducote, by any chance?"

"Yes, I am." Dickce decided that was enough until she knew what the stranger wanted.

"Then I found the right place." The man nodded as if to emphasize the point. "My name is Wade Thurmond, and I'm looking for my mother, Rosabelle. Is she here by any chance?"

CHAPTER 3

Dickce dithered over how to respond. If Rosabelle's fears were true, the last person she would want to see was one of the relatives she suspected. Telling the truth could put Rosabelle in danger, though the thought of lying, even to a stranger, made Dickce uncomfortable.

Instead of answering Wade Thurmond's query, Dickce posed one of her own. "Why should Rosabelle be here, of all places?" *There*, she thought, *that might put him off the scent.*

Thurmond scowled. "Because coming here to Mississippi all the way from California is exactly the harebrained kind of thing my mother would do. She talks about the wealthy Ducote sisters all the dang time, about how wonderful and hospitable you are." He paused for a breath. "So when she bolted in the middle of the night, we all figured this is where she would head."

Dickce felt a presence behind her and moved aside. An'gel

stepped onto the porch. Thurmond offered an uncertain smile.

"Good evening, sir," An'gel said, her tone polite but not welcoming. "Do I take it you are Rosabelle Sultan's son, Wade Thurmond?"

"Yes, ma'am, I am." Thurmond's expression turned mulish. "I take it you're the other Ducote sister. Well, I'm not intending to barge in on anybody, but me and my family are worried about my mother. She ran off, like I was telling your sister here, and we figured she came to see the two of you."

Before An'gel could respond, Rosabelle yelled, "Hold on a minute," from a point behind Dickce. Both sisters turned to see their guest coming down the stairs at a fast pace, her expression stormy.

By the time Rosabelle reached the front door, her bony chest heaved from exertion, and Dickce motioned for An'gel to move out of the way to give Rosabelle plenty of room to confront her son.

"What in the blue blazes are you doing here? Didn't you read my note?"

Thurmond hung his head but cut a sideways glance at his parent. "Aw, now, Mama, we read your note, but what did you think we were going to do? Just let you ride off into the sunset and not try to find you? Besides, saying that one of us was trying to kill you is out-and-out nuts."

Rosabelle snorted. "It is *not* nuts. One of you put poison in my food the other night, and I'd be willing to bet it was that white-trash woman you got yourself married to."

Thurmond's head snapped back, and his expression turned ugly. "Now, you listen here, Mama; you stop that talk about Marla. All she's ever done is be good to you, and you're always putting her down."

"If that's what you think, son, then you're even dumber than I realized. Marla doesn't care about anybody but Marla, and you're too old not to have figured that out by now." Rosabelle's face turned so red that Dickce feared she might stroke out right there on the veranda.

"That is quite enough from the both of you," An'gel's voice rang out, and mother and son flinched, then she turned to glare at the elder sister. "This appalling behavior has to stop, right this minute, or I will be forced to call the sheriff and have him come take charge of the situation."

Dickce knew this mood of her sister's, and if Rosabelle and Thurmond had any sense, they would shut right up. An'gel never threatened idly, and Rosabelle ought to remember that from their sorority days.

Either Rosabelle *didn't* remember or didn't *care* to because she turned back to her son and spoke again. "Don't think I'm going to pack up and go back to California with you. I am staying right here while An'gel and Dickce help me figure out who's trying to kill me."

Thurmond's short, heavyset wife had left the car and was making her way onto the veranda. "Wade, I'm tired of sitting in that car, and I need to use the bathroom." Without waiting for a response from Thurmond or any kind of invitation from Dickce or An'gel, she brushed past her husband and into the house. "Where's the toilet?"

"You see the kind of uncouth behavior I have had to put up with for the past thirteen years?" Rosabelle's fists clenched at her sides. "This is what happens when your son marries trash from the wrong side of the tracks."

Thurmond's wife appeared to take no notice of her mother-in-law. She stared at An'gel and Dickce. "Well, isn't one of you going to show me, or do I have to go find it myself?"

At the barest nod from An'gel, Dickce stepped forward. "Allow me, Mrs. Thurmond." She was tempted to take the woman up to the third floor, to the bathroom the farthest away from the front door, but decided she shouldn't behave as badly as this latest visitor to Riverhill. Instead she headed down the hall to the downstairs powder room near the kitchen.

When they were near enough, Dickce gestured to the door, and Mrs. Thurmond barely nodded before she disappeared into the bathroom.

Dickce turned and walked back toward the front of the house. As she approached the others, she heard Rosabelle tell her son, "You might as well stay. I'm sure An'gel and Dickce have a lot of questions for you." Rosabelle headed for the stairs. "I'm going back to my room to try and get in a little nap before dinner."

Dickce stopped in her tracks and stared aghast at her sister. Had Rosabelle really just invited her son and daughter-in-law to stay with her and An'gel? Surely An'gel would put her foot down now and throw them all out of the house. Dickce couldn't wait to see it.

Wade Thurmond gazed at his prospective hostess. "That would be mighty kind of you, Miss Ducote. What with the expense of flying here and the rental car, well, I'm kinda tapped out."

An'gel glanced at Dickce, her expression enigmatic. Dickce knew her sister could occasionally be unpredictable, and she figured this was going to be one of those times.

"My sister and I will be happy to put you up for a few days," An'gel said. Dickce thought her sister's tone sounded anything but welcoming, despite her words.

Thurmond didn't appear to notice. A relieved smile crossed his face. "Thank you, ma'am. I'll go get our bags and be right back. Is it okay if I leave the car where it is?"

An'gel nodded.

Dickce waited until Thurmond reached the car before she poked her sister's arm. "What on earth are you doing, letting them stay here? Why don't you throw them all out?"

"Stop hissing at me, Sister." An'gel smiled grimly. "That was my first impulse, but then I thought it might be better to have them here where we can watch them. I know Rosabelle is prone to overdramatize herself, but I think for once she's telling us the truth. She's frightened, and we can't simply ignore a plea for help." She paused for a breath. "I'd never forgive myself if I sent them packing and Rosabelle ended up dead at the hands of a family member."

An'gel was in one of her noblesse oblige moods, and Dickce knew better than to argue with her. Besides, she had the sinking feeling that her sibling was right. Rosabelle *did* seem afraid. "If you say so," she muttered. Maybe all that time she and An'gel had spent reading Nancy Drew in their younger years would finally pay off.

"Excuse me." Marla Thurmond spoke from behind Dickce. "I see Wade's got our bags, so I guess you're going to put us up here. I hope the room is clean, because I have terrible allergies."

Dickce felt like slapping her for such rudeness. She eyed Mrs. Thurmond and decided that a woman with a face like a petulant bulldog simply didn't know any better.

An'gel stared at Mrs. Thurmond. "What a horrible burden for you." She paused. "If you find you need medication, I'm sure the pharmacy in town will be happy to help you."

Dickce smothered a giggle at Mrs. Thurmond's uncertain expression. The woman obviously didn't know how to interpret An'gel's reply.

Wade Thurmond clumped onto the veranda, weighed

down by a bag strapped over one shoulder, a large suitcase in each hand, and a smaller bag tucked under one arm.

When Marla Thurmond made no move to assist her husband, Dickce offered to take the smaller bag.

"This way." An'gel headed for the stairs, and Marla Thurmond with her short, stubby legs hurried to keep pace with her hostess. Dickce and Wade Thurmond followed more slowly. Dickce wondered which room An'gel would allot to the Thurmonds. Rosabelle already occupied the most spacious one, and of the two remaining, the room on the third floor—really part of the attic—was barely large enough to accommodate a double bed, dresser, and one chair. An'gel was just ornery enough to put the Thurmonds in that one, Dickce knew, and she was tickled when An'gel marched across the landing on the second floor and headed up the attic stairs.

An'gel opened the bedroom door and stepped aside to allow the Thurmonds to enter, then she and Dickce stood in the doorway. Thurmond dropped the bags—on a rug, Dickce was happy to note, and not on the bare hardwood floor. She stepped in to set her burden down beside them while Mrs. Thurmond stared around the small room, sniffing loudly.

"It smells okay, but why did you put us all the way up here?" Marla Thurmond glared at An'gel.

"I thought you might prefer to have your own bathroom." An'gel gestured toward a door near the dresser. "Otherwise you would have to share one downstairs."

"That sounds just fine to me." Wade Thurmond glanced at his wife. "Don't you think so, honey?"

"It will do," Marla replied.

"I hope you will be comfortable here, Mrs. Thurmond," An'gel said, her tone mild.

"Not Thurmond." The woman stared hard at An'gel. "I don't use my married name because of my career. My name is Stephens."

"I will endeavor to remember that, Ms. Stephens." An'gel turned to leave. "If you need anything, please let either my sister or me know." She departed.

Dickce lingered a moment, her curiosity piqued. "What is your profession, if you don't mind my asking, Ms. Stephens?"

"Personnel management or human relations, whatever you want to call it."

Dickce wanted to laugh at the thought of this rude, clueless woman working in human relations. How did she manage to keep a job with her lack of manners?

"I see, how interesting," Dickce said. "Now, if you'll excuse me, I must go check on preparations for dinner. We'll be dining at seven thirty."

Dickce pulled the door shut behind her before either of the couple could engage her in further conversation. She headed down the stairs and was halfway to the kitchen when the doorbell rang.

Again.

CHAPTER 4

"I did *not* just hear the doorbell," Dickce muttered as she neared the kitchen. "But if I did, it's An'gel's turn to answer it."

"Are you talking to yourself again?" An'gel's tart tone stopped her sister three steps into the room.

"I do enjoy intelligent conversation," Dickce said, "so I suppose I must have been." She crossed her arms and stared at her sister.

Diesel sat at An'gel's feet, too entranced by the piece of chicken breast his hostess held to pay attention to the new arrival. He chirped and extended a paw to tap An'gel's hand.

"The poor boy has been hiding in here," An'gel said as she tore off another bite and dropped it for the cat. Diesel snapped it up before it could hit the floor. "I thought he deserved a treat. I certainly can't blame him for wanting to hide from our visitors."

"If I hide in here, will you feed me, too?" Dickce giggled. "Maybe Diesel and I will move into the kitchen until they're gone."

Diesel batted at An'gel's hand again, for she was obviously too slow in dispensing his treat. An'gel gazed down at him, her expression stern. "Now, would a true gentleman behave that way?"

The cat warbled and tapped An'gel's foot with his paw.

"I think he just apologized," Dickce said, trying hard not to laugh.

"I'll take it as such." An'gel brandished another bite of chicken. "This is it."

Diesel waited silently, and after a moment An'gel gave him the last piece. He made it disappear almost immediately and then began to purr.

An'gel moved to the sink to wash her hands. As she rinsed them, she said, "Didn't I hear the doorbell?"

Dickce nodded as a second soft peal of chimes reached them. "I decided it was your turn to answer it."

"Honestly, Sister." An'gel shook her head. She finished drying her hands and dropped the cloth on the counter. "One would think you were ten years old sometimes instead of almost eighty." She headed out of the kitchen as Clementine emerged from the back porch.

Both Dickce and Diesel sniffed as they caught the scent of Clementine's cigarette. She had cut way back, Dickce knew, because An'gel had fussed at her, concerned for the housekeeper's health, but she refused to give up smoking completely.

While Diesel rubbed against her legs, Dickce said, "I think we may have even more company. The doorbell rang a minute ago, and I sent An'gel to answer it."

"More of Miss Rosabelle's family?" Clementine went to

the sink to wash her hands. She glanced over her shoulder at Dickce, who shrugged in response. "Miss An'gel's been telling me some of Miss Rosabelle's troubles. Why does Miss An'gel want all those people in the house, you reckon?"

"I think she wants to pretend she's Jessica Fletcher." Dickce smiled. Clementine was as big a fan of *Murder, She Wrote* as Dickce and An'gel were.

Clementine frowned. "Well, Miss Dickce, you know when Jessica Fletcher comes to the house, something bad's gonna happen." Her hands clean and dry, she turned to face Dickce.

"I'm trying not to think about that." Dickce smiled. "I'm hoping this turns out to be an overactive imagination on Rosabelle's part, and we can send them all on their way back to California in a couple of days."

Diesel warbled loudly as if in agreement, and both women laughed.

"He may be spending a lot of time in the kitchen with you," Dickce said. "I don't think he's going to take too well to Rosabelle's clan."

"I don't mind the company." Clementine went to the refrigerator and pulled out a large bowl with a chicken marinating inside it. She set it on the counter. "I'd best get to cutting this up and get it ready to fry. I sure hope it's enough because it's the only one I got ready." She glanced at Dickce. "Though I reckon there's a casserole or two I could defrost."

"Go ahead and defrost them, and if casseroles and chicken aren't enough, our guests will just have to fill up on bread or vegetables." Dickce scratched Diesel's head, happy to hear the cat's rumbling purr.

An'gel stepped into the kitchen and called, "Sister, come meet the latest arrivals." Without waiting for a response, she disappeared out the door, and Dickce sighed. She knew she had no choice.

"The rest of the family, no doubt," Dickce muttered. Diesel chirped as he accompanied her out of the kitchen and down the hall toward the front door. "I hope you don't regret leaving the kitchen," Dickce told the cat.

Four people—two women who looked to be in their late fifties and a younger man and woman—stood near the front door conversing with An'gel. As Dickce and Diesel approached, An'gel said brightly, "And here is my sister, Dickce, and our feline houseguest, Diesel. Sister, these are Rosabelle's daughters and grandchildren." She paused. "They came in search of Rosabelle, and I assured them she is fine. They will be staying with us for a day or two."

"How do you do?" Dickce said as she and the cat halted near An'gel. She examined the group as closely as she could without appearing to stare. Rosabelle's daughters favored their mother, though both were plumper and better dressed. The grandson, a tall, weedy-looking specimen of about twenty-five, blinked at Dickce through rimless glasses and offered a shy smile. The granddaughter, the one beauty in the family, as far as Dickce could see, had a lovely hourglass figure, auburn hair, green eyes, and a peaches-and-cream complexion. She did not resemble her mother, aunt, or cousin much, and Dickce reckoned her father must be a mighty handsome man to overcome the Sultan family genes.

The granddaughter, who looked to be about the same age as her cousin, stepped forward, hand extended. "How do you do, Miss Ducote? I'm Juanita Cameron."

Dickce shook her hand. "My pleasure, Miss Cameron." She thought it odd that the granddaughter spoke first, rather than Rosabelle's elder daughter.

Juanita Cameron smiled, and Dickce couldn't help but respond in kind. Juanita turned and indicated one of the women behind her. "This is my mother, Bernice Cameron."

The slightly plumper, slightly taller of the two women nodded and murmured a greeting.

"And this is my aunt, Maudine Pittman, and her son, my cousin, Newton. We call him Junior, because he's named after my uncle."

Newton stepped forward, ostensibly to shake Dickce's hand, but he stumbled—over nothing that Dickce could see—and barely missed stepping on the cat at her feet. Diesel jumped out of the way in time.

Newton muttered an apology, and his mother spoke over him. "You'll have to forgive my son, Miss Ducote. His intentions are good, but he could trip over a piece of lint on the floor."

The young man flushed unbecomingly at his mother's sharp words, and Dickce felt sorry for him. She offered Maudine Pittman her frostiest of glances and said, "Good manners never harmed anyone." She held out her hand. "I'm pleased to meet you, Mr. Pittman."

Newton's eyes widened as he gazed at Dickce. "Thank you, ma'am," he said as he took her hand. Dickce heard the genuine gratitude in his voice and smiled again. He blushed and stepped back, narrowly missing his cousin.

"What kind of cat is Diesel, Miss Ducote?" Juanita shook her head. "I don't think I've ever seen a house cat that large. Have you, Mother?" Diesel chirped and moved closer to rub himself against the young woman's legs.

Bernice Cameron sniffed. "No, can't say as I have. Be careful about getting hair all over your stockings. Those animals shed terribly."

Juanita Cameron laughed. "A little cat hair isn't going

to hurt anyone, Mother. Diesel is absolutely beautiful, don't you think so, Junior?"

Her cousin nodded, and Dickce decided that Rosabelle's grandchildren had by some miracle turned out well. She couldn't say the same for Rosabelle's children, however. They didn't have the manners the good Lord gave a billy goat.

"I'd like to speak to Mother and assure myself that she came to no harm during the drive here," Maudine announced. "Which room is hers?" She took a step forward past her sister.

"Rosabelle was a bit tired when she arrived," An'gel said, her tone chilly. "She is now resting comfortably in her room, and I am sure she would much prefer *not* to be disturbed until dinnertime."

"*Well.*" Maudine packed a lot of irritation and affront into that one syllable. Dickce had to stifle a laugh.

An'gel regarded the four impassively. "Mr. and Mrs. Thurmond arrived a little while ago and are upstairs in their room." She paused. "I am afraid that Mrs. Cameron and Mrs. Pittman will need to share a room. Mr. Pittman, there is a small apartment over the garage out back that should suit you."

"Sounds fine to me. Thank you, ma'am," Junior said. He actually looked relieved, Dickce thought. *Probably glad to be as far away from his mother as possible.*

"What about my daughter?" Bernice Cameron frowned at An'gel. "Isn't there a bedroom for her?"

"Unfortunately there isn't," An'gel said. "There is, however, a trundle bed in Rosabelle's room that should suffice. If Mr. Pittman and Mr. Thurmond won't mind, I'll ask them to move it into your room, Mrs. Pittman."

"The trundle bed sounds like fun." Juanita Cameron smiled. "No, Mother, really, I've always wondered what one is like. But perhaps it could stay in Granny's room, and I could sleep there? I'm a nurse, and I can look after Granny when she isn't feeling well."

Dickce was relieved that An'gel hadn't suggested she move in with her sister. They had not shared a bedroom since they were young girls, and she didn't relish the thought of doing it now. But would Rosabelle want her granddaughter in her room with her? she wondered.

"If Rosabelle has no objection," An'gel said, "that is fine with me. I will ask her once she has finished resting. Now, if you will follow me, I will show the ladies to their room. Dickce will be happy to go with you, Mr. Pittman, to the garage apartment and check it out." She did not wait for a reply but turned and headed for the stairs.

Bernice and Maudine glanced at each other, then followed their hostess. Juanita paused to smile at Dickce before she trailed after them.

Dickce turned to Junior Pittman. "If you will come with me, I'll show you where you'll be staying."

Junior blushed. "Thank you, ma'am. It's awfully kind of you and your sister to put us up like this. I know it's a terrible imposition." He stared at the floor.

Dickce could tell he was embarrassed by his family. "That's quite all right. Don't you even think about it." At her feet, Diesel warbled as if he agreed with her.

The young man smiled at the cat. "He sounds like he's trying to talk."

"He is," Dickce said. "He can be pretty chatty. Now let's go out the front." She thought it better not to disturb Clementine in the kitchen just now.

Cat and man followed her outside, and they walked without speaking along the driveway as it branched off behind the house. The garage, converted from the cookhouse it had been until the end of the Civil War, stood about fifty yards behind the mansion. It had room for three cars, and at the moment it held the sisters' late-model Lexus and Rosabelle's dusty Cadillac.

Dickce headed for a door near the empty slot and tugged it open. She reached in and flipped the light switch to illuminate the cramped staircase. Diesel scampered ahead of her and was about halfway up the stairs when he stopped, head extended, sniffing.

Probably mice, Dickce thought. It had been a few months since anyone had checked the place.

She turned to offer an apology for the apartment's likely condition but instead froze, her mouth open.

Above them, the floorboards creaked, the sound much too loud to be caused by a mouse.

CHAPTER 5

An'gel opened the door of the second guest room and stood aside to let the women enter. Maudine brushed past her, still obviously rankled by An'gel's refusal to let her check on Rosabelle.

"I suppose this will do," Maudine said. Bernice nodded with a tentative smile at her hostess.

Annoyed by the rude tone, An'gel suspected that Maudine, as the elder of the two, took the lead in everything, leaving Bernice to follow meekly in her wake. Thank goodness Dickce had more gumption. An'gel couldn't abide women who didn't speak up for themselves.

Juanita slipped past An'gel to stand beside her mother. "What a lovely room," she said, her face alight with obvious pleasure. "Miss Ducote, does all the furniture date from the antebellum period?"

An'gel noted that Maudine frowned at her niece's

enthusiasm. "Yes, it does, although the mattress is modern, I can assure you. You should find it comfortable."

"What about the bathroom?" Maudine glanced around the room. "There's only one door in here, and that has to be a closet."

"The bathroom is next door," An'gel replied, her tone pleasant despite the other woman's rudeness. "You will be sharing it with your mother."

"Oh, dear," Bernice muttered with a glance at her sister.

"I suppose you have to expect it in an old house like this." Maudine sniffed. "My house in California has four bedrooms, and each one has its own bathroom."

Juanita frowned at her aunt. "Before this, I've never had the opportunity to be a guest in a house with such a long history, Miss Ducote. I'm sure I'll enjoy every minute I spend here."

An'gel smiled at the young woman. At least one member of Rosabelle's family had manners, though An'gel had to wonder how on earth Juanita had learned them. Miss Manners would have a field day with the rest of the clan.

"Thank you." An'gel noted that Maudine didn't appear to have paid any attention to Juanita's rebuke, although Bernice at least had the grace to appear slightly abashed.

"Where did you put Wade and Marla?" Maudine asked.

"They have the guest room upstairs," An'gel said.

"Don't tell me we have to share the bathroom with them, too?" Maudine glowered at An'gel.

"No, there is a bathroom upstairs," An'gel said, already anticipating Maudine's sour reaction to this bit of news.

"I can't believe Marla gets a private bathroom while we have to share one."

The way Maudine's nostrils flared, An'gel thought, she

looked like an irritated horse. Dickce was hard put not to laugh.

Bernice touched her sister's arm. "Now, Maudine, it won't be that bad. It wouldn't be right for Wade to have to share a bathroom with Mother, after all."

Maudine frowned at her sister. Before she could speak, however, Juanita intervened. "Perhaps it would be better if we went to a hotel. I'm sure you can recommend a good one in town, Miss Ducote?"

Both Maudine and Bernice appeared aghast at Juanita's suggestion. Maudine opened her mouth but nothing came out.

Appreciative of the young woman's tactics, An'gel nodded and smiled. "The Farrington House is the oldest and most highly regarded hotel in Athena. I'd be more than happy to call and make a reservation."

"No, that won't be necessary. I'm sure we'll be perfectly comfortable here." Maudine smiled weakly. "After all, it is really kind of you to open your home to us like this."

Maudine changed her mind pretty quickly, An'gel was amused to note. She was also pleased that the woman finally made an effort to behave in a more polite fashion.

"My sister and I are delighted to help our old friend and her family. I'm sure you all must be in need of refreshment," An'gel said briskly. "If you would care to join me in the front parlor in about ten minutes, there will be iced tea for you. Miss Cameron, we'll get you settled once your grandmother is finished resting." She paused long enough to get nods from the sisters and a broad grin from Juanita before she left the room, pulling the door closed behind her.

An'gel had begun to descend the stairs when she heard whistling from nearby. Startled, she turned to her left to see Rosabelle, her door cracked about two inches, mouth pursed to whistle again.

An'gel approached the room, and Rosabelle stood back to let her enter. She closed the door and leaned against it.

"What are *they* doing here?" she asked.

"The same as the rest of your family, I suppose," An'gel replied tartly. "They've come to check on you."

"To murder me, you mean," Rosabelle muttered. She moved away from the door and sank into a chair in front of the vanity. "I have nowhere else to go and no money to get anywhere either. So I guess I'm stuck." She closed her eyes and sighed.

"You ought to be safe enough here," An'gel said. "They'd have to be crazy to try to harm you while you're our guest." Given what she had observed thus far of Rosabelle's family, she couldn't put a lot of conviction in her tone. She felt she had to try to reassure her old sorority sister, though.

Rosabelle's eyes popped open. "You don't know how desperate they are." She shuddered. "They would throw me to a pack of ravenous dogs if they thought they could get away with it."

An'gel wanted to shake her. She understood that Rosabelle was badly frightened, but her tendency to overdramatize got old quickly.

"There's no pack of ravenous dogs here, and you're certainly not Jezebel," she said in a mild tone. "So you're safe from that."

Rosabelle glowered at her, and An'gel thought how much Maudine resembled her mother. "I'm glad you find my situation so humorous."

All at once An'gel felt tired, so she went over and sat on the bed. Maybe Dickce had been right to suggest that she throw the whole clan out. Why had she even agreed to let them stay in the first place?

Because I am accustomed to thinking that I can fix

anything I set my mind to, she acknowledged ruefully to herself. *And in my arrogance I just might have mixed Sister and me up in something nasty.*

She realized Rosabelle was still waiting for her to acknowledge her last remark. *Get a hold of yourself, An'gel Ducote. You* can *help Rosabelle, so stop trying to borrow trouble.* "I didn't mean to make light of your plight," she said. "You're still tired, and I'm sure everything looks grim to you. Dickce and I will do our best to help you sort it all out, and you'll be able to go home and not worry anymore."

Rosabelle appeared mollified by An'gel's reply. "That would be wonderful. I could sleep the night through without being terrified."

"Why do you think one of them is so desperate to do away with you?" An'gel asked. "You told us that your house goes to Wade, but is that all? Would your daughters and grandchildren inherit anything significant?"

Rosabelle shook her head. "I don't have anything to my name really, not even the house. It's mine for my lifetime, but then it goes to Wade. I get a barely adequate income for life from a trust set up by my first husband, but I can't touch the capital. When I'm gone, however, the trust is dissolved, and the money goes to Maudine and Bernice." She paused. "My second husband, Wade's father, also left me a small income from a trust. Same situation, though. When I'm dead, Wade gets everything."

Though she had no idea how large the trusts were, An'gel suspected they were huge. Rosabelle wouldn't have married poor men, or even moderately wealthy ones. Rosabelle liked money too much to settle for anyone less than a multimillionaire. An'gel also thought both men shrewd to set up trusts for Rosabelle; otherwise, she might have burned through the money and been left with nothing. Evidently the third husband had nothing to leave. She thought it odd Rosabelle didn't mention him.

Now that she was aware of Rosabelle's financial position, however, An'gel could understand why the woman was frightened. Her children and grandchildren stood to inherit significant sums of money, and one of them might be tired of waiting to get hold of it. The question was, who was the most desperate? She and Dickce would have to ascertain what they could of the younger generation's finances.

An'gel reached over and patted Rosabelle's hand. "Dickce and I will get to the bottom of this. In the meantime, you try to relax. I believe you'll be safe here. I will let your family know, discreetly, of course, that Sister and I will be guarding your welfare closely."

"Thank you," Rosabelle said, her eyes suddenly wet. "I don't deserve such good friends."

An'gel forbore to respond to that comment. Instead she stood, her energy coming back. "Don't think any more about it. I do have a question for you, however. Would you allow your granddaughter to share your room? There's a trundle bed she can use, and we can move it across the hall to your daughters' room if you'd prefer to be alone."

Rosabelle shook her head. "Juanita can stay with me. She and Junior aren't like their parents, thank the Lord. They're both sweet and loving." She shrugged. "Anyway, I'll feel safer with Juanita in the room with me at night."

"Very well, then. When you're ready, you can let Juanita know. In the meantime I'm going downstairs to prepare iced tea for everyone. You can join us in the front parlor when you feel like it."

Rosabelle nodded, and An'gel left her, still ensconced in the chair, staring down at her hands.

On the way to the kitchen, An'gel resolved to get to the heart of Rosabelle's troubles quickly. She wanted the whole clan out of her house as soon as possible.

CHAPTER 6

Dickce stood still. Had she imagined the creaking floorboards overhead? Right now all she heard was the faint whirring of the air-conditioning.

One glance at Junior Pittman's face assured her she hadn't imagined the sounds.

She felt sweat forming on her forehead and scalp despite the cool, slightly dank air. The musty odor made her want to sneeze, and she pinched her nose to stop the tickle.

Ahead of her, Diesel slowly climbed the stairs, body low, obviously in hunting mode.

"Let me go first," Junior whispered and motioned for her to let him pass.

Dickce stepped back, and the young man moved upward, hardly making a sound. He laid a hand on the cat's head, and Diesel stopped. When Junior's head reached a point where he could see the upper room through the railing, he paused.

Dickce saw his tensed shoulders relax.

"Dang it, Benjy, what the heck are you doing here?" Junior sounded exasperated.

Dickce waited on the stairs. Was the mysterious Benjy dangerous?

"I didn't have a lot of choice. You know what my mother's like." The petulant tones of a young man's voice carried down to her. Diesel chirped but didn't move.

Junior turned to look down at Dickce and frowned. "It's okay, ma'am. It's only Benjy." He disappeared from the stairway.

Diesel climbed the rest of the way up to the landing with Dickce. Her left hand rested on the newel post at the head of the stairs as she paused to catch her breath and give her pulse time to stop racing.

The apartment occupied the full second story of the garage. The bathroom was at the far end, along with a large closet. Otherwise, the space, which included a small kitchen and dining area, was open. The shabby but still serviceable furniture dated from the 1960s.

We really need to replace all this, Dickce thought, before her attention settled on the newcomer.

A youth of perhaps nineteen or twenty, clad in ragged jeans and a garishly colored T-shirt, regarded her with an uncertain smile. His shaggy blond hair, an inch past shoulder length, reminded Dickce of the pageboy style all the young people wore in the 1950s. Each ear sported two earrings, and each eyebrow had a small ring at the outer edge. Dickce was surprised there were no visible tattoos, given his other adornments and choice of clothing. He looked like young men she saw on the street whenever she and An'gel went to Memphis to shop.

Junior Pittman said, "Miss Ducote, this is Benjy Stephens, Marla's son. Benjy, Miss Dickce Ducote."

Benjy shook her proffered hand gently. "Nice to meet you, ma'am."

"You are quite a surprise, young man," Dickce said, her tone prim. "Before we go any further, we need more air." *How did Benjy know about the garage apartment?* She marched across the room to a window that overlooked the woods behind the mansion and set the air conditioner on high.

Dickce turned back to the two men. Diesel was rubbing himself against Benjy's legs, and the youth grinned as he scratched the cat's head.

"Why didn't you come in with your parents when you arrived?" Dickce felt embarrassed when she saw the layer of dust that coated everything in the apartment. Motes floated in the air, disturbed by the force of the air conditioner blower. She wasn't thrilled to discover yet another guest, but she noted that at least Diesel seemed to approve of him. She had to wonder also whether there were any more family members who might pop up. The situation was beginning to border on the ridiculous.

Benjy's face darkened as he pulled his hand away from Diesel. "Mom told me there probably wouldn't be room in the house for me. She said I should stay out here. The Wart's mother told them about the apartment over the garage, I guess." He shrugged. "The door wasn't locked anyway, so I figured nobody would mind."

Diesel chirped to remind Benjy that he needed attention, and Benjy resumed scratching the cat's head.

Dickce assumed that the nickname referred to the boy's stepfather, Wade Thurmond. *No love lost there*, she reckoned.

Then she wondered what kind of mother would tell her child such a thing. Her already low opinion of Marla Stephens plummeted even further.

"We don't usually lock it," Dickce said, her tone gentle. "I'm afraid there is no more room in the house. You're welcome to stay here, but you'll have to share with Mr. Pittman." The apartment contained a double bed and a large sofa, and the two ought to be comfortable enough here. "I'm sorry about the dust, but we haven't had the place aired and cleaned in months."

"Don't you worry about that," Junior said. "A little dust isn't going to bother me. I don't have any allergies."

Benjy snorted. "Me either. Mom would have a fit, though, if she had to sleep in here. She's allergic to all kinds of weird stuff."

Dickce nodded. "Yes, I believe she did mention her allergies."

"She would." Benjy rolled his eyes before gesturing at Diesel. "What's his name, and what kind of cat is he?"

"His name is Diesel, and he's a Maine Coon." Dickce smiled fondly at the cat. "He is visiting with my sister and me while his family vacations in France."

"I've never seen a house cat that big before," Junior said. "Does he have some kind of glandular problem?"

"Your grandmother asked the same question. No, he's perfectly healthy," Dickce replied. "Maine Coons are generally larger than most breeds, but Diesel is exceptional, and not just because of his size."

The cat warbled, his gaze fixed on Dickce, and the two men laughed.

"He agrees with you," Benjy said.

"He's smarter than some people I know," Dickce said. "He certainly seems to like you." She found it interesting that the cat had taken to Benjy so quickly. Diesel had an excellent record as a judge of character, and Dickce hoped he hadn't made an error in this case.

"He can tell I like animals," Benjy replied. "I want to be a veterinarian, if I can get enough money to finish college."

"He has two spiders," Junior said. He shook his head. "They give me the creeps."

"They're tarantulas, and they're not poisonous," Benjy said, his tone sharp. "How many times do I have to tell you?" He rolled his eyes at Dickce. "Bert and Ernie wouldn't hurt anyone, as long as they're left alone. At least my mother isn't allergic to them, like she is with dogs and cats."

Dickce wasn't that fond of spiders herself, but she admired Benjy's willingness to care for such creatures. "You'll probably find a few spiders here," she said. She glanced at Junior and wasn't surprised to see him grimace.

"Don't worry, Junior." Benjy grinned. "I won't let them bite you."

Junior muttered under his breath, and Dickce figured it was just as well she couldn't make out the words. "You'll need fresh linens for the bed and towels for the bathroom. If one of you would like to come back to the house with me, I'll get them for you."

"We'll both come," Junior said with a stern glance at Benjy. "My mother and Aunt Bernice need help with their bags, and I have to get my own."

Benjy shrugged. "Might as well."

"Come along, then, and we'll all have something cold to drink before you have to start carrying bags." Dickce turned for the stairs. Diesel, ever alert, scampered down ahead of her.

"That sounds great," Benjy said from right behind her. "Any chance of a snack before dinner?"

Diesel warbled, and Dickce giggled. "I'm sure we can find you something, Benjy," she said as she stepped outside. "Diesel would like a snack, too. Wouldn't you?"

The cat chirped with enthusiasm, and the men laughed. Satisfied that Junior had shut the apartment door properly, Dickce led men and feline across the drive toward the kitchen door. In the kitchen, she found Clementine busy preparing dinner.

"Something smells awesome." Benjy sniffed appreciatively.

Clementine glanced at the newcomers curiously but didn't respond. An'gel, busy at another counter filling glasses with ice, stopped when she realized there was a stranger with Dickce.

Dickce grinned at her sister. "An'gel, we have another guest. This is Benjy Stephens, Marla's son. We found him in the garage apartment." She paused. "Evidently his mother told him he should go there instead of coming into the house with her and her husband."

An'gel frowned as Benjy stepped forward, hand extended. "Nice to meet you, Miss Ducote," he said. "Sorry if I caused any trouble."

An'gel accepted the young man's hand. "Mr. Stephens, I don't see how *you* could be at fault by simply doing as your mother told you. I trust my sister made you feel welcome."

"I brought them over to fetch fresh linens and towels," Dickce said, her tone bright and cheery. "Mr. Pittman mentioned also that he wanted to help his mother and his aunts with their luggage."

"There will be time enough for that later," An'gel said as she reached into the nearby cabinet for more glasses. "Why don't you join me and your family in the front parlor? I thought we could all use a cold drink about now."

"That sounds good to me," Benjy said, and Junior nodded.

"May I carry that for you?" Benjy stepped forward and reached for the tray An'gel had picked up.

An'gel smiled as she relinquished her burden. "Thank you. I'll show you the way."

Dickce felt oddly pleased at this show of manners on Benjy's part. She had taken a liking to this young man, despite his uncouth manner of dressing.

"I'll be along in a minute," she said. She wanted to find a snack for Benjy. She knew young men his age often had voracious appetites, and she wouldn't mind a few nibbles herself.

Benjy, An'gel, and Junior left the room. Diesel stayed behind. He sat near her feet and stared up expectantly.

Dickce grinned. "You know what I'm doing, you rascal. But I'm afraid there won't be any tidbits for you."

Diesel chirped and then turned to sit with his back to her.

Clementine chuckled. "Cats sure have a funny way of pouting, don't they? My grandbaby Lawanna does the same thing."

"It's so cute," Dickce said. "Are there any of those oatmeal raisin cookies left?"

"Should be, unless Miss An'gel got into them last night." Clementine gestured toward the counter, where a cookie jar in the shape of a potbellied dog sat.

"She didn't, as far as I know." Dickce walked over to pull off the lid and peer inside. Her sister had a weakness for Clementine's cookies, but she had also been watching her weight lately. Dickce was pleased to see the jar was still nearly full.

She found a serving tray and a paper doily, then arranged two dozen cookies on it. She noticed Diesel at her feet, gazing expectantly up at her. "No, sir, these are not for you. I think you'd better stay in the kitchen with Clementine so you won't be begging." She glanced at the housekeeper. "You don't mind, do you?"

Clementine smiled. "No, he's fine here with me. Besides, he's gonna be more interested in the fried c-h-i-c-k-e-n anyway."

Diesel warbled and transferred his attention to the housekeeper.

Dickce laughed. "I have a feeling he knows how to spell." She headed out the door and down the hall to the front parlor.

She had neared the foot of the stairs when she heard a woman cry out from above her. Startled, she looked up the staircase in time to see Marla Stephens rolling down.

CHAPTER 7

An'gel found Maudine and Bernice in the front parlor near the fireplace when she ushered Benjy and Junior inside. Maudine had the Ming Dynasty goldfish vase upside down in her hands, peering at the bottom. "I'll bet it's a fake," she told her sister in a waspish tone. "Or else they're even richer than Mother has always claimed."

Bernice's eyes widened when she caught sight of An'gel. She hissed at Maudine. "Put that down."

"Yes, please do put it back as it was." An'gel strode forward, momentarily forgetting about Benjy and the tray he bore. Maudine grimaced but complied with her hostess's request. Annoyed by her guest's obnoxious comments, An'gel adjusted the position of the vase on the mantel until it met with her satisfaction, then stepped back. "When my great-grandfather purchased the vase in China on his honeymoon in 1853, he was assured that it was authentic. I have never had cause to doubt that, nor did the appraiser from Christie's in New York twenty years ago."

Maudine appeared to wither under An'gel's unyielding gaze. "I suppose you would know," she said. "It's beautiful."

Benjy cleared his throat. "Miss Ducote, where would you like me to put the tray?"

An'gel, recalled to her duties, turned to smile at the young man. "Right over here." She indicated a side table next to one of the sofas, and Benjy set the tray gently down.

"Please help yourselves," An'gel said. If Maudine wanted tea, she could darn well get it for herself.

Benjy complied with alacrity and had nearly drained his glass by the time Maudine, Bernice, and Junior each claimed their own. An'gel gestured for him to refill his glass, and he thanked her.

"Maudie, Bernie, what are you two doing here?" Wade Thurmond nodded at his half siblings as he joined them beside the tea tray. "I see you found your way inside the house, Benjy. Afternoon, Junior. Marla will be down in a minute." He helped himself to iced tea.

Benjy shrugged at his stepfather, and Junior nodded in response. An'gel noted with interest that, although Wade spoke to the other two men, his gaze remained fixed on his sisters.

Maudine glared at Wade. "We came to assure ourselves that Mother is well. I can't believe she would simply take off in the night like that and drive across the country away from her family."

"Yeah, well, Mama is unpredictable." Wade stared into his glass. "I think she's getting a bit mental, if you know what I mean. All this goofy talk about somebody putting something in her food." He shook his head. "Marla thinks

Mama has developed a food allergy and needs to be tested. Of course, Mama won't accept a rational explanation."

"I'm sure Marla would like us to believe it's something that simple," Maudine replied tartly. "But I wouldn't put it past her to add something to Mother's food just to make her sick. She hates Mother, even after all the kindness Mother has shown the two of you, letting you both live in her house rent-free." She pointed at Benjy. "Not to mention letting that juvenile delinquent son of Marla's live there, too."

Appalled at the spite in the woman's voice, An'gel glanced at Benjy to witness his reaction to Maudine's words. He appeared not to have heard. Instead he seemed to be engrossed in enjoying the view out the front window.

"You stop talking like that right this instant." Wade's tone betrayed his fury. "You know as well as I do that house is rightfully mine. And the idea of Marla spiking Mama's food, well, it's just plain outrageous."

An'gel found it interesting that Wade did not defend Benjy in his impassioned reply. She glanced toward the window again. Benjy's shoulders were hunched up, and she suddenly felt sympathy for the young man, despite the fact that she had no idea whether Maudine's accusation was truth or hyperbole.

"Pardon me," An'gel said, suddenly tired of the squabbling. She needed to get out of the room for a few minutes. "I'll check on Dickce and be right back." Really, these people had no manners whatsoever. She would never dream of airing family troubles in front of a stranger the way Rosabelle's children were doing. She wondered whether they would continue to behave this way in front of Rosabelle.

As she headed for the door, Bernice spoke up. "Hush, you two, you shouldn't be carrying on like this."

Too little, too late, An'gel thought. When she stepped out of the front parlor, she heard someone cry out, then saw a blur of motion as Marla Stephens landed with a loud thud on her back at the bottom of the stairs. One foot was bare, the other wore a spike-heeled shoe. *Did she trip wearing those high heels?* An'gel wondered.

"Ms. Stephens, are you okay?" As she hurried forward, she raised her voice. "Mr. Thurmond, come quickly. Your wife fell down the stairs."

Wade responded immediately and came bustling out of the parlor. He brushed past An'gel to kneel beside the unmoving form of his wife. He grasped her left arm and patted her hand, his expression anxious. "Marla, honey, speak to me. Say something. *Marla.*" His breath caught on a sob.

There was no response.

Marla Stephens's head was twisted at an unnatural angle, and An'gel couldn't detect any signs of breathing. *Was she dead?*

Suddenly shaky, An'gel looked up to see her sister standing nearby, food tray trembling in her hands. An'gel moved closer and placed an unsteady hand on Dickce's shoulder. "Did you see what happened?"

"She just came rolling down the stairs." Dickce shook her head, her eyes wide with shock. "There was nothing I could do to stop it."

"Put down that tray before you drop everything," An'gel said. She felt faint herself, and the hall seemed suddenly chilly. "Someone should call for an ambulance." Her feet wouldn't move when she tried to turn back toward the front parlor.

Dickce quickly set the tray upon a small table against the wall between the parlor and the library. She took An'gel's arm and began to lead her back to the parlor.

"Sister, you look like you're going to faint any second now. I'm not feeling all that steady myself."

An'gel halted for a moment to observe the scene continuing to unfold in the area near the foot of the stairs.

Junior stood in the parlor doorway, cell phone in hand. Dimly An'gel heard him talking and realized he was conversing with the emergency operator.

"Yes, a fall down some stairs," Junior said, the impatience obvious in his tone. "No, I don't know the address. I'm not from around here." He paused. "The house belongs to the Ducote sisters. Yeah, Riverhill, that's it."

Satisfied that Junior was handling the emergency call, An'gel glanced at the activity nearby.

Wade Thurmond was performing CPR on his inert wife. From what An'gel could see, however, his attempts were fruitless. Maudine and Bernice remained nearby, their faces pale as they watched. They clutched each other, their breathing agitated. Benjy knelt beside Wade, his mother's limp right hand clasped between both of his. He held the hand to his cheek, his eyes bright with unshed tears, as he watched his stepfather. An'gel could see his lips moving, perhaps in prayer.

"What on earth is going on? Did she fall down the stairs?"

An'gel looked up to see Juanita Cameron hurrying down the staircase to join Wade beside his wife's body. "Here, let me take over," she said. She pushed an unprotesting Wade to one side and went to work.

Wade collapsed into a sitting position, his eyes, now streaming with tears, fixed on Marla. He pulled a handkerchief from his pocket and held it against his mouth.

An'gel glanced up again. Rosabelle stood at the top of the stairs, both hands to her mouth, staring at everyone below. An'gel couldn't read her expression from this far away. Rosabelle made no move to descend. Instead she appeared rooted to the spot.

"Come on, Sister," Dickce said, her tone agitated. "I don't know about you, but I need to sit down." An'gel tore her gaze away and allowed her sister to lead her into the parlor.

Dickce got An'gel seated on the sofa. An'gel still felt shaky, and she could see that Dickce was as white as she no doubt was. She watched as Dickce headed for the liquor cabinet, pulled out the whiskey and a couple of glasses, then poured two healthy shots. She handed one to An'gel and urged her to drink. An'gel accepted the glass, eyed it for a moment, then knocked it back while Dickce did the same.

An'gel felt the warmth spread through her body, and her head cleared. "Thank you, Sister," she said. "I needed that."

"Me, too," Dickce replied as she sank down on the sofa by An'gel. "That poor woman. So awful." She paused for a steadying breath. "What the heck have we gotten ourselves into?"

"Please, Lord, let it be an accident, and not murder," An'gel said in response. "She simply tripped in those heels and fell."

Dickce squeezed her hand, but An'gel took little comfort from the gesture. She had the uneasy feeling that the horror had only just begun.

From the hallway they could hear the muted sounds of conversation in short bursts. After a moment An'gel pushed herself up. "We'd better see what's happening. The others are likely to need a restorative as well." Dickce grimaced but followed her sister to the hall.

Juanita continued her efforts to revive Marla, but from what An'gel could see, Marla remained unresponsive.

Benjy and Wade remained close by, their gazes focused on the motionless body. Maudine and Bernice still huddled together, several feet away.

Junior, cell phone still stuck to his ear, spoke in low tones to the emergency dispatcher. "No, she's not responding. How long is it going to take that ambulance to get here?"

An'gel glanced up at the second-floor landing. Rosabelle no longer had her hands to her mouth, but her gaze appeared focused on the scene below. An'gel waved to catch her attention and then motioned for Rosabelle to come downstairs. Rosabelle stared at her hostess for a moment before she slowly began to descend, her body tightly against the right banister.

When she reached the foot of the stairs, Rosabelle stepped around the supine form of her daughter-in-law, barely glancing at her granddaughter still hard at work. She ignored her daughters, even though Maudine held out her hand toward Rosabelle.

She stopped beside An'gel and Dickce. "We need to talk. In private."

"Come into the parlor," An'gel said. She figured Rosabelle was in shock and would benefit from a shot of whiskey as she and Dickce had. She took Rosabelle's arm and led her into the room. She heard the siren of the ambulance as it neared Riverhill and was glad the professionals would soon be on the scene.

An'gel seated Rosabelle on the sofa while Dickce went to the liquor cabinet to pour the whiskey.

Rosabelle didn't speak again until she had downed the liquor. She set the glass on the coffee table and leaned back. She turned to stare at An'gel, seated beside her.

"That was supposed to be me out there, dead on the floor, not Marla."

CHAPTER 8

"Does that mean you think Marla's fall was no accident?" An'gel watched Rosabelle's face intently even as her stomach began to churn from anxiety.

Rosabelle nodded.

"And that *you* were the intended victim of whoever caused her to fall," Dickce said.

"Yes," Rosabelle replied.

"How can you be sure it *wasn't* simply an accident?" An'gel hoped fervently that it was and that Rosabelle was imagining things.

Rosabelle glared at her. "There's water on a couple of stairs on the left side of the staircase near the top. Unless you have a leak in the ceiling, someone had to put it there."

An'gel felt cold to the bone at those words. She could think of no innocent reason that there would be water at the head of the stairs. Water on marble was dangerous, as she had occasion to know, having slipped herself a few times when mopping the stairs.

"On the *left* side?" Dickce frowned. "Why on the left side? Most people descend on the right, don't they? I know I always go up and down on my right side."

"That's because you're right-handed," Rosabelle said. "I'm left-handed." She paused. "And so was Marla. It was just her bad luck she got there ahead of me; otherwise, I would be the one lying dead." She shuddered. "Just as my murderer intended."

So *that* was why Rosabelle pressed herself so tightly against the banister to her right when she came downstairs a few minutes ago, An'gel thought. She glanced at her sister and could see her horror mirrored in Dickce's expression. It had to be murder after all, if Marla really was dead.

Rosabelle appeared not to care much that Marla was probably dead. An'gel thought that was cold, even for someone as generally self-absorbed as Rosabelle.

The doorbell rang before An'gel could question Rosabelle further. *Pull it together*, she scolded herself. *You have to deal with this, and sitting here quivering isn't going to do one little bit of good to anybody.*

An'gel pushed herself to her feet. "I'd better go see who that is." She shot her sister a glance and knew that Dickce would understand she was to stay with Rosabelle.

When An'gel stepped into the hall, she saw that someone had admitted the emergency personnel. Rosabelle's family stood out of the way near the wall opposite the parlor. Wade was talking to one of the EMTs while two others examined Marla.

An'gel glanced toward the front door. It stood open, and as she watched, Kanesha Berry, the chief deputy of the

Athena County Sheriff's Department, strode into the hall, followed by another deputy. *Bates*, An'gel said to herself, pleased that she could recall the name when her brain felt so sluggish.

Chief Deputy Berry glanced her way after surveying the scene. She walked over. "Miss An'gel. Looks like a bad fall."

An'gel had known Kanesha Berry since the deputy was a small child, and had watched her grow into a seasoned professional who was outstanding at her job. An'gel was thankful that a person she knew and trusted would be in charge of the investigation into this dreadful event.

Her mouth suddenly felt dry. "I'm glad you're here." She hesitated over her next words. "It might not have been an accident."

Kanesha's gaze sharpened. "What do you mean?"

Before An'gel could answer, Deputy Bates claimed Kanesha's attention. He motioned for her to join him where he waited with one of the EMTs.

"Excuse me a moment." Kanesha walked over to the two men.

An'gel wished she could hear what they were saying. The EMT shook his head in response to something Kanesha said. She then spoke to Bates, who stepped away and pulled out his cell phone.

Probably calling for backup, An'gel thought. The churning in her stomach grew worse. As she watched, the two EMTs who had been working on Marla stood and moved away. One of them approached Wade and the rest of the family. An'gel averted her gaze. She couldn't bear to watch as the EMT confirmed to them that Marla was beyond help now.

Kanesha approached An'gel again, while Bates joined the EMT talking to Wade and the others.

"She's dead." An'gel said it flatly, and Kanesha nodded.

"What did you mean when you said it might not have been an accident?"

An'gel hesitated. "Take a look at the head of the stairs. Left side, coming down. Go up on your left."

Kanesha frowned, then nodded.

An'gel watched the chief deputy ascend the stairs, staying close to the banister. When she reached the top, she took a couple of paces into the hall before she turned and came close to the left side of the stairs. She squatted, elbows on knees, and peered closely at the top steps. After a moment she rose and came back down to rejoin An'gel.

"Water, third and fourth steps down," she said.

An'gel nodded. "Plus she was wearing high heels. She must have slipped and fallen down the stairs." She shuddered.

"Miss An'gel, you look a bit shaky," Kanesha said, obviously concerned. "Can I get you something?"

"Maybe a little more whiskey," An'gel said with a faint smile. "If it's okay with you, I'll rejoin Dickce and our guest in the parlor and have a bit more."

"You go right ahead," Kanesha said. "I'll be along in a few minutes to ask you two what you know about this. One thing, though, before you go. Who is the deceased?"

"Her name is Marla Stephens," An'gel replied. "She's married, or she *was* married, to the gentleman over there." She gestured toward Wade where he leaned against the opposite wall, eyes closed, while his half sisters clucked around him. Juanita had her arms around Benjy, who rested his head on her shoulder. "That's her son, the young blond man. She was the daughter-in-law of an old friend of mine and Dickce's, Rosabelle Sultan. She's in the parlor with Dickce right now."

"Thanks," Kanesha said.

"If you need to, use the library," An'gel said, indicating the room across the hall.

Kanesha nodded. "You go on and get that whiskey."

An'gel was happy to comply. Rosabelle and Dickce turned to look at her when she entered the parlor.

Dickce stood and motioned for An'gel to sit. "You look like you need another shot." She didn't wait for a response from her sister and went to pour more whiskey.

An'gel settled herself on the sofa beside Rosabelle. "I just spoke to the deputy, and she told me Marla is dead." She patted her guest's hand. "I'm so sorry."

Rosabelle sniffed. "If you're expecting to hear any weeping and wailing and gnashing of teeth from me, you'll be waiting until hell freezes over. I'm no hypocrite. I didn't like the woman, but I am sorry for her son. For Wade, too. He loved her, and I think she loved him in her own way."

An'gel wasn't much surprised by these words from her self-centered friend. She accepted a glass of whiskey from Dickce and took a healthy sip. She felt the warmth spread through her and settle in her empty stomach. She decided she should eat something before she had any more alcohol. Otherwise, she could end up tipsy, and that would never do.

Dickce took a seat opposite her sister and Rosabelle. She frowned at the latter. "You almost sound like you're glad she's dead."

"I am not glad she's dead. I'm not a monster," Rosabelle said in a firm tone. "I am glad, however, that I'm alive and that the murderer failed to kill me. It was Marla's bad luck she died in my place."

An'gel raised her eyebrows at her sister. "It appears that

Marla wasn't the one trying to kill you." She glanced at Rosabelle to gauge the effect of her statement.

"True." Rosabelle cocked her head to one side, rather like a parrot, An'gel thought. She had to suppress a laugh. The whiskey was making her slightly giddy, she realized.

"That means she might not have been the one to doctor your food," Dickce said.

"I suppose so." Rosabelle shrugged. "If Wade was behind it, then it's poetic justice."

An'gel was confused. "If Wade was behind what? The doctored food or the water on the stairs?"

"Either, or both, I suppose." Rosabelle shifted her head to the other side. "He might have gotten Marla to doctor the food, and when that didn't work, he put water on the stairs. His tough luck the wrong woman slipped and broke her neck." She sniffed.

Did Rosabelle have no maternal instincts whatsoever? An'gel wondered. She exchanged an appalled glance with Dickce. Clearly Wade couldn't expect much sympathy from his mother. Nor could poor Benjy, An'gel decided. She felt sad for the young man. What a tragedy for him to lose his mother at his age, and in such a terrible fashion.

An'gel also wondered what Kanesha would make of Rosabelle. Should she try to talk to the deputy herself, give her a little of Rosabelle's history, before Kanesha questioned her old friend? She thought about that for a moment before she concluded it was a bad idea. Kanesha was smart. It wouldn't take her long to figure out exactly what she was dealing with in Rosabelle Sultan.

An'gel couldn't think of anything else to say to Rosabelle now, and evidently Dickce couldn't either. Rosabelle didn't speak again and instead sat staring at her hands and picking at something on her dress.

The silence lengthened, and An'gel wondered impatiently how long it would be before Kanesha came to talk to her, Dickce, and Rosabelle. The giddiness she'd experienced just moments ago had passed, and now she felt her hunger more keenly. She remembered the tray of food Dickce had been bringing to their guests, but the tray was sitting on a table in the hall. Perhaps she should retrieve it and take it to the library. She should probably ask Clementine to make coffee or hot tea to offer everyone. Something hot and sweet would be good for all of them about now.

Before she could act on these thoughts, Kanesha entered the room. She closed the door behind her and then stopped only a couple of paces into the room.

"Miss An'gel, could I speak to you for a moment?" She indicated with a nod that An'gel should join her.

"Certainly." An'gel rose from the sofa and walked over to the deputy. Kanesha's gloomy expression made her nervous. *What else could have happened?* she wondered.

"I wanted to let you know that the body has been removed," Kanesha said. "I'll be talking to the family in a moment, but first I wanted to ask you something."

"Of course," An'gel said. "What is it?"

"Is there any reason for Vaseline to be all over the banister?"

CHAPTER 9

For a moment An'gel wasn't sure she had heard correctly. "Vaseline?" She shook her head. "No, no earthly reason that I can imagine."

"That's what I thought." Kanesha's mouth set in a grim line. "One of the techs found it moments after the body was taken away. I'm betting there's also residue on the hands from where she clutched at the banister to keep from falling."

An'gel felt sick to her stomach at the mental image. She could see Marla Stephens make a frantic grab for the banister when she first started to slip. Her hands encounter the Vaseline and slide right off, and the momentum of that desperate reach further unbalance her. So down she went, with nothing to break her fall except cold, unyielding marble.

"Miss An'gel," Kanesha said, her concern obvious, "how well do you know these people?"

"Not well at all," An'gel said, her throat suddenly dry.

She coughed. "Dickce and I have known Rosabelle since our college days. We were sorority sisters at Athena College. I never met any of her family, however, until today, when they all just showed up here. Rosabelle first, then the rest of them followed right behind her."

"Did you invite them here?"

An'gel shook her head. "No, Rosabelle came to us because she has a problem she wanted us to help her with. Her family turned up soon after because they're worried about her."

Kanesha frowned. "Can you tell me the nature of her problem?"

"I think you should ask Rosabelle about that yourself." An'gel nodded in the direction of the sofa. "Let me introduce you, and then Dickce and I will make a discreet withdrawal so you can talk to her alone."

An'gel turned and approached the couch. "Rosabelle, this is Chief Deputy Kanesha Berry from the sheriff's department. She will be in charge of the investigation, and she needs to talk to you." She turned to Kanesha. "This is Rosabelle Sultan, our old sorority sister."

"Ma'am." Kanesha inclined her head. "I know this is a distressing time for you and your family, but I'm afraid there are questions I need to ask you."

Rosabelle stared at the deputy, and for a moment An'gel feared her old friend was going to be rude. She recalled that, when they were younger, Rosabelle's attitudes about race hadn't been all that enlightened. She could only hope that in the intervening years Rosabelle had become more tolerant.

"Of course, Deputy," Rosabelle finally said. "I have much to tell you, and I can assure you that you'll have my complete cooperation."

"Then Dickce and I will leave you for now," An'gel said, greatly relieved. "If you need us, we'll be in the kitchen."

Dickce didn't say anything until she and An'gel reached the hall. "Do you think I should take the food I was bringing to the library right now?"

An'gel nodded. "While you do that, I'll get started on a pot of coffee. I'm sure everyone could use a hot drink." She glanced across the hall toward the library. The door stood open, and she could see a deputy she didn't recognize standing in profile inside the room.

Dickce picked up the tray and headed for the library. An'gel watched for a moment before turning down the hall toward the kitchen.

Diesel greeted her with reproachful warbles when she stepped inside. She scratched his head, and the warbles turned into purrs.

"He's been talking like that for five minutes, I swear," Clementine said as she wiped her hands on a dishcloth. "What's all the noise I keep hearing out there? I've been too busy to come take a look-see. Besides, I thought I'd best keep the cat in here out of the way."

Diesel rubbed himself against An'gel's legs while she gave the housekeeper a quick rundown of the events of the past hour. Clementine's eyes widened, and she started shaking her head as if in disbelief. When An'gel concluded her summary, Clementine closed her eyes for a moment. An'gel could see her lips moving and figured Clementine was praying.

An'gel closed her own eyes and did the same, mentally sending a plea heavenward for patience, understanding, and protection. Beside her Diesel had stilled, and when she opened her eyes and glanced at him, he had his head down, too. She couldn't decide whether the cat was also praying, imitating her behavior, or simply examining his front paws.

Then An'gel noticed an ant crawling across the floor. Diesel appeared intent on stalking it, so she left him to it while she got busy making enough coffee for nine people. She ate three cookies during the time it took for the machine to brew. Clementine helped by assembling cups and saucers, spoons and sweeteners, and a pitcher of half-and-half.

All the while Diesel toyed with the ant, until it finally escaped under a cabinet. The cat scratched at the woodwork until An'gel told him to stop. He turned his head in her direction and uttered a reproachful-sounding warble, and An'gel and Clementine exchanged amused glances. *He really is a wonderful tonic when things are stressful*, An'gel thought.

Clementine wheeled out the wooden serving cart, and An'gel poured the coffee into a large carafe. "Would you go ahead and make another pot?" she said to Clementine. "I'm sure we'll be wanting more before too long." She looked down at Diesel, who had climbed into the bottom shelf of the cart. He was so large he barely fit. His long plume of a tail hung out one end and his head the other.

"I really think you ought to stay here with Clementine. You'll just be in the way of all that's going on outside the kitchen."

Cat and woman stared at each other for a moment.

An'gel put on a stern expression. "Come now, Diesel, be a good boy, and get out of there."

Diesel chirped three times but remained where he was.

An'gel debated whether she should attempt to pull him out. She didn't think he would try to scratch or bite, but she was reluctant to remove him forcibly. She really didn't feel like getting down on her knees to wrestle the cat loose, and she certainly wasn't going to ask Clementine to do it. Their knees were far too old for such antics, she reflected wryly.

"Oh, very well." An'gel glanced at Clementine, who was smiling broadly. "I guess he's going with me." She took hold of the cart and headed for the door. "I'll be back in a few minutes for the second pot."

Diesel's tail stuck out of the back of the cart and swished against her legs as An'gel pushed forward slowly. *Good thing I'm not ticklish there*, she thought.

When they reached the library, the young deputy at the door moved aside to let her pass. He glanced down at the cat and grinned, but he quickly sobered. An'gel nodded politely.

Inside she surveyed the room for a moment, struck by the silence broken only by the muted sounds of breathing. Maudine and Bernice occupied the single sofa, while Wade sat behind the large desk that dominated one part of the room. Juanita and Junior accounted for the other two chairs, and Dickce and Benjy huddled together in the window seat that overlooked the front lawn. No one spoke, and An'gel felt the tension.

Three of the four walls were covered nearly floor to ceiling with bookshelves. The Ducotes had been readers and book collectors, one generation after another. Windows in the two outside walls offered the only breaks, except for the fireplace, which shared a wall with the room next to it. Several small, elderly Axminster rugs dotted the floor.

An'gel wheeled the cart, with its double load of coffee and feline, to the area in front of the window seat. "I've brought coffee. I thought we could all use a hot drink. Please, come and help yourselves." She twisted the lid of the carafe and started pouring the liquid into cups.

Diesel climbed from his perch on the bottom shelf, stretched, and then jumped onto the window seat into the spot Dickce had vacated. He butted his head against Benjy's arm, and the young man rubbed the cat's head, his gaze averted from An'gel.

Maudine and Bernice crowded close and helped themselves to coffee. "Thank you." Maudine dumped three heaping spoons of sugar in her cup along with a dollop of the half-and-half. Bernice did the same, then both women retreated to their spots on the sofa.

Juanita and Junior came next. Juanita carried the cup she prepared to her uncle and then returned to the cart to pour her own.

"This is just what we need." The young woman smiled at An'gel. "We're all still in a state of shock over this terrible accident." She cut her eyes toward Benjy, still engrossed in stroking Diesel.

The young man seemed oblivious to what was going on around him, An'gel thought. She felt sorry for him. She wondered whether anyone besides Dickce had made any effort to comfort him over the death of his mother.

Dickce poured coffee and added a couple of spoons of sugar, then enough half-and-half to turn the brew light brown. "Here, Benjy, you should drink this." She held the cup out to the young man, and he stared up at her.

An'gel wondered whether he had taken in what Dickce said. He nodded and accepted the cup. Diesel stuck his nose near the coffee, and Benjy smiled briefly. "I don't think this would be good for you, kitty." He sipped while the cat watched closely.

An'gel and Dickce took their own cups and stepped away from the window toward the inside corner of the front wall.

"Has anyone been talking?" An'gel asked.

Dickce shook her head. "Not at all. It seems strange to me, but maybe having the deputy in here with them has put them off." She nodded in the direction of the young man at the door.

"Clementine is making another pot of coffee," An'gel said. "I'll go back in a moment to see if it's ready." She drained her cup.

Kanesha Berry strode into the room. All heads swung in her direction, and An'gel tensed as the deputy prepared to speak.

"Folks, my name is Kanesha Berry, and I'm the chief deputy in the Athena County Sheriff's Department. I'll be in charge of the investigation, and I'm going to need to ask you all some questions. I hope you'll bear with me, because this is going to take some time. I know you are all distressed by what has happened, and I'm sorry for your loss." She paused a moment to glance around the room. "I must inform you, also, that we are treating this as a suspicious death."

Wade rose from his chair behind the desk, the shock evident on his face. An'gel feared that he would faint, the way he was swaying on his feet. "Suspicious? Do you mean you think this was deliberate and not an accident?"

"That's what we have to determine, sir," Kanesha replied.

"If it wasn't an accident," Junior said, his expression thoughtful, "then that means one of us is a murderer."

An'gel was startled by a shriek. She turned in time to see Maudine topple off the sofa in a dead faint.

CHAPTER 10

Junior scrambled out of his chair to kneel by his mother. Maudine lay on her right side, moaning.

An'gel noted with relief that Maudine somehow managed to miss the low table with the Sèvres vase in front of the sofa. The vase was a souvenir of her grandmother's honeymoon in Europe in 1900. Then she felt a bit ashamed of herself for worrying more about the vase than about Maudine—although she suspected Maudine of deliberately staging the incident. She *was* Rosabelle's daughter, after all.

"Mother, are you okay?" Junior grabbed his mother's left arm and began chafing her wrist.

As An'gel watched, Maudine's eyelids fluttered, and she moaned yet again. Her eyes opened and focused on her son's face. "What happened?"

Juanita appeared beside Maudine's head. "You fainted, Aunt Maud. Come now, Junior and I will help you up, and you can sit on the sofa while someone brings you water."

Kanesha's young subordinate, whose name An'gel still didn't know, responded to a signal from the chief deputy and came forward to assist. Juanita smiled and stood back. The deputy slipped his hands under Maudine's right shoulder while Junior pulled his mother into a sitting position on the floor.

Taking the hint about the water, An'gel started toward the door, but Dickce darted out ahead of her. An'gel turned back in time to see Junior and the deputy lift Maudine and set her on the sofa.

Junior muttered "thank you" to the deputy, who stepped back. Junior continued to pat his mother's hands and stare at her face. "Come on, Mother, everything will be okay. I didn't mean to frighten you with what I said. I wasn't thinking."

"Do you think I should call a doctor?" An'gel asked Kanesha. She thought she spoke quietly enough that no one else could hear, but Juanita came over, evidently in response to her question.

"My aunt has these little *spells* occasionally. There's no need to call a doctor. She'll be right as rain in a few minutes." Juanita winked. "I'll keep an eye on her, of course."

"Thank you, my dear," An'gel said, relieved. "Deputy Berry, this is Rosabelle's granddaughter, Juanita Cameron. Miss Cameron is a registered nurse."

"It's fortunate you're here, then," Kanesha said. "If you need any more medical assistance, though, just ask the deputy there to call."

"Thank you, Deputy Berry. I'm sure it won't be necessary, though," Juanita said. She returned to stand by her mother. An'gel thought Bernice looked a bit peaky herself, but evidently she wasn't the fainting type, unlike her sister.

"As I was saying earlier," Kanesha said, claiming the attention of the group, "I'm going to need to meet with each one of you in turn. Please remain in this room until that time."

An'gel was surprised there were no objections. She fully expected Rosabelle's family to make a fuss, but perhaps they were all still subdued by the tragedy of the occasion.

Dickce returned with a glass of water and a wet cloth. She handed them over to Juanita, who began ministering to her aunt. Dickce went back to the window seat, where Benjy and Diesel sat. An'gel could tell from her sister's actions that Dickce was concerned about the young man. She was pleased that someone was paying attention to the poor boy.

"Miss An'gel, I'd like to start with you, if you don't mind," Kanesha said.

"Certainly," An'gel replied and preceded the deputy from the room.

Kanesha didn't speak again until she and An'gel were alone in the front parlor. "I asked Mrs. Sultan to move to your study. One of my deputies is with her."

"That's fine." An'gel went to the sofa and sat. Kanesha took a chair opposite.

"Two deputies are upstairs right now, searching for the source of the Vaseline. That's why I want to keep everyone downstairs for a while." Kanesha shook her head. "I sure am sorry to put you and Miss Dickce through all this, but it has to be done."

"You're not the reason behind what's happened here," An'gel said with a slight smile. "Rosabelle is. Of course you have to search. I expected it. I think you'll find that the Vaseline came from either my bathroom or my sister's. Unless the perpetrator is not too bright."

"I wouldn't be surprised either way. You wouldn't believe some of the stupid things criminals do that make it easy to catch them." Kanesha pulled out a notebook and pen. "Now, if you don't mind, can you give me a rundown on what happened since Mrs. Sultan arrived this afternoon?"

Heavens, was it only this afternoon that they all descended upon us? An'gel took a moment to organize her thoughts before she launched into her summary of events. "Dickce and I were sitting here in the front parlor, enjoying the quiet, until I heard a car pull up out front . . ."

Kanesha occasionally jotted something down as An'gel talked but did not interrupt the narrative with questions. When An'gel finished, Kanesha thanked her and glanced over her notes.

"After Mrs. Sultan and her family members began arriving, neither you nor your sister went upstairs, except to show them to their rooms. Is that correct?"

An'gel thought for a moment. "Yes, that's correct."

"That means that Mrs. Sultan, her two daughters, her granddaughter, and her son and daughter-in-law were all upstairs for a period of time without you or Miss Dickce." When An'gel nodded, Kanesha continued, "How long do you estimate they were upstairs on their own, so to speak?"

"Let me see." An'gel frowned. "Fifteen or twenty minutes, I reckon. Rosabelle was up there longer, more like thirty to forty minutes."

"Did Mr. Pittman or Benjy Stephens have an opportunity to go upstairs that you're aware of?"

"No, I'm pretty sure they didn't. Dickce took Mr. Pittman out to the garage apartment, where they found Benjy Stephens." She paused as a thought struck her. "I suppose it's possible that Benjy could have entered the house and then returned to the garage apartment before Dickce and Mr. Pittman found him there. I don't think it's likely, though."

"Thanks," Kanesha said. She consulted her notebook again. "I want to get another sequence fixed in my mind. When you came into the front parlor with the tea, you were accompanied by Mr. Pittman and Mr. Stephens. You found Mrs. Pittman and Mrs. Cameron already here. Is that correct?"

"Yes," An'gel said. "I have no idea how long they'd been here, though. At least a couple of minutes, at a guess, because Mrs. Pittman was examining that vase and commenting on it to her sister." She pointed to the Ming Dynasty piece. She didn't think it necessary to repeat Maudine's catty remark, nor her own comeback.

"How long was it after you came into the room that Mr. Thurmond joined you?"

"No more than five minutes," An'gel said.

"That left Mrs. Sultan, Miss Cameron, and Ms. Stephens the only ones upstairs at that point." Kanesha tapped the notebook with her pen.

"Then the question has to be, when did someone put water on the stairs and Vaseline on the banister?" An'gel said.

Kanesha nodded. "I'm thinking it was most likely done either before any of them came downstairs, or between the time Mrs. Pittman, Mrs. Cameron, and Mr. Thurmond came down and when Ms. Stephens fell."

An'gel pondered that a moment. "I suppose Mr. Thurmond *could* have done it on his way downstairs." She shrugged. "But he wouldn't have had much time, unless his sisters had come down several minutes before him. He would have had to use a container for the water and then gotten rid of the Vaseline and cleaned off his hands before he came into the parlor." She paused. "I think I would have noticed if he had been wiping his hands or if they had been visibly greasy."

"Exactly what I was thinking." Kanesha set her notebook and pen down on the table near her chair. "We really need to find that Vaseline and whatever was used to hold the water."

"That latter bit may be tough," An'gel said. "There are a number of vases upstairs in the hall and in the bedrooms, not to mention cups in the bathroom cabinets for guests to use. Dickce and I also have cups in our bathrooms."

"Are they the disposable kind?"

"In the guest rooms, yes," An'gel said. "Dickce and I have glasses, actually, not cups."

"So we could be looking for a disposable cup," Kanesha said. "Or possibly two, since the person responsible for this might have put the Vaseline into one, rather than take the entire container to the banister and then have to return it."

"I hadn't thought of that," An'gel said. Kanesha was so sharp, she thought. *I'm sure she'll get this sorted out as quickly as possible.*

"How big are the cups?" Kanesha asked. "Would one of them hold enough water to make small puddles on a couple of stairs? If not, something larger would have been used."

"They're not that big," An'gel said. "They're about big enough for a mouthful of water, to rinse out toothpaste or take a pill. No more than that."

"Not big enough then for the amount of water needed, I'm thinking. At least not without more than one trip, and I don't think that's likely."

An'gel nodded. "Must be something else." She thought for a moment. "There are no fresh flowers upstairs, so it wouldn't be a vase with water already in it."

Kanesha added that information to her notebook. Then she looked up and frowned. "This is highly irregular."

"What do you mean?" The remark confused An'gel.

"Talking over the case with you like this." Kanesha sighed. "By rights I should consider both you and Miss Dickce suspects, and I wouldn't be talking like this with a suspect." She shrugged. "No way in the world, though, that I'd ever think you and Miss Dickce deliberately injured a guest in your home."

An'gel understood the chief deputy's dilemma and appreciated the consideration for her and Dickce. She did not want Kanesha to get in any trouble, however, for not following proper procedure.

"Thank you for that," she said lightly. "Dickce and I know you have a job to do, and it's important to do it right. We'll go along with whatever you need."

"Thank you," Kanesha said. "That brings me to one final question I have for you." She paused. "Are you willing to let these people continue to stay with you and your sister until the investigation is complete?"

CHAPTER 11

Dickce wished she could have gone with An'gel and Kanesha. She wanted to be doing something instead of just sitting here in the window seat. Her curiosity about what An'gel and Kanesha were discussing was making her restless, she realized, along with the fact that she was stuck in a roomful of people she had met for the first time within the past few hours.

Her gaze fell on the young man beside her, and her fidgeting ceased. Benjy had lost his mother, violently, less than an hour ago. Dickce was glad Diesel was here to comfort the boy, because none of Rosabelle's family had paid any attention to him.

Except Juanita, Dickce reminded herself. Rosabelle's granddaughter appeared to have a kind heart, but now Juanita's attention was focused on her mother and her aunt. Dickce glanced over at the sisters, and to her mind, they both still looked a bit peaky. Wade Thurmond remained behind the desk, staring into space. Junior Pittman squirmed in his chair while he watched his mother.

Dickce wanted to reach out to Benjy but realized that, under the watchful eye of the young deputy, it probably wasn't a good idea right now. Besides, Benjy might prefer Diesel to a strange elderly woman like herself.

Elderly. Dickce suppressed a shudder. She hated thinking of herself that way. Most days she felt fifty, maybe fifty-five tops. The about-to-be eighty-year-old woman who stared back at her in the mirror in the mornings had to be someone else.

Dickce continued to sit in the window seat with Benjy and Diesel and watched as, one after another, Rosabelle's daughters, son, and grandchildren were called out of the room to talk to Kanesha. Finally, only she and Benjy, along with the cat, remained.

All this time—and Dickce estimated that at least an hour had passed since An'gel left with Kanesha—Benjy had given little indication he was aware of his surroundings, other than to stroke the cat's head. Dickce was amazed by Diesel's patience. He lay with his head, chest, and front legs in Benjy's lap the whole time. He purred on and off, and seemed content to remain with the boy.

When the deputy came to take Benjy across the hall to the parlor, the young man rose after gently sliding Diesel from his lap. "You stay here, kitty." He gave the cat's head one last stroke and followed the deputy from the room.

Diesel stood and stretched on the window seat. He turned to look at Dickce, his head nearly on level with hers. She touched a finger to his nose. He warbled, and she told him, "It won't be much longer, and we'll be out of here. Better settle down with me until it's my turn to talk to Kanesha."

The cat warbled again and arranged himself so that his head lay against her thigh and the rest of him spread out to cover the remainder of the window seat. He closed his eyes, and Dickce thought he went to sleep right away. She leaned back and stared out the window, but her gaze focused inward.

For the past hour Dickce had purposely let her mind flit around, like a bee in a field of clover, because she really didn't want to think about the death of Marla Stephens. Alone in the room now, except for the deputy who had resumed his position by the door, she found she could no longer keep the tragic event out of her mind.

The premeditation disturbed her. The fact that someone had poured water on the stairs with the intention of causing an accident—fatal as it turned out—sickened her. Suddenly she wished they were all out of the house and had never come in the first place. An'gel should have sent Rosabelle packing. *She should never have let her in the door,* Dickce thought. *But no, Sister* had *to play the great and generous lady to an old friend in need. Bet Sister's regretting it now.* She allowed herself a small, spiteful grin before her thoughts shifted inevitably back to the crime.

Crime. The word resonated in her head for a moment. Yes, it was a crime. Murder, in fact. There was no way that water got on the stairs by accident.

Dickce shivered. Which member of Rosabelle's family hated her enough to want to kill her? None of them, except Juanita and perhaps Junior, had any manners to speak of, but being rude didn't identify a person as a murderer.

Junior and Benjy were out of the running, she decided. Neither of them had an opportunity to put water on the stairs. Junior had meant to help his mother and aunt with their bags, but there had been no time. He and Benjy had gone straight to the parlor with An'gel and remained there until both Dickce and An'gel witnessed the final moments of Marla Stephens's fall.

Dickce felt pleased by what she determined was proof of innocence in Benjy's case. She couldn't explain why, but she felt drawn to the boy despite his appearance. *Why would anyone want rings in his eyebrows?* Rebellion, she supposed, happy that part of her life was over long ago. She glanced down at the cat beside her. Diesel obviously sensed goodness in Benjy as well; otherwise, he wouldn't have taken so quickly to him. The cat seemed to be an excellent judge of character, and Dickce decided she would trust the cat's instincts and her own.

The deputy interrupted her reverie with a cough. "Miss Ducote, Chief Deputy Berry would like you to join her in the other room now."

Dickce smiled at the earnest expression. "I'm ready, Deputy," she said as she stood. Diesel stretched again before he jumped to the floor to follow her.

The deputy escorted her and the cat across the hall to the parlor and opened the door for them. Dickce thought Diesel might go in search of Benjy or head to the kitchen, but he came into the parlor with her.

Dickce wasn't surprised to see An'gel ensconced on the sofa. She wondered whether her sister had been there the entire time Kanesha was interviewing Rosabelle's family. *Trust An'gel to be in the middle of it all*, she thought with a tinge of resentment.

Kanesha stood. "Miss Dickce, I'm sorry I had to leave you for last. I know it must have been pretty tedious having to wait for so long." She glanced down at Diesel. "I'm assuming you had company, though."

Dickce smiled. "Yes, Diesel was there the whole time."

She took a seat beside her sister. The cat climbed up into the space between them and arranged himself across both their laps. "Have you been here all along?"

An'gel shook her head. "No, of course not. Kanesha called me back in just now so the three of us could talk."

"First," Kanesha said, "I'd like Miss Dickce to take me through what happened this afternoon from her perspective." She flipped to a new page in her notebook.

Dickce took a moment to marshal her thoughts. "It all started when An'gel made the mistake of letting Rosabelle in the house." She cut a sideways glance at her sister. She could see that An'gel was not amused. Dickce was tempted to stick out her tongue, but she knew this was a serious matter. She focused on complying with the chief deputy's request.

"Thank you," Kanesha said when Dickce finished. "Now, I'd like to clarify a point or two. To your knowledge, did either Mr. Pittman or Mr. Stephens have an opportunity to go upstairs today?"

"I was thinking about that while I was waiting," Dickce said. "I'm sure that neither of them did. I took Junior Pittman out to the garage apartment while An'gel took his aunt, his mother, and his cousin upstairs. He was with me the entire time until we came back to the house. That's when he accompanied An'gel to the parlor."

"And Mr. Stephens?" Kanesha prompted.

"Mr. Pittman and I found him in the garage apartment. I don't see any way he could have gotten into the house without our knowing it. He came with Junior and me into the kitchen, and then he went with An'gel and Junior to the parlor."

"Thank you, ma'am," Kanesha said. She closed the notebook and put it aside on the table near her chair. "At this point I'm reasonably certain we can rule out Mr. Pittman and Mr. Stephens as being responsible for what happened. And the two of you, of course." Kanesha smiled briefly.

Dickce was pleased to hear that Kanesha didn't regard Benjy as a suspect. Or Junior either, she thought. He seemed like a nice young man.

Kanesha continued, "Earlier I asked Miss An'gel how she felt about allowing your guests to remain here. We discussed the situation, and I told her I would arrange for them to be accommodated at one of the hotels in the area."

"I said I thought it best to keep them all here," An'gel said.

"Why on earth?" Dickce asked. She wasn't really surprised, but she wanted to hear her sister's reasoning.

"It will be easier for us to keep an eye on Rosabelle," An'gel said, her tone firm. "I am not happy harboring a murderer in this house, but I don't think he or she will try again as long as they're here. I would fear for Rosabelle's safety if they moved into a hotel."

And out of your control, Dickce thought somewhat snidely. Except that An'gel hadn't been able to stop the killer the first time.

"Besides," An'gel said, her gaze narrowing as she looked at Dickce, "I've arranged with Kanesha to hire off-duty deputies to remain in the house with us for a few days until the case is solved."

"What a good idea," Dickce replied. "Whoever arranged that nasty fall for Rosabelle will probably think twice about trying something funny with an officer of the law in the house."

"I should certainly hope so." An'gel gave an unladylike snort. She turned to Kanesha. "Is there anything else you need from us right now?"

"No, ma'am," Kanesha said. "I need to check on the status of the evidence search, and as soon as it's done, I will let your guests go to their rooms." She glanced at her watch. "I imagine you'll be ready to have dinner before long. It's nearly seven o'clock."

"Goodness, yes," Dickce said. Now that she thought about food, she realized she was ravenous. Lunch was a long time ago, and she had eaten only a few bites of the snacks she took to the library for Rosabelle's family members. "I should go see how Clementine's getting along. I'm sure she's wondering when we're going to serve dinner." She slid Diesel gently off her lap and stood. The cat chirped in protest at being disturbed, but An'gel patted his head to reassure him.

In the hall Dickce remembered the serving cart and food tray in the library. She decided she might as well retrieve them and take them to the kitchen. She found Rosabelle and her family in the room, watched over by the same young deputy. She was slightly surprised but then realized that this room was larger and more comfortable than the office where each person was sent after the interview with Kanesha.

Dickce explained her errand to the deputy, and he nodded. Then Dickce addressed the assembled guests. "I'm about to go check on dinner. I'm sure it won't be long before we're able to eat. For whoever might be hungry," she said.

Rosabelle nodded, and Dickce could see interest in the faces of several others. She smiled at them before she picked up the food tray and placed it on the middle shelf of the serving cart. As she did so, she spotted something odd.

She straightened, her heart beating faster as the implications of what she found sank in. Her hands trembled as she grasped the cart's handle and began to wheel it out of the room. She headed back across the hall to the parlor. The moment she had the cart and its contents far enough inside, she closed the door behind her.

An'gel and Kanesha glanced up from their conversation, and Dickce could see they were startled by her sudden entrance.

"There's something here you need to see," she said.

CHAPTER 12

"What did you find?"

Dickce ignored An'gel's imperious tone. "Come see for yourself."

Kanesha reached the cart while An'gel was still rising from the sofa. "Show me, please," she said, her tone firm.

Dickce pointed to the food tray. "Look under that."

Kanesha squatted beside the cart and used her pen to lift the paper towel Dickce indicated. Beneath it was a plastic tube labeled *Vaseline*.

An'gel approached and peered over Kanesha's shoulder. "Brazen," she said.

"Imagine the nerve it took to keep that on your person and then somehow manage to drop it on the tray when nobody was looking." Dickce shook her head. "It makes my blood run cold."

Kanesha stood and pulled out her cell phone. She stepped away from the cart and punched in a number. "Bates, I'm in the parlor. Miss Dickce found something we need to bag, and I don't have what I need." She paused. "Right. Thanks." She ended the call and put away her phone.

"I didn't touch it," Dickce said. "I left it the way I found it, except of course for moving the tray onto the cart."

Kanesha nodded. "Yes, ma'am. About the paper towel. I don't see any others here. Where do you think it came from?"

"There's a roll in each of the bathrooms upstairs," An'gel replied.

"In the cupboard under the sink," Dickce added.

"Thank you, that's helpful." Kanesha thought for a moment. "Did either of you have a tube like that upstairs in your rooms? Or was there one in any of the guest rooms or bathrooms?"

"I have one of those little containers of it in my bathroom. You know, the kind with the lid?" Dickce said. "I don't recall putting any in the guest areas." She glanced at her sister. "Did you?"

An'gel shook her head. "To my knowledge there wasn't any in the guest rooms. Like my sister, though, I have a container in my bathroom."

"Thank you," Kanesha said. She looked toward the door. "Ladies, if you don't mind stepping back, Deputy Bates will take care of this now."

Bates nodded at Dickce and An'gel as they moved away from the serving cart. "Evening, ladies."

Dickce watched with great interest as Bates pulled on plastic gloves. He pulled out a pair of mid-sized tweezers and proceeded to put the tube and the paper towel in separate plastic evidence bags.

"Are you going to dust the cart for fingerprints?" Dickce hoped Bates would do it so she could watch. She felt guilty even thinking it, but it was a bit thrilling to be this close to an actual investigation.

"No, ma'am," Bates said. "We wouldn't gain any real helpful information, because probably every one of you touched the cart today. We will be testing the tube and the paper towel, of course, but they'll have to go to the state crime lab."

"Surely you didn't think he was going to whip out his fingerprint kit and do it right here?" An'gel glared at Dickce. "You need to stop watching all those forensic shows on television. You're getting positively morbid about such things."

Well, someone is obviously tired and cranky, Dickce thought. An'gel always got this way when she wasn't in control of a situation. Dickce once again had the urge to stick her tongue out at her sister but knew she would be embarrassed if either of the deputies saw her do it.

Instead she settled for a tart rejoinder. "What I watch is certainly more educational than those trashy reality shows about trashy people."

An'gel drew back at that, and Dickce would have sworn for a moment that her sister started to blush. But decades of training asserted itself, and An'gel maintained her composure.

"Excuse me, ladies," Kanesha said. "I think we are done here for the moment. I'll just go across the hall to speak with your guests, and then we will be leaving. Except, of course, for the deputy, who will remain here until he can be relieved by an off-duty deputy."

"Thank you," An'gel said. "I know I will certainly rest easier tonight knowing that one of your men is on guard here."

Kanesha nodded before she headed for the door. Bates

hesitated a moment before he followed his boss, and in that moment, Dickce thought he winked at her.

She wanted to giggle. He was such an attractive man. Broad-shouldered with a trim waist, he had the chiseled face of a movie star. She had heard an interesting rumor about him and Stewart Delacorte recently. She wondered if it was true, and if it was, she was happy for Stewart because he deserved a nice man.

"If you're done mooning over that deputy," An'gel said, "let's get this out to the kitchen and see about helping Clementine with dinner." She grabbed the cart handles and started pushing.

This time Dickce did stick out her tongue—at her sister's retreating back.

Maudine and Bernice were the first of the guests to appear at the dining room table. Dickce thought cynically there probably wasn't much that would put Maudine off her food. The avid gleam in her eyes as Maudine surveyed the table told Dickce she was probably right. Dickce had to admit, however, that a table full of Clementine's wonderful Southern cooking was a sight to gladden anyone's eye. *Anyone who isn't a health nut*, she amended.

An'gel invited them to sit, and moments later, Wade and Junior came in. They took chairs opposite the women. An'gel sat at the head of the table, her usual place, while Dickce decided for once to sit at the foot, instead of at An'gel's right. Three places remained unclaimed.

Dickce wondered whether An'gel would insist on the usual saying of grace before anyone was allowed to eat. Then she noticed that Maudine and Wade were already helping themselves to the food. Dickce caught An'gel's eye and shrugged. She could tell her sister wasn't pleased, but given their experiences with these people so far, she thought An'gel shouldn't be surprised by the lack of manners at the dinner table.

Juanita entered the dining room and went straight to An'gel. "Miss Ducote, Grandmother asked me to express her regrets, but she doesn't feel well and really isn't up to sitting down to dinner. Would it be okay if I take a plate up to her?"

"Of course, my dear." An'gel actually looked relieved, Dickce thought. She certainly was, because she hadn't relished the idea of listening to Rosabelle carry on over the dinner table. Everyone else seemed relieved as well, Dickce would have been willing to bet.

Juanita prepared a plate of chicken and vegetables for her grandmother while An'gel went to find a bed tray for her.

"Thank you," the young woman said when An'gel returned. "I'll take this up and be back down shortly for my own dinner."

Dickce had picked up her fork, ready to eat, when she realized there was still one person unaccounted for. Benjy was missing. She hesitated but decided after brief thought that he would turn up soon. A boy his age was always hungry, and he wouldn't miss a meal.

Ten minutes later, when Benjy still hadn't turned up, Dickce began to worry. There was no conversation at the table, other than the "would you pass the corn" variety. Juanita had rejoined them, but no one else seemed to notice that Benjy wasn't there.

"Mr. Pittman," Dickce said, "do you know why Benjy hasn't come to dinner?"

Junior looked up from his plate with a frown. "Oh, he said he wasn't hungry. I tried to get him to come, but he wouldn't." He returned his attention to his food.

Dickce glanced at her sister. She could tell An'gel was concerned, too. Dickce decided that she would go check on Benjy. She hadn't meant to forget about him, but until now there hadn't been a chance to talk to him.

"Excuse me," Dickce said as she pushed back her chair and stood.

An'gel nodded, as if giving permission for her to leave the table, and Dickce shrugged. She was going to check on that young man whether An'gel approved or not.

The kitchen was empty. Clementine had gone home, and An'gel had insisted that Diesel be put upstairs in her bedroom during dinner. Dickce knew the cat was not happy being isolated like that, but she supposed An'gel was right. They weren't used to having an animal begging for food while they ate, and An'gel certainly wouldn't allow it with guests at the table.

The evening sun hung low in the sky as Dickce stepped outside. The heat and humidity hadn't abated with the approach of darkness, and Dickce was glowing with perspiration by the time she reached the door to the garage apartment.

She opened the door and stepped inside. "Benjy, is it okay for me to come up? It's Dickce Ducote."

For a moment she thought the apartment must be empty, then she heard a familiar chirping.

What on earth is Diesel doing here? she thought, startled.

Benjy appeared at the head of the stairs with the cat beside him. "Sure, you can come up here if you want to." He turned and moved away, but Diesel remained where he was.

"How did you get here, you rascal?" Dickce tapped the cat on the head when she reached him.

"I heard something scratching at the door downstairs a

little while ago," Benjy said, his tone defensive. "When I went down there, I found him trying to pull the door open. He had one paw in the crack, but that door kinda sticks, and he couldn't budge it."

Dickce had to laugh at the mental image. "Charlie—that's his owner, Charlie Harris—told us Diesel could open doors on his own, but I don't think I really believed him until now. He wouldn't have had much trouble getting out of An'gel's room, or out the back door, I guess, because those doors are in better shape."

Diesel warbled several times, as if he knew he was being discussed. Benjy smiled slightly as he indicated a chair. "He sure is one smart cat. Please sit."

Dickce noted that Benjy waited until she was seated before he plopped on the couch across from her. Diesel joined him, his head butting the young man's upper arm. Benjy put his arm around the cat and hugged him close. Diesel started purring.

"I'm glad he found his way to you," Dickce said. "He always seems to know when someone needs a little comfort."

"I'm okay," Benjy muttered and ducked his head.

Dickce waited a moment, but he didn't continue. "I was a little concerned when you didn't join us for dinner. I know you must be terribly upset by what's happened, but you need to keep up your strength. Clementine is a wonderful cook, and hot food will help you feel better."

"Miss Clementine gave me some food." Benjy pointed toward the table across the room. "I just didn't feel like being in the same room with the Wart and his family."

Dickce glanced over at the table. She could see a plate, cutlery, napkin, and glass. Plate and glass were empty. Knowing Clementine, that plate had been heaped with food.

Unless Benjy had fed most of it to Diesel—and she sincerely hoped he hadn't, because the cat would undoubtedly get sick—he had eaten well.

Dickce wasn't quite sure what to say next. Benjy was obviously distressed, but he was a stranger, and she didn't know what would help him the most. Instead, she asked him the first thing that popped into her head.

"Benjy, how old are you?"

He glanced up, obviously startled. "I was nineteen in June. What's that got to do with anything?"

"I just wondered," Dickce said. She had figured his age correctly, but she thought he sometimes seemed young for nineteen. "I'm sorry about your mother."

To her dismay, he burst into tears. Diesel warbled anxiously, and for a moment Dickce didn't know what to do. Then she got up from her chair and sat on the sofa by Benjy and pulled him into her arms. He sobbed on her shoulder while she held him and Diesel rubbed his head against the boy's side.

CHAPTER 13

After a few minutes the storm of tears abated, and Dickce could feel Benjy trying gently to pull away. She released him, and he rose on unsteady legs to make his way to the sink in the kitchen area. Diesel followed him and twined himself around the young man's legs. Benjy splashed his face with water, dried off with paper towels, then blew his nose twice.

Dickce moved back to the chair to allow Benjy his space on the sofa when he returned. He smiled shyly at her. "Sorry about that," he said. "Guess I kinda freaked for a minute."

"No need to apologize," Dickce replied. Given the circumstances, she would have been surprised if the boy hadn't broken down.

Diesel climbed onto the sofa beside Benjy, who rubbed the cat's head and back. "You're such a sweet kitty." He looked up at Dickce. "He really seems concerned. Isn't that funny?"

"He has a big heart," Dickce said. Her throat tightened as she examined Benjy. With his red nose and pink eyes, he looked vulnerable and much younger than nineteen. He also looked a little bit lost right now. She wondered whether he had any family besides his mother. She hesitated to ask, because it was really none of her business. She couldn't walk away now, however, and leave him on his own.

"I loved her," Benjy said, startling Dickce with the sorrowful tone of his words. "Even though she was rotten to me a lot of the time."

Dickce decided to venture the question she was burning to ask. "What about your father?"

"He walked out when I was two or three," Benjy said. "So it was just my mom and me until a few years ago. That's when she met the Wart."

"It doesn't sound like you think much of your stepfather," Dickce said.

Benjy shrugged. "He doesn't think much of me either. Couldn't wait to get me out of his house when they got married, so he sent me to boarding school in New York. I was stuck in that place for three years, but I graduated last year."

Dickce heard the pain and anger behind the pose of indifference. At a time in his life when Benjy needed a strong father figure, Wade Thurmond couldn't be bothered and shunted the boy off to boarding school. *Wart, indeed.* Dickce could think of a worse name for him. She also didn't think much of Marla for rejecting her son—because that was exactly what it amounted to—in favor of a new husband. That kind of woman disgusted her.

"So you're on your own now, other than your stepfather," Dickce said. *A stepfather who obviously isn't much interested in your welfare*, she added silently. She wondered if

Benjy would be left to fend for himself now that his mother was gone.

Benjy nodded.

He was obviously miserable and frightened, Dickce realized.

"I have friends in California," Benjy said. "I think one of them will let me move in with him. He has his own apartment, and I have a part-time job." He didn't sound happy about the prospect, Dickce thought.

"I didn't push her down the stairs," Benjy said out of the blue. "I hated her sometimes, but I wouldn't have done something like that." He stared at Dickce, his eyes imploring her to believe him.

"I know you didn't," Dickce said gently. "You never went upstairs."

"No, I didn't." Benjy's face cleared. "That deputy woman was pretty scary when she asked me questions. Sure made me feel guilty, even though I knew I hadn't done anything."

"She's tough and comes across as pretty intimidating," Dickce said. "I've known her since she was a little girl. She's smart, dedicated, and thorough. She'll find out who caused your mother to fall down the stairs, and that will be the end of it. She knows by now that you couldn't have done it."

Diesel warbled, and Benjy smiled. "Guess he agrees."

"He's known Kanesha for a few years, too." Dickce stood. "I'd better get back and help clear the table. Is there anything else you need?"

"No, ma'am," Benjy said. He rubbed Diesel's head. "Do you think it would be okay if he stayed here with me tonight? I don't think Junior will mind. He's an okay kind of guy."

"I imagine I'd have a hard time keeping him in the house." Dickce grinned. "He's made it pretty obvious that he wants to stay with you, at least for tonight. If you think of anything you need, you be sure to let me know. Or if you just need to talk to someone. Okay?"

"I will." Benjy smiled. "Thank you."

"You're quite welcome." Dickce wagged a finger at Diesel. "You be a good kitty, and I'll see you in the morning."

Diesel chirped in response, and Benjy laughed.

Smiling, Dickce walked down the stairs and into the sultry evening. She didn't particularly look forward to going back to the dining room. She'd had about enough of Rosabelle's family for one day, if not for a lifetime. Was it too much to hope that they would all have gone upstairs to their rooms by now?

~

An'gel was glad that Dickce went to check on Marla Stephens's son. She was worried about the boy herself, but since Dickce seemed to have established some sort of rapport with him, it was better that she dealt with him.

Even if it meant An'gel was now on her own with Rosabelle's family. She was heartily sick of the lot of them but, at the same time, determined to see this thing through. Marla's was the second violent death at Riverhill in less than a year and that was two too many. She wanted the murder solved and these people out of her house as soon as possible. The previous murder, which took place during a fundraiser for the Friends of the Library, had been resolved quickly. She prayed this one would be too.

There was not a morsel of food left by the time her guests finished their meals. An'gel reflected that at least it would make the cleanup easier. Before any of them left the table, however, An'gel had a few things to tell them.

"If I could have your attention for a moment," she said.

"I know you all must be tired and eager to get some sleep, and I suggest that you do so right away. I have arranged for a deputy to remain with us here in the house at all times until this dreadful situation is resolved. I'm sure we will all rest easier knowing that help is so close at hand." She paused for reactions to this news and was surprised that no one chose to comment. She continued, "Breakfast will be served at eight, and if you should need anything during the night, please let me or my sister know."

"I usually sleep until eight or nine," Maudine said with a frown. "Will I still be able to get breakfast?"

"If there is anything left after the others finish, certainly you will," An'gel replied in a pleasant tone. "The housekeeper, however, will not have time to prepare multiple breakfasts. I suggest you consider rising early enough to be downstairs at eight."

An'gel could see that Maudine was peeved at her response but did not protest further. An'gel rose. "If there are no other questions or requests, then I will bid you all good night."

Her guests muttered their good nights, and An'gel was not surprised that none of them volunteered to stay and help clear the table.

"Miss Cameron," An'gel said, "if you could stay a moment. I'd like to talk to you, if you don't mind."

Juanita, the last to exit, turned and came back toward the table. "Yes, ma'am, certainly."

"How is Rosabelle?" An'gel asked. "Is there anything she needs?"

"Grandmother is distressed, naturally," Juanita replied. "She is convinced that one of the family is trying to kill her, and I'm finding that hard to believe, even with what happened to Marla." She shuddered.

"That was no accident," An'gel said. "Rosabelle is right to be afraid, if she really was the intended target."

"I know you're right." Juanita hesitated before finishing her reply. "It's frightening to think that one of my relatives hates Grandmother so much."

"Do you have any idea who is behind this?"

Juanita shook her head. "I wouldn't have said any of them could be capable of this. I know my mother isn't. I know she's high-handed and rude, but she does love Grandmother in her own way." She paused. "At first I thought Grandmother was making all this up because she wanted attention. Ever since her husband died, she's been fretful. She's used to having a man around to cater to her, and let's face it, at her age, she's not likely to find another husband."

An'gel was struck by the young woman's insight into Rosabelle's character. Juanita evidently had few illusions about her grandmother.

Juanita stared hard at An'gel. "Miss Ducote, I'm really worried, and I have to confide in someone." She hesitated for a moment. "You're going to think I'm crazy, but I'm wondering whether my grandmother isn't responsible for Marla's accident."

CHAPTER 14

An'gel wasn't sure she had heard Juanita correctly. Then the import of the young woman's words sank in. "That's monstrous. Surely you don't think your grandmother is a murderer?"

Juanita's eyes widened, and she held up her hands as if to ward off a blow. "No, that's not what I meant at all. Please, let me explain."

"I surely hope you will," An'gel said. She pulled out a chair and sank into it. She felt her pulse racing from the shock.

"I'm so sorry if that upset you badly," Juanita said. "Can I get anything for you?"

An'gel shook her head. "No, I'll be fine. Please explain what you meant."

"First, let me say that I don't believe Grandmother would have intentionally harmed anyone." Juanita paused. "This is a difficult thing to say about my own grandmother, but I think she might have planned it so she could pretend to fall and continue with the charade that one of us was deliberately trying to harm her. She put the water on the stairs, but for some reason Marla got there first. And, well, the unthinkable happened."

An'gel felt the tension radiating from the young woman as Juanita awaited her response. She was in no rush to respond because she needed to choose her words carefully.

Perhaps bothered by the silence, Juanita spoke again. "I know it must sound like I think she's a terrible person, but I really don't. Grandmother is impulsive and doesn't always think things through. She's a bit like a child sometimes. She does whatever enters her head without considering the consequences."

An'gel had no trouble believing that part. Rosabelle had been exactly like that during their college days. An'gel and Dickce had helped the headstrong girl out of more than one scrape that resulted from lack of foresight. Age and experience apparently hadn't taught Rosabelle much, An'gel reflected sourly.

Even so, she balked at the notion of Rosabelle's having put water on the stairs so she could fake an accident. An'gel realized she had knowledge that could allay Juanita's fears, but she couldn't share it with the young woman. In An'gel's mind, the use of the Vaseline on the banister was proof of intent to kill. She could see that Rosabelle might put water on the stairs, but she wouldn't put the petroleum jelly on the banister. The risk would be too great.

An'gel knew she had to speak at this point. "I've known your grandmother for over sixty years, child. I can't argue with you over Rosabelle's need to be the center of attention all the time, because she has always been that way. I just don't happen to think that this was one of her stunts gone badly wrong." She paused to gauge Juanita's reaction.

The young woman looked relieved for a moment, but then the full implications of An'gel's statement appeared to sink in.

Juanita paled. "Then you think someone really *is* trying to kill Grandmother?" She groped for a chair and lowered herself into it.

"I'm afraid so." An'gel touched Juanita's arm lightly. "We have to protect her until Deputy Berry and her men get to the bottom of this."

Juanita shook her head, as if she was still in shock. "I almost wish this was one of Grandmother's little schemes for attention." Suddenly she stood. "If you'll excuse me, I think I'd better get upstairs right away and keep an eye on her." Without waiting for a response, she hurried from the room.

An'gel sat back in her chair and pondered the conversation. One possibility had struck her that she didn't want to bring up to Juanita. It was a terrible thought, but one that had to be faced.

What if Rosabelle was responsible for the water and the Vaseline? What if she had deliberately set a trap for one of her family members? Even Rosabelle, who blithely tended to ignore the consequences of her actions, would have had to realize her target could be seriously injured or die as a result.

An'gel didn't want to think her friend capable of such a terrible deed, but she had never been one to shy away from the truth, no matter how disturbing.

Dickce walked into the dining room and interrupted her reflections. "Sitting down on the job, I see. I don't suppose any of them volunteered to help clear away?"

"Do you *see* one of them helping?" An'gel got to her feet and started piling plates.

"Well, who put the fly in *your* mashed potatoes?" Dickce shook her head as she began to help her sister.

"Oh, don't mind me," An'gel said in a milder tone. "Tired and upset, that's all."

"I know." Dickce picked up her stack and headed for the kitchen. "These people are enough to make you want to put your head through a brick wall."

An'gel followed behind her. "We need to talk, but I am just too tired to do it now." She set her pile of dishes on the counter near the dishwasher. "Let's leave all this for the morning."

"I don't feel right leaving it for Clementine to have to deal with." Dickce opened the dishwasher and pulled the rack out. "You go on up to bed, and I'll handle this."

"You don't have to," An'gel said. "I talked to Clementine before she left, and she agreed we need extra help as long as Rosabelle and her family are here. She's going to get her granddaughter Antoinette to come. Antoinette isn't due back to college for another two weeks, and Clementine said she'd be glad of the money for schoolbooks."

"All right then." Dickce closed the dishwasher. "I wish I had half the energy that girl has. She makes that battery bunny look like he's walking through molasses."

"Being sixty years younger doesn't hurt," An'gel said wryly.

"Or in your case, sixty-four." Dickce grinned on her way out of the kitchen.

"Touché." An'gel turned off the kitchen light and shut the door. "I told our guests breakfast would be served at eight."

An'gel decided they should leave a couple of lights burning downstairs, one in the hall and another in the parlor, where the off-duty deputy named Kilgore was keeping watch. "There are sandwiches and iced tea in the refrigerator for you," An'gel told him. She was happy to see that he was young, tall, and muscular. He ought to be able to handle any situation that might arise.

"Thank you, ma'am," Kilgore said, his voice deep and calm. "Y'all have an easy night. I'll be moving around the house every so often, and I'll do my best not to disturb anyone."

An'gel and Dickce thanked him before they made their way upstairs on the left. An'gel averted her gaze as she neared the top. It would be a long while before she could look at the staircase without seeing Marla Stephens falling down it.

The second floor was quiet. Two lamps with low-wattage bulbs along the wall provided a dim but adequate glow as An'gel and Dickce strode down the hall to their rooms at the back of the house. No light shone under the doors as they passed, and An'gel hoped that meant all their guests were in bed and asleep.

At the end of the hall An'gel whispered "good night" before she opened her door, and Dickce responded in kind.

An'gel closed and locked her door. She didn't fear for her safety—the lock was old and easily broken through—but at least the sound of a person attempting to get into her room would wake her up.

After she cleaned and washed her face and donned her nightgown, An'gel climbed into her four-poster bed with a grateful sigh. She couldn't remember when she had been this tired. Having a houseful of guests—and unwelcome ones to boot—was exhausting.

She smiled in the darkness. She had thought having a *cat* as a houseguest would be a burden.

The cat.

An'gel's heart skipped a beat. She pushed aside the covers and slid to the floor. Where was Diesel?

She turned on the lights and began a frantic search through her bedroom, closet, and bathroom. She had left him here before dinner and then forgotten all about him.

She called him, softly at first, then with increasing urgency. After five minutes she had to conclude that he was not in her room. Her heart skipped a few more beats.

An'gel's legs trembled as she unlocked her door and stumbled across the hall to Dickce's room. She called Dickce's name as she tapped on the door, then tried to open it. Locked. She tapped again, harder this time.

The door swung open to reveal her sister's scowling face. "What on earth is it?"

"Diesel is missing," An'gel said. "He's not in my room anywhere."

Dickce's scowl turned to an expression of dismay. "Oh, dear, I knew I forgot something."

"What did you forget?" An'gel glared at her sister. "Is Diesel all right?"

Dickce took hold of her arm and pulled An'gel into the bedroom. "Yes, Diesel is fine. He managed to get out of your room a couple of hours ago *and* out of the house, too. I found him in the garage apartment when I went there to check on Benjy."

"If I weren't so relieved," An'gel said, her heart rate beginning to slow, "I'd snatch you bald-headed. Do you realize what a scare you gave me?"

"I'm sorry, Sister," Dickce said, obviously contrite. "I meant to tell you, but I forgot. I'm just as tired as you are."

An'gel nodded. "All right. I forgive you. Do you think

Diesel will be okay with that young man? After all, we don't know anything about him."

"I'm sure he'll be fine. Benjy wants to be a veterinarian, or so he said earlier today. Besides, Diesel obviously thinks he's a good person; otherwise, he wouldn't have gone to such lengths to be with him."

"I can't believe we're accepting a character reference from a cat," An'gel said, shaking her head. "But I'm too tired to argue. If anything happens to Diesel, though, you'll be the one to explain it to Charlie."

"I'm not worried in the least." Dickce glared at her.

An'gel knew that mulish expression all too well. There was no point in further argument. "Good night, again."

Back in her room, door once again locked, An'gel got comfortable in bed. She decided she was not going to worry about the cat, nor about Rosabelle and her family and their assorted troubles. She decided for once to take the advice of the South's most notorious belle. *After all, tomorrow is another day.*

CHAPTER 15

Thunder rumbled in the distance, and the overcast skies promised rain. Ordinarily Dickce enjoyed such days, so long as the storm wasn't violent. Today, however, she didn't relish being cooped up inside with Rosabelle and her family during a downpour. At least a good rain might break the oppressive heat for a while. That thought cheered her slightly as she finished setting the table for breakfast.

Dickce checked her watch. Quarter to eight. Their guests would start turning up any minute. She scanned the room. The orange juice and coffee carafes were on the sideboard, and Clementine and Antoinette ought to be bringing in the large chafing dishes with scrambled eggs, sausages, and biscuits any minute now. An'gel had prepared a small platter with grapes, pineapple, sliced apples, and two kinds of cheese for those who wanted a lighter repast.

"Surely that will be enough," Dickce said.

"Beg your pardon?"

Startled, Dickce turned toward the door, where Junior Pittman stood, his expression puzzled.

Dickce laughed. "Sorry, talking to myself. Bad habit." She waved a hand toward the table and the sideboard. "Please help yourself to coffee and orange juice. The hot food will be here in a few minutes, I'm sure."

"Thank you." Junior headed straight for the coffee. "I've been dying for caffeine."

Dickce smiled at that. "I hope you found your bed comfortable."

"I sure did." Junior stirred cream and sugar into his mug. "I was pretty much tapped out last night, and I think I was asleep as soon as my head hit the pillow."

"Good. Was Benjy up when you left to come over here?" Dickce had thought a lot about the bereft young man before she was finally able to sleep.

"He was taking a shower," Junior replied. "Ought to be here soon. Said he was hungry." He sipped his coffee.

"Miss Dickce, Miss An'gel wants you in the kitchen."

Dickce turned to see Clementine wheeling in the serving cart, followed by her granddaughter Antoinette carrying the fruit and cheese tray. Once the two women were clear of the doorway, Dickce headed out. What did An'gel want now? Dickce had already polished the dining room table and the sideboard, before setting them up for the meal, at her sister's insistence. *You'd think we were entertaining the Queen of England*, Dickce thought grumpily.

When she walked into the kitchen, she found An'gel chatting with Benjy. Diesel sat beside the young man, his eyes focused on Benjy.

An'gel looked up. "This young man was asking for you." Diesel warbled in agreement.

"Good morning, Benjy. You, too, Diesel." Dickce smiled. She was pleased to see that Benjy looked clean and rested this morning. He wore pants with no holes in them and a tucked-in button-down shirt. Diesel looked just fine, too. Spending the night with Benjy in the garage apartment didn't seem to have done him any harm.

"Good morning, Miss Dickce," he said. He glanced sideways at An'gel. Dickce got the impression he wasn't keen to talk in front of the elder Miss Ducote.

Diesel chose that moment to head to the butler's pantry, where Clementine had put down a water bowl, a litter box, and a bowl of dry food. A few seconds later Dickce could hear him crunching away.

"Is there anything I can do for you, Benjy?" Dickce asked. She stared hard at her sister, and An'gel appeared to realize what Dickce wanted, made her excuses, and left the kitchen.

Benjy waited until An'gel was gone before he spoke. "I was wondering if it would be okay for me to eat in here. I don't really feel like dealing with the Wart and his family right now."

"If that's what you'd prefer," Dickce said, "then of course you can." She paused. "You're going to have to face them all at some point, though."

He shrugged. "I wish I could hit the road right now and get away from all of them. They didn't like my mom, and they don't want me hanging around."

"I know it's difficult for you because you don't think of them as family," Dickce said. "But I like you, and so does An'gel." She hoped the latter statement sounded convincing, because she actually wasn't sure of her sister's attitude toward Benjy. "We want you to stay. Besides, don't you want to be here to find out who is responsible for what happened?"

Benjy looked away. He didn't appear convinced by her words.

Dickce decided to press a little harder. "An'gel and I want to see this figured out so the person who harmed your mother won't be able to harm anyone else. With the exception of Rosabelle, whom we haven't seen in probably twenty years, we don't know *any* of those people. You do, however, and you could help us with your knowledge of them so we'll know the right questions to ask."

"Isn't that the sheriff lady's job?" Benjy regarded her with obvious skepticism.

"It is," Dickce said. "But Deputy Berry can't be here every moment. I think the others are likely to talk more freely to An'gel and me than they are to the deputy. We might be able to find out important information that could help solve this." She paused. If that wasn't enough to persuade him, she didn't know what else to say. She didn't think his trying to isolate himself was a good idea.

Clementine and Antoinette returned, and the housekeeper said, "Don't be letting that food get cold, Miss Dickce. Y'all go in there and have something to eat." She glanced around. "Where's the kitty?"

As if on cue, Diesel padded back into the kitchen and meowed loudly three times. Antoinette laughed as he came up to her and rubbed his head against her jeans-clad leg. "Gram, he's answering you."

"He sure does like to talk," Clementine said. "He can stay in here while y'all finish breakfast." She glanced pointedly toward the door.

"Thank you," Dickce said. "I *am* hungry, now that I

think about it. How about you, Benjy? Will you join me in the dining room?"

Benjy hesitated a moment before nodding. He followed when Dickce left the room.

Rosabelle and her family were at the table. Dickce wasn't sure whether she was ready to have them all in the room at the same time, but at the moment they appeared to be concentrating on their food.

Juanita, seated next to Rosabelle on An'gel's left, looked up when Dickce and Benjy entered. She pushed back her chair and came around to Benjy. She put her hand on his shoulder and gave it a squeeze. "How are you doing?"

Dickce watched the interaction between the two, trying not to be too obvious about it, while she began to load her plate. She saw Benjy shrug.

"I really am sorry about your mother," Juanita said softly. "If there's anything I can do, let me know."

Benjy nodded, and Dickce heard him say "thank you," though his voice was hardly above a whisper.

Dickce wondered whether she should have let the boy remain in the kitchen to eat as he had asked. Perhaps she shouldn't have urged him to join everyone in the dining room. Accepting sympathy could cause emotions to well up, she knew from past experience.

No one besides Juanita, however, made any approach to Benjy. After the girl resumed her seat, Benjy came over to the sideboard and picked up a plate. He stared for a moment at the eggs but then added two large spoonfuls to his plate, followed by three sausages and three biscuits.

Dickce, her own plate full, chose a seat at the end of the table opposite her sister, a couple of chairs away from any of Rosabelle's clan. Benjy took the chair to her right.

The room remained quiet except for the sounds of

eating. Dickce exchanged glances with her sister. An'gel gave a slight shrug. Even with their extensive experience in social situations, they had never had to sit down to breakfast after a murder and try to make polite conversation with a group that included a murderer.

What would Miss Manners do? Dickce suppressed a giggle at the irreverent thought. She checked on Benjy and was pleased to see that he was eating, and not simply picking at his food.

An'gel cleared her throat, and Dickce, along with everyone else, faced her.

"I trust that you are all enjoying your breakfast." An'gel paused but no comments were forthcoming. "Clementine will be serving a light lunch at one o'clock. In the meantime there will be light food and drinks in the front parlor if you have need of them." She had a sip of orange juice before she continued.

"I have spoken this morning with Chief Deputy Berry. She has informed me that she will return at nine thirty to talk to each of us again about the events of yesterday. She will be using the library for this purpose. She would like everyone to remain in the house until she has finished her interviews sometime later this morning. The weather will be inclement today. In fact, there is a strong chance of thunderstorms and high winds, so it is advisable that everyone remain in the house."

An'gel sounded like a prison warden or a school principal—Dickce couldn't decide between the two. At times like this, she was happy that An'gel was the elder. Acting the heavy came so much more naturally to her. Dickce glanced around the table to gauge the reactions to her sister's words.

"I suppose we have to sit around twiddling our thumbs

while we wait for our turn?" Maudine glowered at An'gel. "I don't knit, and I don't play cards. There doesn't seem to be anything else to do." She snorted. "Don't you even have a television set in this house, or is it too modern?"

Maudine could hardly be more ungracious if she tried, Dickce thought. "There is a television," she said in a pleasant tone. "It is in the library, however, so I'm afraid you won't be able to watch it until after the chief deputy has finished her interviews." She paused, as if struck by an idea. "The library does have shelves and shelves of books, though. You're welcome to choose one to read." *If you know how,* she wanted to add.

Dickce kept her expression bland as Maudine turned to her. "I'm far too upset to read, thank you very much. This situation is intolerable. I think you people are making a big fuss over what was simply a terrible accident."

"That's enough, Maudine." Rosabelle's tone brooked no argument. She folded her napkin and set it down by her empty plate. "You were a stupid child, and I'm sorry to say you've learned very little since. If you think what happened yesterday was an accident, then you have even fewer brain cells than I realized."

Dickce exchanged an appalled glance with An'gel.

"Mother, how could you?" Maudine's face crumpled, and she began to cry.

"Mother, you should apologize to her right this minute." Bernice shook a finger at Rosabelle. "You're not in your right mind. I think Marla and Wade were right, you need to be committed to a psychiatric facility."

CHAPTER 16

The string of profanities with which Wade responded to his half sister's ill-considered remark sent An'gel's blood pressure skyward. She gripped the arms of her chair to stop herself from picking up the remains of her orange juice and pitching them in the man's face.

Bernice shrank in her chair, and for a moment An'gel thought the poor woman was going to hide under the table.

"Wade Thurmond," Rosabelle said, her face suffused with blood, "is this true? Were you plotting behind my back to have me committed to a mental hospital?"

An'gel feared Rosabelle might have a stroke. She had never seen the woman in such a rage.

Wade didn't shrink from his mother's fury. "No, Mother, we weren't going to try having you committed. We do think you need to be evaluated by a psychiatrist, however. We all agreed that you may no longer be competent enough to care for yourself."

"You *all* agreed?" Rosabelle glanced at each member of her family in turn. "Maudine, Bernice, are you part of this attempt? Juanita, Junior, you two as well?"

"No, Grandmother, I wasn't part of it." Juanita shook her head. "You know I don't think you're incompetent. I tried to argue with Aunt Maudie and Uncle Wade, but they wouldn't listen to me."

"Viper." Maudine stared at her niece. "Weak, just like my sister. Bernice doesn't want to admit the truth about Mother, and neither do you."

"Now, Maudine," Bernice said softly. "I told you I thought you and Wade were jumping the gun. Mother has some strange notions, but that doesn't mean she needs to be put in a mental hospital."

"Thank you for that heartfelt testimonial, Bernice," Rosabelle said. She turned to An'gel. "Now do you understand what I've been trying to tell you about my family? You see how they are plotting to destroy me. First it's a loony bin, and then one of them decided on a more permanent solution."

An'gel felt shell-shocked. Had she and Dickce been dropped somehow into the middle of an episode of *All My Children*? She had never heard such goings-on in her life outside of a soap opera. She didn't feel capable of answering.

Instead she glanced down the table at Dickce and Benjy. The boy had lowered his head, evidently fascinated by the pattern of the china. Dickce rolled her eyes and shrugged. An'gel had a sneaking suspicion that her sister was, in some odd way, enjoying the melodrama.

Rosabelle didn't appear to need a response. "*How sharper than a serpent's tooth it is to have a thankless child.*" She closed her eyes, leaned back in her chair, and in a moment tears trickled down. Then her eyes popped open, and Rosabelle dabbed away the tears with a linen napkin. "You all should be ashamed of your treatment of me, your own mother."

She declaimed that quotation with all the drama of a Sarah Bernhardt wannabe, An'gel thought cynically.

"Come off it, Mother," Wade said, obviously disgusted. "When we were children, we saw our nannies more often than we saw you. If we'd been left to your tender mercies, we'd all have been naked and starving to death. You were too busy living the high life and spending your husband's money." He stood, dropped his napkin on the table, and walked out of the room.

"He's right," Maudine said. "You're a vicious old cow, and I for one am sorry it wasn't you who fell down those stairs. Marla was a horrible woman, but you make her seem like Miss Congeniality." She pushed her chair back and lumbered to her feet. "When we get back to California, we're going to get you put away where you should have been years ago." She cast her mother a glance of loathing as she headed from the room.

"Maudie, no," Bernice whimpered as she scurried after her sister.

"And so ends the latest episode of *As the Stomach Turns*." Junior shook his head. "Grandmother, I'm sorry you had to endure all that. But you bring it on yourself. Juanita and I know you aren't crazy or incompetent, but you act like a five-year-old brat sometimes." He came around the table and kissed Rosabelle's cheek. "Don't pay any attention to them. Juanita and I won't let them put you away."

Rosabelle did not appear mollified by her grandson's words, An'gel thought. Privately she couldn't help but agree with Junior's assessment of her. She could have told him Rosabelle had been a brat all her life, but now didn't seem to be the time, she thought wryly.

"Newton Aloysius Pittman Junior, you've never spoken to me like that in your life." Rosabelle sounded hurt, and An'gel wondered if, for once, real emotion was coming through.

Junior patted her hand. Juanita leaned in her chair to slip an arm around Rosabelle's shoulder. Her head close to her grandmother's, Juanita said, "Junior is right, Gran. You can't treat Mother and the others so harshly and not expect them to make a fuss." She sighed. "Junior and I will talk to them again and see if we can calm them down. But you might try being nicer to them."

Juanita followed her cousin from the room, and now An'gel, Dickce, Benjy, and Rosabelle were the only ones still at the table.

"Can you believe how they talked to me? My own grandchildren." Rosabelle appeared stunned, and again An'gel wondered whether she was acting or if she truly was upset.

An'gel took a deep breath. She might regret this later, but now was probably the time for Rosabelle to hear a few home truths from a person who had known her for much of her life.

She patted Rosabelle's hand and shot Dickce a warning glance. "Honey, I know this is upsetting, but your grandchildren are right. There's only one thing you've ever wanted to be, besides a rich man's wife, and that's the Center of Attention. It's usually a lonely place, because to get there and stay there, you have to care more about yourself and what you want than about what others want. You were that way when I met you during rush week at Athena College all those years ago, and you've never changed."

An'gel sat back and waited for the explosion. She glanced at Dickce and was not much surprised to see her giving a thumbs-up. Poor Benjy looked like he wanted to crawl under the table. An'gel realized she should probably have sent him out of the room before she said what she had to Rosabelle.

One look at Rosabelle's face, and An'gel could tell her words hadn't sat well with her old sorority sister. An'gel had hoped that, given the seriousness of the situation, Rosabelle might finally take responsibility for her own behavior.

Evidently those hopes were not to be realized. Rosabelle stared at An'gel—as she remarked to Dickce later—like Hercules seeing the Aegean stables for the first time.

Rosabelle stood. "I seem to have made many mistakes in my life, and one of the biggest ones was thinking you were my friend. I didn't realize you despised me so much."

Before she could continue, Dickce spoke. "We don't despise you. We don't always *like* you very much, but *despise* is too strong a word. Stop acting like a brat and grow up."

Rosabelle's head turned, and she looked at Dickce, eyebrows raised. "That's the peanut gallery heard from." She sat. "Well, if I have to choose between my family and the Ducote sisters, I guess I'm better off with you." She glanced toward the sideboard. "Is there any more coffee?"

An'gel couldn't help herself. She laughed, and she heard Dickce giggle. When she looked down the table, she saw her sister and Benjy with their heads together. Perhaps Dickce was attempting to explain Rosabelle's mercurial behavior to the boy. An'gel wished someone would explain it to her.

She got up and refilled Rosabelle's coffee. Seated once again, she waited to hear what her friend would say next.

After a couple of long sips, Rosabelle set her mug down.

"My first husband had to entertain a lot. That's how it is in Hollywood. Luncheons, dinners, premieres, and all sorts of public appearances. He wanted me with him at every single one. That's why we hired a nanny for Maudine. I didn't have a lot of time to spend with her, and when I was home, I was so exhausted from the socializing, I didn't have much left over for a child."

She frowned. "Maudine was not a pleasant child either. Always cross and fussy. Then Bernice came along. She was much more biddable, rather sweet actually, but I didn't have much time for her either."

"How old were they when your first husband died?" An'gel asked.

Rosabelle thought for a moment. "Maudine was almost seven, and Bernice had just turned five."

"What exactly happened to him?" Dickce asked.

"He was producing a film on location in Africa. He either drank water that was bad or washed in it. Or maybe it was a mosquito bite. They never really did know how, but he came down with dysentery. A violent case, apparently, and he died before they could get him to a hospital."

"That's awful," An'gel said. "I know you were devastated."

Rosabelle nodded. "Jack Carson was the love of my life. I tried to talk him out of producing that film, but he was bull-headed. It ended up costing him his life, and I thought I would die from grief myself."

After a moment, Dickce spoke. "When did you meet your second husband?"

Rosabelle glanced at her, then away. When she spoke, her tone was cool. "I'd known him all along. He was our banker. Tom Thurmond and Jack had been friends before Jack and I married. I always knew he was in love with me, but of course as long as Jack was alive, I ignored that." She fiddled with a spoon, drawing invisible patterns on the tablecloth. "I married him, after a decent interval. Eleven months later, Wade was born. We hired another nanny, and I kept up the kind of life I'd had before, but this time as the wife of a financier-turned-producer."

An'gel was about to ask about the third husband when Rosabelle stood again after glancing at her watch. "It's nearly nine thirty. The deputy should be here." She smiled, and that smile made An'gel uneasy. "I intend to talk to her before my loving children fill her head with the idea that I'm off my rocker."

CHAPTER 17

"This is going to be a long day." An'gel sighed. "I suppose I'd better go see if Kanesha has arrived, in case she needs our help in any way."

She paused in the doorway to look back at Dickce and Benjy, still at the table. "Will you check with Clementine to see if one of us should run into town? I suspect a trip to the grocery store is on the agenda for today."

Dickce nodded, but waited until An'gel was gone before she remarked to Benjy, "It will be yours truly who goes to the grocery store. Would you like to go with me?" She thought it would do them both a world of good to be out of the oppressive atmosphere at Riverhill, even for a brief time.

Benjy nodded eagerly. "The more I can stay out of the Wart's way, the better. I can carry stuff, anything you want me to do."

"Thank you. I appreciate that." Dickce rose and surveyed

the table. "Do you mind helping me clear the table? We can stack the dishes on the cart."

"Not at all," Benjy said. He immediately started stacking dishes, scraping any leftover food onto one plate. "I worked in a restaurant last summer to earn money for college."

Dickce was delighted to see how quickly and efficiently Benjy cleared the table. She was far slower, and thus he did the bulk of the work. Within a few minutes, the table was cleared, the cart stacked with all the dishes, glasses, and utensils. Benjy grasped the handle and started steering the cart out of the dining room. Dickce moved ahead of him so that she could open the kitchen door.

"Goodness, Miss Dickce," Antoinette said with a smile, "I was just coming to do that." She motioned for Benjy to let her have the cart. "I'll take it from here."

"I had experienced help," Dickce said. "Benjy did most of the work."

Diesel rose from his resting place beneath the kitchen table, stretched, and then padded over to greet the newcomers with a few meows. Dickce rubbed his head for a moment before the cat switched his attentions to Benjy.

"If he's that good, I might put him to work myself." Clementine laughed. "Antoinette would rather have someone her age to talk to instead of her old gram."

"You hush that talk," Antoinette admonished her grandmother with a smile as she wheeled the cart to the dishwasher. She had to steer with some care around Diesel, who attempted to rub against her legs. "I'll be gone back to school soon and won't get to see you much until Thanksgiving."

"My granddaughter is a student at Vanderbilt," Clementine told Benjy with obvious pride. "She wants to be a doctor."

"That's great," Benjy said. "Do you like college?"

Dickce thought his tone seemed wistful. He had mentioned college himself a few times, but evidently money was an issue.

Antoinette dimpled. "I sure do. There's a lot of hard work, but I don't mind. Are you going to school?"

Benjy shook his head. "I'd like to, but I don't have the money right now. I want to be a veterinarian." He scratched Diesel's head. "I like animals a lot."

"That one sure seems to like you," Antoinette said. "He is the sweetest thing I've ever seen."

Benjy blushed and nodded. "I wish I could take him back to California with me." He wandered toward Antoinette and the dishwasher with Diesel at his side.

While the two young people chatted about California, Dickce talked to Clementine about shopping. "An'gel told me I probably need to go into town and buy some groceries. Especially since we don't know how long this swarm of locusts is going to be staying with us."

Clementine pulled a small notebook from the pocket of her apron and tore out a couple of pages. "This is what I'm guessing we're gonna need for the next three or four days. I think that's all, but you may want to check for anything I missed."

Dickce almost groaned as she scanned the list. She was glad Benjy wanted to go with her. Clementine's requests would fill at least two shopping carts, if not three.

"I'll have to check with Kanesha Berry to see if it's okay for Benjy and me to go," Dickce said. "And then, hopefully, we'll be on our way."

Clementine shook her head. "I sure do appreciate it. That pantry is as bare as I've ever seen it, except for those jars of muscadine jelly and tomatoes I put up."

Dickce nodded. They couldn't feed their guests on jelly and tomatoes alone. "I'll go find out about going into town." She glanced over at Benjy and Antoinette, still chatting by the dishwasher. "If you do have something Benjy can help with for a little while, that would be a small blessing. If he can keep busy, I'm hoping he won't have time to brood much about his mother."

"Don't you worry, Miss Dickce," Clementine said. "Me and Antoinette will look after that poor child. That cat, too. I'm not used to having so much company in here, but right now I'm liking it pretty fine."

Dickce left the kitchen in search of An'gel and Kanesha, well aware that Clementine, one of the most kind-hearted women she knew, would look after Benjy. Dickce wasn't sure why she herself was so determined to see to the boy's welfare. She had always liked young people and occasionally regretted that neither she nor her sister had married and had children of their own.

You are not taking that child to raise. She could hear An'gel scolding her already. She had no intention of taking Benjy to raise, but she didn't see any harm in keeping an eye on him. Nobody else was, as far as she could tell, and he was too young to weather all this on his own. If An'gel made an issue of it, that was exactly what Dickce would tell her.

Dickce walked into the parlor while Kanesha was addressing the assembled family, all of whom were seated on the sofas and chairs near the fireplace. Kanesha had her back to the door, and Dickce walked around to the left where An'gel stood to one side of the fireplace.

". . . you'll understand that I have further questions to ask. I have to reiterate that we are treating this as a suspicious death. I can't say any more about that right now, until we have the results of various tests. I have to work on the assumption that this was a deliberate act, and not an accident."

"It certainly wasn't an accident," Rosabelle said. "No matter what my children might think. Deputy, I would like to talk to you first, before you interview the rest of my family." She rose from her chair.

"That's fine, Mrs. Sultan," Kanesha said. "If you'll come with me to the library, we'll get started. I would appreciate it if the rest of you would be on hand during this process. It will make everything go smoother and quicker that way. If at any time you need to talk to me, one of my deputies will be here to assist you."

Dickce hadn't noticed him before, but now she spotted a man in uniform positioned by the front window. He looked vaguely familiar, but he was not the young man who had spent the night keeping watch.

"Mrs. Sultan, if you'll come with me now, please." Kanesha stood back to allow Rosabelle to pass, then turned to follow her.

"Deputy Berry," Dickce said, stepping forward. "If I could ask a quick question."

"Certainly, Miss Dickce," Kanesha said. "You can go on ahead, Mrs. Sultan. Deputy Bates is in the library. I won't be long."

Rosabelle nodded, though she frowned at Dickce. Dickce ignored that and approached Kanesha. She spoke in an undertone. "I need to go grocery shopping, and I'd like to take Benjy Stephens with me. I know you will want to talk to him first, though."

Kanesha nodded. "Yes, ma'am, I do need to interview him. I will put him next after Mrs. Sultan. I suppose it will be all right for him to accompany you. Are you sure you will be okay with him?"

"Yes," Dickce said firmly. "These people really aren't his family, and he and his stepfather don't get along. Benjy needs distraction, and I thought it would do him good to get away from all this, even for an hour."

"Okay, then. I will finish with him as soon as I can." Kanesha nodded once more before she headed out of the room.

"I hope this isn't going to take all day," Maudine said. "I can't stand to be cooped up in one room like this."

"I heard thunder a few minutes ago," Wade said. "Why don't you go out for a walk and see if you can get lightning to strike you? Stand under a tree."

Maudine's face turned so purple Dickce thought she might burst right there.

"Wade, don't talk to Maudine like that." Bernice shook a finger at her half brother. "You're going to make us all upset, and that's the last thing we need right now."

"Tell Maudine to stop complaining, then." Wade crossed his arms over his chest and glared at Bernice. "Mother is in there now with that deputy saying who knows what about all of us, and I am tired of hearing the sound of Maudine's whining."

Dickce wondered whether she should offer to lead them in a sing-along. Maybe that would get them to settle down.

No, she decided, they would only argue about what song to sing. She had seldom encountered a family so determined not to be civil with one another.

"Uncle Wade, please." Juanita held out a hand toward him in a clear entreaty. "We're all on edge right now.

Deputy Berry impresses me as a smart professional. Whatever Grandmother tells her, I'm sure the deputy is shrewd enough to see through any attempts to mislead her."

"That is certainly true," An'gel said. "Deputy Berry is an experienced officer. She has handled several investigations like this in the past couple of years. I can assure you she will treat everyone fairly and not be prejudiced by anything Rosabelle might say to her."

"How about something to drink?" Dickce said. "I think Clementine has the iced tea ready by now. I'll just go and see about it." She was eager to get out of the room.

"How about something stronger?" Wade asked, his tone still strident. "I need a real drink."

Dickce decided An'gel could handle that request. She scooted out of the parlor and headed for the kitchen.

When she returned ten minutes later with the serving cart, An'gel was talking about the history of their house, Riverhill, and the Ducote family. Dickce tuned it out. She knew it every bit as well as An'gel and could recite it in her sleep. She presumed one of their guests must have asked a question, because it wasn't like An'gel to talk at such length about family history without being prompted.

Dickce placed the cart near one of the sofas. She figured their guests could help themselves when they were ready. An'gel had seen her, she knew, but her appearance hadn't stopped the flow of words.

She decided she might as well sit for now because there was no telling how long she would have to wait for An'gel to stop. She took the one empty chair near the sofas and settled back.

Then she squirmed. There seemed to be something under the cushion. She could feel the lump under her right side. She stuck her hand down between the cushion and the base of the chair and felt for the object.

Her fingers encountered what felt like plastic. She tried to get a good grip on it but couldn't. She stood, turned, and pulled up the cushion.

She blinked. *A water pistol?*

CHAPTER 18

What in the name of Sam Hill was Dickce doing?

With one part of her brain, An'gel registered that her sister was standing over a chair, cushion in hand, staring down at the seat. The other part kept her spiel about the house's history running right on course. She had given this talk so many times, she felt like she had a tiny on-off switch for it in her brain and connected to her tongue.

No one else seemed to have noticed Dickce's odd behavior. No one, that is, except for the deputy by the front window. Dickce evidently called him over, An'gel realized, because he moved quickly to join her sister by the chair.

An'gel kept going, but Juanita Cameron must have noticed something about her expression because she turned toward where Dickce stood with the deputy. Once Juanita's head turned, other heads began to turn as well, until everyone in the room was looking at Dickce and the deputy.

An'gel stopped in the middle of a sentence about repairs

to the house after a fire in 1893. "What's going on over there?" She stepped forward.

Dickce dropped the cushion back in place and turned to An'gel with a smile. The deputy left the room. "I found something—sat on it, actually—that I think Deputy Berry will want to see."

"What is it?" Wade asked.

"Yeah, what is it?" Junior said, followed by similar inquiries from his cousin and his mother.

"I think the deputy should see it first." Dickce stood in front of the chair.

An'gel was determined to find out, and she approached her sister. She reached down to pull up the cushion, but Dickce smacked her hand lightly.

"You have to wait, too," Dickce said with a smarmy grin.

An'gel frowned at her. Dickce was being childish. It was one thing to keep her discovery from their guests, but surely she had as much right as Dickce to know what it was.

Before An'gel could protest, Kanesha returned with the deputy. She did not speak as she motioned for the deputy to remove the cushion. An'gel noticed that both Kanesha and her subordinate now wore plastic gloves.

She peered around Dickce's shoulder to see what the cushion had hidden. Her eyes widened when she saw the water pistol. How on earth had it come to be under the cushion of that chair? Where had it come from in the first place?

One of the guests had to have brought it, An'gel decided after a moment's reflection. There was no reason she or Dickce would have one in the house—although with Dickce's occasionally odd sense of humor, she couldn't be completely sure of that. She would be interested to hear what her sister had to say.

Kanesha indicated that her deputy should replace the

cushion. "Thank you, Miss Dickce," she said. "I'll want to talk to you and Miss An'gel about this later, along with everyone else. Deputy Rhodes here is going to remove the chair for a little while to have a little closer look at it. He'll be really careful with it"—she shot an admonitory look at the deputy—"because he knows it's a valuable antique. Now, if you'll excuse me, I need to get back to Mrs. Sultan."

An'gel nodded. She turned back to face the curious glances of her guests as Kanesha and Deputy Rhodes left with the chair. Dickce found another chair farther away from the sofas while An'gel resumed her spot in front of the fireplace.

"What was so interesting about that chair?" Maudine's voice was strained. "Was there blood in it?"

An'gel wanted to snap at the woman for such a ridiculous question. She held on to her temper as she replied, "No, it wasn't blood. I'm not at liberty to say what it was, because Deputy Berry prefers to examine it first. I'm sure she will talk to each of you about it when it's your turn with her."

She barely registered the frowns of her guests. Her mind was busy grappling with the implications of her sister's discovery. She realized that one person in the room, other than she herself and Dickce, knew about the water pistol because one of them had hidden it there.

After using it to squirt water on the stairs.

In a sense that water pistol was the murder weapon—along with the petroleum jelly on the banister. An'gel marveled at the devious mind that had come up with such a simple yet effective method of killing someone.

She glanced at each of her guests in turn. Which of them possessed that devious mind? She didn't think Maudine was smart enough to think up such a plan—but perhaps that stemmed from her dislike of the woman. Maudine could be far more clever than she appeared.

Bernice didn't impress her as being any more intelligent than Maudine, but that mousy demeanor could be the perfect cover for a cunning mind. An'gel thought that either Wade or Juanita was a more obvious choice. Junior appeared to be an innocuous young man, about as dim as his mother.

She also considered Rosabelle, mindful of the discussion last night with Juanita. The girl's concern that her grandmother had dreamed up the *prank* in order to dramatize her imagined persecution had stuck with An'gel. She had told Dickce about the conversation this morning before Dickce had gone to set the table for breakfast. Her sister had been as troubled by the idea as An'gel herself was. After Rosabelle's performance at the breakfast table, An'gel decided, she couldn't dismiss Juanita's worries.

She realized with a start that her guests were staring at her expectantly. Should she continue with her mini dissertation on the house? At the moment she couldn't think of any other innocuous subject for conversation, and she wanted to forestall further questions about the water pistol.

"Now, where was I? Oh, yes, the fire of 1893. It started, I believe I told you, because a guest was smoking in bed, despite warnings not to." An'gel glared for a moment. Thus far she had no evidence that any of Rosabelle's family smoked, but if one of them did, she wanted it clearly understood that smoking was not allowed inside the house. She resumed her narrative. "Fortunately the fire was quickly contained, and the resulting damage wasn't extensive." She went on autopilot from that point.

During her lecture An'gel had been vaguely aware of the occasional flash of lightning, followed by a boom of thunder, but had paid them little heed since they appeared to be several miles away. Now, however, lightning struck somewhere nearby, and she heard thunder two seconds later. She felt the house shudder and heard the parlor windows rattle. She also noted the alarmed expressions of her guests. "I suggest that we move out of the parlor now, and gather under the back side of the stairs. The area between there and the kitchen. Now, please."

The deputy had already moved away from the front window, and he held the parlor door open as An'gel and Dickce shepherded their guests out into the hall and toward the area An'gel suggested.

Their mother had been afraid of storms, particularly of violent ones, and she had passed that fear on to An'gel. Dickce was less bothered by them, but even she turned cautious during conditions like they were currently experiencing.

"Do you think there will be a tornado?" Bernice's voice trembled. "Don't you have a storm cellar?"

"There is a storm cellar," An'gel said, "but I don't believe there's any need for us to get into it." She worked hard to keep her voice calm. "The storm seems to be moving quickly, and I'm sure it will be out of here in a few minutes."

"Thank goodness," Maudine said with a shudder. "There are bound to be spiders in a storm cellar, and I can't abide spiders. I'm not going in there no matter what."

An'gel didn't care much for spiders herself, but she'd rather share quarters with a few spiders than end up dead in a tree somewhere from the deadly force of a tornado.

Thunder rolled again, and it sounded like the storm was right over the house. An'gel felt the vibrations under her feet. Their position under the stairs should be safe enough, An'gel thought. They stood roughly in the center of the ground floor with no windows nearby and were protected by the house around them. She knew Clementine would have taken refuge in the pantry, along with her granddaughter, Benjy, and Diesel. An'gel prayed the storm would pass quickly.

For now they huddled close together as the thunder sounded loudly yet again.

CHAPTER 19

Half an hour after the storm had passed over Riverhill, Kanesha finished with Benjy. Dickce was waiting for him in the hallway when he came out of the library.

"Ready to go to town?" she asked. He nodded, and she gestured toward the front door. "I've got the car out on the drive."

She waited until they were settled and seat-belted in the late-model white Lexus before she asked him how the interview with Kanesha had gone.

"Okay, I guess. I really didn't know anything about what happened to my mom, but she asked a lot of questions about how my mom got along with the Wart and his family. Fine with the Wart, but not too good with the others, that's what I told her," Benjy said as Dickce shifted into drive and hit the accelerator.

The car jumped forward, and Dickce glanced over to see Benjy gripping the straps of his seat belt. "It's not far into town. We'll be there in a few minutes." She accelerated, and the car sped down the drive toward the highway. An'gel had had the driveway resurfaced back in the spring, and Dickce liked the smoothness of it. She wished the highway into Athena were as nice as this.

Dickce slowed the car when they reached the highway and flipped the signal for a left turn. She glanced both ways to determine there was nothing coming and hit the gas again. She noticed Benjy was still holding on to his seat belt, and he looked a little pale. The poor boy must not ride in cars very often, she decided. She wondered if he knew how to drive.

"I've got quite a list from Clementine." Dickce decided to keep the conversation away from what was going on back at Riverhill. "She's a wonderful cook, good old-fashioned Southern food. It's a wonder An'gel and I don't weigh three hundred pounds apiece, the way she feeds us."

She was about to launch into a description of the desserts Clementine often prepared when Benjy said, "Miss Dickce, stop the car. Please."

Dickce immediately complied, slowing the car until she could safely pull to the side of the road and stop. He looked upset. "What's wrong? Are you sick?" She hit the button to lower his window. "Just stick your head out the window."

Benjy shook his head as he unbuckled his seat belt. "No, I'm not sick. I saw something back there. It looked like a dog. It might be hurt." He opened the door and hopped out of the car before Dickce had time to respond.

She glanced in the rearview mirror and saw him walking fast back down the road the way they had come. She killed the engine and looked both ways before opening her door and getting out of the car. She started to follow Benjy slowly. If he had seen a dog, she hoped it hadn't been hit by a car. She wasn't sure she could handle seeing a badly injured animal.

About a hundred feet back she watched as Benjy slowed and then sank down on his knees in the grass verge. He held out a hand, and she heard him calling out in a gentle tone, "It's okay. I won't hurt you. Miss Dickce, don't come any closer, okay?" He repeated his assurances to the dog, and Dickce stood rooted to the spot as Benjy requested.

Benjy kept talking, and as Dickce watched, she could see the dog slowly coming closer. It wasn't very big, perhaps about twenty-five pounds, she thought. Its coat was a warm cream color, and the hair looked soft and fleecy, but wet from the recent storm. It didn't look much like any dog she remembered seeing around the area.

Dickce wasn't sure how long she had been standing there when the dog finally came close enough for Benjy to touch it on the head. She held her breath. Would the dog bite? Or turn and run away?

"What a good puppy you are," Benjy crooned to the dog. "See, Benjy isn't going to hurt you. Benjy only wants to be your friend and get you warm and dry, with some food to eat. You'd like that, wouldn't you?"

The dog sat in front of the boy and allowed Benjy to rub its head. "He doesn't have a collar," Benjy said in the same singsong voice. "I'm going to see if he'll let me pick him up and put him in the car. Is that okay with you?"

"Of course," Dickce said as she started to back away slowly. She was thankful there was no traffic on the road just now. She couldn't bear the thought of the dog getting excited or upset and dashing out into the road in the path of an oncoming vehicle.

Benjy put his arms around the dog, and Dickce saw the dog lick the boy's ear. She smiled and turned toward the car.

She opened the back hatch and moved out of the way so Benjy could get the dog inside. The rear seats were already down, in anticipation of the large number of groceries she planned to purchase.

The dog barked several times as Benjy neared the car. It didn't seem reluctant to get into the car, but there was a certain urgency in the tone of the barking, Dickce thought. She glanced back in the direction from where Benjy first approached the dog. Was there perhaps another dog out there?

She saw a sudden flash of reddish brown moving in the undergrowth a few feet from the grass verge. Maybe a puppy?

The dog barked again, and suddenly a small creature streaked out of the undergrowth to jump into the back of the car beside the dog.

Benjy spoke in singsong again. "Well, hello there, kitty. Where did you come from? Are you and Mr. Dog here buddies?"

Dickce stayed where she was, afraid that any movement might spook the animals into jumping out of the car. She held her breath again as Benjy talked to the animals while he slowly climbed into the back with them. When he was settled, his arm around the dog and the cat in his lap, he called out to Dickce. "Can you close the door now? I think they'll be okay until we can get them to a vet."

Dickce hit the button on her remote to close the hatch. She waited to be sure nothing jumped out before she got back in the car and started it up. She pulled out onto the highway after checking for traffic, but now she drove a bit more slowly. Her foot, however, itched to mash down on the accelerator. She hated driving at a snail's pace.

"I'm sorry to cause all this trouble," Benjy said, "but

when I saw the dog out there, I just couldn't go by and not try to do something. I didn't see the cat at all."

"Don't you worry about it," Dickce said. "I'm glad you spotted the poor dog. I wonder if someone just dumped them by the side of the road. People who do that to animals ought to be flogged. I can't stand cruelty to the poor things."

"I agree with you," Benjy said. "There are so many animals out there without good homes. If people would only get their pets spayed or neutered, but they're so irresponsible sometimes."

Dickce heard the passion in the boy's voice, and it made her warm to him all the more. A boy who cared for animals as much as Benjy did was obviously a good person, one who deserved better treatment from his stepfather and his family.

"There's a wonderful vet in Athena, Dr. Devon Romano," Dickce said. "Our friend Charlie Harris takes Diesel to her, and that's where we'll take our two new friends. Dr. Romano might know whom they belong to."

"Whoever it is shouldn't get them back," Benjy said heatedly. "I bet they were abandoned on the road."

Dickce thought he was probably right. This cat and dog weren't the only animals she and An'gel had picked up from the side of the road over the years. They had rescued a number of animals and taken them to the vet's office, and the veterinarian usually found good homes for them. She and An'gel hadn't ever had pets, but having Diesel with them made her aware of how nice it was to have one around the house.

While Dickce drove, Benjy continued to talk in a reassuring tone to the two animals. She glanced in the rearview mirror a few times, and each time she saw that the animals appeared content. She was afraid they might be frightened and try to get out, but evidently Benjy knew how to keep them calm. She was grateful he was with her, because she doubted she could have managed on her own. She would have had to find someone to help, and who knows what could have happened to the poor things in the meantime.

A few minutes later she pulled up in front of Dr. Romano's clinic, Athena Veterinary Hospital. "Here we are," she announced.

"Great," Benjy said. "Miss Dickce, do you think you could see if the kitty will let you hold her? I don't think I can get them both inside on my own."

"Surely," Dickce said. She got out and shut her door, stuck the keys in her jacket pocket, then opened the back passenger door. Benjy held tight to the dog and the cat while Dickce reached in to stroke the cat. "Hello, kitty. You sure are a pretty thing. I've never seen a kitty your color before."

The cat seemed docile and allowed her to stroke its head. Taking this as a good sign, Dickce slipped one hand beneath the cat's small body and lifted it. The cat didn't protest. So far so good. Dickce brought the cat to her chest, surprised at how little it weighed—five pounds at the most, she judged. Compared to Diesel, this little girl was a Lilliputian.

The cat purred when it was completely in her arms, and Dickce looked down into a small, sweet face. "How could anyone ever abandon you? You are the cutest little thing." Dickce felt her heart melt at the trust the cat displayed. Someone had loved it, she realized. What had happened to that person?

Dickce moved away to allow Benjy to crawl out and then bring the dog with him. He bumped the door with his body to shut it, then followed Dickce into the clinic.

The waiting room was empty, and Dickce was glad of that. The last thing they needed was to expose these two rescues to strange animals. Dickce approached the reception desk, the cat nestled contentedly in her arms.

"Good morning, Wendy," she said to the young woman behind the desk. "How are you today?"

"Just fine, Miss Dickce. What are you doing out on a day like this?" Wendy smiled. "And where did you get that beautiful Abyssinian?"

"Is that what it is?" Dickce glanced at the cat. "I've never seen an Abyssinian before or even a cat this particular color." She stepped aside to let Benjy come closer. "This is my friend Benjy. We just found these two by the side of the road out near Riverhill."

"Hi, Benjy," Wendy said. "Your friend looks kind of like a labradoodle. They were together, you say?"

"Yes, ma'am," Benjy said. "I saw the dog and asked Miss Dickce to stop. When I got him in the car, the cat came streaking out of the woods and jumped in the car with us." He shifted the dog in his arms slightly. "They seem to be friends."

"So sweet," Wendy said. Then her tone turned brisk. "Y'all have a seat in the waiting room there, and I'll check with Dr. Romano. I'm sure she can see you in a few minutes."

"Thank you, Wendy," Dickce said. She found a seat and put the cat in her lap. She stroked its head, and the cat purred. "I can't get over how calm she is."

Benjy sat next to her with the dog. "I guess she knows that good people found her and are going to take care of her. Same thing with this guy here." The dog licked the side of Benjy's face, and the boy smiled.

They sat in silence for a moment. Benjy turned to her,

his expression now worried. "I wish I knew what was going to happen to them. If they belong to someone awful, surely the vet won't let them go back to a bad person."

Dickce smiled. "Don't you worry about that. I'm not about to let that happen." She had already made up her mind who was going to take these poor animals.

And if An'gel didn't like it, well, that was just too bad.

CHAPTER 20

An'gel checked her watch again. Quarter to one. Where was Dickce? She should have been home half an hour ago. A run to the grocery store shouldn't take nearly two hours.

Plus she had either turned off her cell phone or was simply ignoring it, like she sometimes did, An'gel knew, when she didn't want to talk.

"I'm sorry, Clementine," An'gel said. "I don't know where Dickce can be. I guess we'll just have to set lunch back an hour."

"Don't fret about it, Miss An'gel," Clementine said. "I made a big batch of potato salad. When Miss Dickce gets here, we can serve a cold lunch. I had sandwich meat on the list, and there ought to be plenty."

"Provided Dickce didn't forget it." An'gel knew stress was making her grouchy, but she was frustrated by the unforeseen hitch in her plans. She had told her guests lunch would be at one thirty, and she didn't want to have to tell them it would be delayed. They were fractious enough as it was, being cooped up in the house and subject to interrogation.

"You go on and stop worrying," Clementine said. "Antoinette ought to be done with the bedrooms soon, and we'll start getting everything ready for when Miss Dickce gets back from town."

"I hope Diesel isn't a hindrance," An'gel said. "I'm not sure it was such a good idea for Antoinette to take him upstairs with her."

"He was getting a bit stir-crazy cooped up in here." Clementine laughed. "He won't be no trouble. He's been real good so far."

"All right," An'gel said. "I'll be back to help when Dickce gets here with the groceries." She headed out of the kitchen to the small room next to it that served as the study. She and Dickce had a desktop computer there that they used for e-mail and Internet searching. An'gel figured she might as well check her e-mail. She was in no hurry to rejoin her guests in the front parlor. A few minutes of quiet would do her good.

She left the door slightly ajar so she could hear her sister when she returned. Seated at the desk, she booted up the computer and logged in to her e-mail account. She stared at the screen for a moment but didn't see anything that demanded an immediate reply.

An'gel leaned back in the chair and closed her eyes. She tried to clear her mind, but to no avail. Her thoughts were full of the morning's activities and her talk with Kanesha.

The chief deputy had departed twenty minutes ago after waiting as long as she could for Dickce to return. She finally told An'gel she would come back later in the day. Kanesha arranged for another off-duty deputy to be on hand through the day, and another would report for overnight duty that evening. On that score, at least, An'gel could rest easy.

She kept thinking about the water pistol. According to Kanesha, none of the guests admitted to having seen it before. One of them was obviously lying, just as he or she had lied about the tube of Vaseline. The problem was, any one of them might have had the Vaseline in his or her luggage. It was a fairly common item in a person's toiletries.

The water pistol, however, was not. Its presence argued premeditation. Someone had brought it to use for a nasty purpose. Otherwise, why would an adult travel with such an item?

From conversations with her guests, An'gel discovered that Rosabelle had described the house to all of them on a number of occasions. They were all therefore aware of the presence of a marble staircase in the house.

A long and potentially deadly marble staircase. An elderly woman like Rosabelle would likely not survive a bad fall on it.

An'gel recalled one story from family lore in which the staircase had claimed another victim less than a year after it was installed. A neighbor's son, part of a group of rowdy young men "with more hair than sense," accepted a dare after a night of drinking to ride his horse bareback up the stairs at Riverhill. While the group cheered, the young man urged his horse up the steps, and all seemed well until they reached the top. One of the servants upstairs, hearing the fearful racket, had come to see what was going on. When she neared the staircase and a horse came lunging at her, she threw up her arms and screamed. The startled horse reared, and the drunken rider lost his grip on the reins. He cracked his head on the way down and died on the spot. The servant, though frightened, was not injured, nor was the horse.

An'gel sat up. What good were these morbid thoughts? *You're hiding in here to avoid Rosabelle and her family. Get up and do something; don't sit there like a big bump of nothing.*

With a heavy sigh she left her chair and headed for the front parlor.

~

Dickce and Benjy stayed at the veterinary clinic for about thirty minutes. The first sign of skittishness the animals betrayed was when they took them into an examination room. At first Dr. Romano was going to separate them, but Benjy protested politely.

"I think they're used to being with each other," he said with a shy smile. "They'll be happier if you can keep them together." Since the dog had whimpered earlier when Dr. Romano started to take the cat from the room, Benjy seemed to be right.

"No problem, then." Dr. Romano, a cheerful, attractive woman in her late thirties, motioned for Benjy to place the dog on the examination table. She then positioned him so that the cat remained in his sight line. "Let's check for a microchip first, since neither of them has a collar and tags." She ran the scanner over the back of the dog's neck.

"No chip?" Benjy said.

"Correct." The vet turned to Dickce. "Miss Dickce, if you don't mind holding the cat in your lap, I'll check her now."

"Certainly," Dickce said. She put one hand under the cat's stomach and patted her head with the other.

Dr. Romano scanned the cat. "No chip here either." She put the scanner aside, then leaned against the cabinet to look at her patients and the humans with them. "From just a cursory glance, neither of them looks malnourished, so

I'd guess they weren't on the roadside long before you found them. No more than a day or two. They're reasonably clean, too, though the dog has a few burrs and other debris in its coat."

"You don't recognize them, do you?" Dickce asked.

Dr. Romano shook her head. "They haven't been in this clinic before, I'm certain. My best guess is either they got loose from a car passing through or someone deliberately dumped them by the road."

"People who would do such a thing should never have animals in the first place," Dickce said. "I'd like to see them dumped on the side of the road and left to fend for themselves."

"I'd take a bat and knock them upside the head myself," Benjy said.

Dr. Romano smiled. "I agree with both of you, though please don't tell anybody I advocated the use of a bat upside the head." She stood and came back to the examination table. "What is the plan for these two? I can call someone from the animal shelter and have them picked up after I've finished examining them."

"That won't be necessary," Dickce said. "They will be coming home with me. If anyone comes looking for them, I want to have a little chat with that person before he tries to take them back. Run whatever tests you need to run, and give them whatever shots they need. How long will all that take?"

"If you'll leave them here overnight, that will be sufficient," Dr. Romano said. "You can pick them up after lunch tomorrow. But give Wendy a call first to check."

"That sounds fine. We'll be back tomorrow." Dickce rose and set the cat on the table with the dog. "Come along,

Benjy. Dr. Romano and her staff will take excellent care of our new friends." The cat rubbed against the dog and purred.

Benjy scratched the dog's head behind an ear. "You'll keep them together, won't you? Let them sleep together, I mean."

"We won't separate them unless we have to," Dr. Romano said. "They'll be fine. After my examination I'll be able to give you a ballpark idea of their age. They both look pretty young to me, I have to say."

"Thank you, Dr. Romano," Dickce said. She laid a hand on Benjy's shoulder. "Let's go now. An'gel will be wondering where we are before long."

"Yes, ma'am." Benjy gave the dog a quick hug and tickled the cat's chin, and then he was ready to go with her. "You two be good, and I'll be back tomorrow."

The dog yipped, as if in acknowledgment, and Benjy smiled.

On the short drive to the grocery store, Benjy was quiet. Dickce knew he had much on his mind in addition to the welfare of the two animals. He would talk if he had something to say.

Forty-five minutes later they stowed the last bags of groceries in the back of the car, and Benjy pushed the two carts over to the cart rack. In the car, Dickce said, "That should be enough to keep us eating for a few days."

Benjy nodded and looked out the window as Dickce backed the car out of the parking space and headed for the street.

She suspected that one of the boy's concerns was where the dog and the cat would live. He seemed attached to the dog already, and he might be thinking about trying to take them both back to California with him. She didn't think that was a practicable solution. For one thing, she didn't think Wade Thurmond would permit it. He might not even want Benjy to remain with him, though since it was Rosabelle's house, it would really be up to her, Dickce supposed. Rosabelle might allow the animals in her house, but Dickce didn't think it likely.

She had already decided that the animals could stay with her and An'gel. That was the simplest solution, but it might be hard for Benjy to accept. In the emotional devastation resulting from his mother's death, he might latch on to the two pets as a lifeline. Dickce was worried about what would happen to him once the investigation was successfully concluded.

Dickce sped along the highway toward Riverhill, and Benjy stared fixedly out the window. When she turned into the driveway, he stirred a bit and glanced over at her.

She had the feeling he was trying to get up the nerve to say something, probably about taking the animals home with him. When he did speak, however, he shocked her.

"Miss Dickce, I know where that water pistol came from."

CHAPTER 21

Dickce hit the brakes a little too hard, and the car started to skid on the still-damp surface of the driveway. She kept control of the car, however, and brought it out of the skid. She eased down the brakes and stopped the vehicle.

"Sorry," Benjy said, his face pale. "I didn't mean to startle you like that."

Dickce waited a moment for her heartbeat to settle down before she responded. "I'm okay. How about you?"

"Okay, too." Benjy loosened his grip on the door handle and the seat belt strap.

"What's this about the water pistol?" Dickce asked.

Benjy glanced sideways at her, then stared out the windshield. "I'm pretty sure I know where it came from. I pretended not to recognize it when the deputy showed it to me. I was too scared."

Dickce reached over and patted his arm. "I can understand

that. You have to remember, though, the deputy knows you couldn't have been the one to use it to squirt water on the stairs. You had no opportunity to get into the house to do it. Now, where did it come from?"

"It's mine. Last time I saw it was a couple years ago, when I used it with a Halloween costume." Benjy leaned against the headrest and closed his eyes. "It was a toy I got when I was about ten. It was in a box of stuff when my mother and I moved into the house where the Wart lives with his mother. After that Halloween I stuck it back in the box in my closet and forgot about it."

"But you're sure it's the same one?" Dickce asked.

"Pretty sure." Benjy turned to look at her, and she could read the fear in his eyes. "I swear I didn't bring it, and I didn't use it to squirt water on the stairs."

"I know you didn't," Dickce said, making her tone as reassuring as she could. "Like I said, you didn't have the opportunity. I've already told Deputy Berry that."

"I hope she really believes you," Benjy said. He looked less fearful now, Dickce thought.

Dickce put the car into gear again and drove on down the driveway. "I do think you need to tell Deputy Berry where the pistol came from, though. She needs to know that, and it will look better if you tell her. Someone else might remember that you had one anyway."

"The Wart probably does," Benjy said. "I used it a few times to play jokes on him. He complained about it to everyone, so they know about it." He sighed. "I'll talk to her next time she's here."

"Good," Dickce said as she halted the car behind the house. "Let's get these bags into the house. I don't know about you, but I'm ready for some lunch."

"Me, too," Benjy said as he unbuckled his seat belt. He met her at the back of the car and picked up several of the plastic bags. "Miss Dickce, are you going to tell your sister about the animals?"

"Yes," Dickce said. She headed for the back door. "But I'm not telling her just yet that they're going to be coming here. I'll tell her we stopped to rescue them and then took them to the vet. She's got enough to think about for now."

"All right, I won't say anything," Benjy promised.

The back door opened, and Antoinette came out, accompanied by Diesel. She stepped forward, hands outstretched. "Here, Miss Dickce, let me have those. You go on in the house, and Benjy and I will unload the car."

Dickce happily gave her bags to the young woman. She went back to the car for her handbag, and on her way toward the house again she saw Diesel sniffing Benjy's pant legs as he walked. She wondered what the cat would make of the strange animal scents on Benjy's clothing.

She continued to think about Diesel and the two rescued pets as she went into the downstairs bathroom to wash her hands. She hadn't really considered the effect on Diesel in bringing two strange animals into the house. She knew Diesel was used to a dog, namely Stewart Delacorte's poodle, Dante. But she didn't know if he had been around other cats that much. She decided the best thing would be for the rescues to stay in the garage apartment with Benjy, and they would have to keep Diesel in the house until they had time to introduce the animals to one another.

Besides, having them in the garage apartment would keep them out of An'gel's way, too. Dickce wasn't sure how her sister would react to the news that she had suddenly acquired a dog and a cat. An'gel was softhearted, despite her often crusty demeanor, but that didn't mean she would welcome two strays into the house.

"If you have to," Dickce told her reflection in the mirror as she dried her hands, "you can move into the garage apartment with them. They're going to stay no matter what An'gel thinks." She turned out the light, opened the door, and almost stepped on her sister's foot.

"Who were you talking to in there?" An'gel asked. "Yourself?"

"I *am* rather fond of intelligent conversation," Dickce said.

An'gel did not look amused. "What took you so long? We're having a cold lunch instead of the hot one Clementine had planned because you were so late getting back with the groceries."

"Sorry about that," Dickce said, "but Benjy and I encountered an emergency on the way."

"What kind of emergency? Was either of you hurt?" An'gel looked her over. "You look fine to me."

"I'm fine, and so is Benjy," Dickce said. "Right after we turned on to the highway, Benjy spotted a stray dog by the side of the road. We stopped to pick it up, and it turned out there was a cat with the dog."

An'gel glared at her. "You didn't bring them back here, did you? The last thing I need right now is stray animals in the house."

"No, I promise you I didn't bring them back with me." Dickce smiled. "We took them straight to the veterinarian's office and left them there." She hadn't lied to her sister. She hoped An'gel would let the subject drop for the moment. "Now, what can I do to help get lunch ready? I'm starved." She headed back to the kitchen.

"Ask Clementine," An'gel called after her. "I'm going to tell our guests that everything will be ready soon."

The front parlor was empty when An'gel checked it. She crossed the hall to the library, and there she found Junior and Wade watching golf on television. She had never understood men's fascination with the sport. She found it tedious in the extreme and much preferred tennis.

"Excuse me, gentlemen," she said to gain their attention.

Wade lowered the volume with the remote, and he and Junior turned in the chairs to face her. "Yes, ma'am?" Junior said.

"Lunch will be served in the dining room in about fifteen minutes," she said. "Sandwiches and potato salad, so go along and help yourselves when you're ready."

Wade grunted and turned back to golf. Junior smiled and said, "Thank you."

An'gel nodded and left them to their golf. She headed for the stairs. Not for the first time she thought about installing an intercom system in the bedrooms as she climbed. That would save wear and tear on the knees. Somehow, though, she never got around to acting on her idea. They didn't have guests that often, after all.

Upstairs, she tapped lightly on Rosabelle's door. She waited a moment, then tapped again. This time it opened, and Juanita stepped into the hall, pulling the door closed behind her.

"Grandmother's still napping," Juanita said. "I had to give her a mild sedative. She was terribly upset over what happened at breakfast." She shook her head. "She's not used to being thwarted or crossed."

"No, she isn't." An'gel sighed. She harbored a bit of guilt over her confrontation with Rosabelle, but at the time she had felt it was the right thing to do. Someone had to call Rosabelle's bluff, and at least she wouldn't have to live with her after this mess was settled. Rosabelle could go back to California, and her family could deal with her. Rosabelle might even learn to behave more kindly toward her family after this if any of them made an effort to do the same toward her.

And I'll go to church wearing a pink tutu.

"Will she be awake anytime soon?" An'gel asked, trying to quell that cynical inner voice. "Lunch will be ready in the dining room in about fifteen minutes. It's basically self-serve, with cold cuts and potato salad."

"She ought to be up soon," Juanita said. "I might just come down and have a bite myself, and then put together a plate for her. You don't mind if she eats in her room?"

"Of course not," An'gel said, feeling relieved. With Rosabelle absent from the dining room, there was less chance for more histrionics.

"Thank you. I'll be down in a few minutes." Juanita smiled before she went back into the bedroom.

An'gel crossed the hall to the bedroom Maudine and Bernice shared. Bernice opened the door before she finished knocking.

"Good afternoon, Bernice," An'gel said. "I came to let you and your sister know that lunch will be served in the dining room in about fifteen minutes." Before she could share the menu with Bernice, Maudine appeared in the door.

"What are we having?" She frowned. "I have an upset stomach. Your cook must have put something in those eggs that didn't agree with me. I'm not sure I can handle anything other than plain food."

An'gel reckoned it was the four helpings of scrambled eggs and seven sausages and biscuits that were to blame for

Maudine's gastric problems. An'gel did not offer her opinion, however. Instead she said, "Plain food, for sure. Cold cuts for sandwiches, with some of my housekeeper's potato salad. Nothing highly spiced to cause you further distress, I can assure you."

"Cold cuts?" Maudine grimaced. "Well, if that's the best you can do." She turned away.

Bernice smiled timidly as she leaned toward An'gel and said in an undertone, "Don't mind Maudie. She's really upset over the things Mother said this morning. We'll be perfectly happy with whatever you have."

An'gel nodded. She pitied Bernice, having to trail around after her sister to make one apology after another for Maudine's rudeness. An'gel suspected it might be a full-time occupation.

When she reached the bottom step, she heard the doorbell ring. She went to the door, expecting to see Kanesha or one of her officers on the other side. Instead there stood a tall, handsome, and distinguished-looking man of perhaps sixty. He was nattily dressed in white linen trousers, a pale blue silk shirt, and a navy blazer. His stylishly cut hair, black with gray streaks, was thick and luxuriant. An'gel caught a hint of a mellow cologne as the stranger proffered a hand.

Slightly bemused, she returned the gesture. He clasped her hand and bowed over it, then straightened.

"Good afternoon, signorina. You must be one of the charming Ducote sisters that my beloved Rosabella has spoken of to me so very often."

CHAPTER 22

"Good afternoon." An'gel wasn't sure how she managed to get the words out, she was so surprised. Who could this courtly gentleman be?

"Allow me to introduce myself," he said with a smile that displayed beautiful, even teeth. "I am Antonio Mingione, the Conte di San Lorenzo, and husband of Rosabella, at your service."

An'gel blurted out the first words that came into her head. "I thought you were dead." Appalled by what she said, she felt her face flushing.

The conte smiled. "Ah, *Rosabella mia*, she is as mischievous as a child sometimes. I am very much alive, as you can see, Signorina Ducote."

"Please, forgive my manners. Do come in." An'gel stepped back and indicated that Rosabelle's husband should enter. She was furious with her old sorority sister for lying about her husband's death. Why on earth had she done it? She had also neglected to mention that the husband had a title. Did this mean Rosabelle was the Contessa di San Lorenzo? An'gel couldn't imagine why Rosabelle wasn't throwing that about.

Another question popped into her head. How had Rosabelle, who was eighty-two if she was a day, landed a man so handsome and so, well, Italian? Off the movie screen An'gel didn't think she had ever encountered a man this attractive.

She still felt off-balance from the surprise but her instincts for hospitality kicked in. "I am An'gel Ducote, Signor Mingione, or should I say Conte?"

"Please, call me Antonio, if I may be so bold as to call you An'gel." He smiled.

My, the way he said *An'gel.* His pleasant baritone washed over her like warm honey. "Please do," she managed to say. "Let's go into the parlor, shall we? Perhaps you would like something to drink?"

"That would be very kind, An'gel." He followed her into the parlor but stopped a few paces inside. "Such a charming room. Rosabella has told me many times about your lovely home and your distinguished family."

"An'gel, who was that at the door? Oh." Dickce, on her way into the parlor, stopped suddenly when she realized there was a stranger present.

"Dickce, this is Rosabelle's husband, Antonio Mingione, the Conte di San Lorenzo. Antonio, my sister, Dickce."

An'gel watched as the man exerted his seemingly effortless charm on her sister. Dickce blushed when he took her hand and bowed over it. *Did I look that foolish when he bowed over mine?* An'gel wondered. She was thankful Dickce didn't blurt out *I thought you were dead* like she had.

With the initial pleasantries complete, An'gel pointed their new guest to a sofa. "What can we offer you to drink, Antonio?"

"A glass of cold water would be *perfetto*, or as you say, perfect." He flashed his beautiful smile.

"Dickce, would you mind seeing to that?" An'gel sat opposite him on the other sofa.

"It would be my pleasure." Dickce hurried out. An'gel knew her sister would be burning with curiosity the whole time she was out of the room.

"Tell me, An'gel, my wife, she is well? I have been most anxious to see her, for in her last communication with me, she said she had been terribly ill." His expression was the epitome of husbandly concern. "I came to her side as quickly as I could."

"She is upstairs resting at the moment," An'gel said. "Her granddaughter is with her. They will all be down soon. We're about to serve lunch, and we would be delighted to have you join us." She winced inwardly at the thought of serving cold cuts to a member of the Italian nobility. Then she chided herself for being a snob. Really, this man had her much too flustered. *What is wrong with me?*

"Yes, Juanita is most capable, and I would be delighted to join you for lunch," he said. "Forgive me, but you said *they will all be down*. Who else is here?"

"All of the family," An'gel said. "There is something I must tell you, I'm afraid. There has been a tragedy."

"Has some harm come to my wife?" Antonio's face darkened. "I did not take seriously these stories of hers that one of her children is trying to harm her. She exaggerates, you know. But perhaps I have been a fool."

"Rosabelle is fine," An'gel said. "I'm afraid the tragedy

involved Marla Stephens. She fell down our stairs yesterday, and well, she died from the fall."

"*Maledizione!* You tell me this. The one who looks like the unhappy bulldog, she is dead? *Santo cielo.*" He shook his head, as if in disbelief.

An'gel had a sudden urge to laugh at his description of Marla Stephens, but she suppressed it quickly. Stress sure was making her behave oddly, she thought.

Dickce returned with the requested glass of water and brought it to their guest. "*Grazie, signorina.*" He accepted it and drank half of it. "That hit the spot, as you say."

"My pleasure." Dickce sank onto the sofa by An'gel.

"What a terrible thing to happen," Antonio said, his expression grave, as he returned to the subject of his conversation with An'gel. "A most unfortunate accident. I must express my sympathies to Wade and, of course, to Rosabella."

"I regret to have to tell you that it was not an accident," An'gel said. "Someone arranged it to look like an accident, but it was not."

"Antonio, what are you doing here?"

Startled, An'gel turned to see Juanita advancing into the room. She did not appear happy to see her grandmother's husband.

Antonio stood and set his glass on the table beside his chair. He moved forward to greet Juanita, both hands extended. "*Bellissima*, I have just been told the terrible news. Here I come to find my lovely wife, and instead it is tragedy I find."

Juanita stopped in her tracks and folded her arms across her chest. She glared at Antonio, whose hands fell to his sides. "You are unbelievable," Juanita said. "You disappear for three months, and then you suddenly turn up here.

Well, you aren't welcome. Grandmother doesn't want to see you or speak to you."

An'gel glanced at her sister, and Dickce shook her head as if to say *what next?*

"Juanita, my dear, I told Rosabella that I must return to Italy for several weeks to attend to business matters. My son, Benedetto, required my assistance, and I had to consult with my lawyers on other matters. Your grandmother knows this as we discussed it thoroughly before I departed last month." He shrugged.

Juanita grimaced. "I should have known Grandmother was making things up again. She said you had abandoned her and vowed never to return. I'm sorry, Antonio." She held out her hands.

"Do not worry, *bellissima*." Antonio smiled and drew her to him. He kissed both her cheeks and then released her. "I, too, know your *nonna*, and she loves to tell these stories. She must have drama, that one, or her day is otherwise so tedious." He turned to smile at An'gel and Dickce. "She told these charming ladies that she was a widow."

"Honestly," Juanita said, "is there nothing she won't say to get attention?"

Antonio laughed. "She is fiery, my Rosabella, and never boring."

He's either a fool or completely besotted, An'gel thought. How did Rosabelle manage to fascinate men to the point of fatuity? An'gel couldn't understand it.

She rose from the sofa. "I believe lunch should be ready in the dining room. Shall we go in?"

"As you wish, signorina." Antonio offered her his left arm, and she accepted. Dickce and Juanita followed them into the dining room.

On the way An'gel explained that the meal would be a

simple one, and Antonio insisted that whatever food he found at her table would be delightful.

The dining room was empty, and An'gel took Antonio straight to the sideboard and urged him to help himself. He smilingly refused. "No, the ladies, they must go first."

"I will, if you don't mind." Juanita smiled as she picked up a plate. "I want to take something to Grandmother. She was just waking up when I left. I think I will let her have her lunch before I break the news of your arrival, Antonio."

He inclined his head. "As you think best, bellissima. Your nonna will want time to prepare herself to receive me. I know her little ways."

An'gel knew those little ways, too, and she suspected that the next time they saw Rosabelle in public, she would barely resemble the weary, frumpy woman who'd arrived yesterday.

Once Juanita finished loading a plate for Rosabelle, An'gel and Dickce helped themselves. Only then would Antonio prepare anything for himself. He accepted a glass of iced tea from An'gel, and the three of them sat, with An'gel in her usual place at the head of the table.

They ate in companionable silence for several minutes, and An'gel wondered where the rest of her guests were—not that she minded being able to enjoy her food without their lowering presence. Moments later she heard voices and footsteps in the hallway, and Wade Thurmond and Junior Pittman strolled into the dining room.

Wade stopped suddenly, and Junior, who was right behind him, almost knocked into him. Junior managed at the last moment to sidestep.

Wade's lip curled. "Well, well, the gigolo returns."

CHAPTER 23

To Dickce's surprise, Antonio laughed heartily at Wade's insult.

"You will have your little joke, Wade." He sobered as he rose from his chair. "But I must not laugh at a time of such tragedy. Signorina Ducote has told me of the sad loss of your wife. I am so sorry to hear of this."

"Save it for my mother." Wade went the long way around the table to the sideboard, where he picked up a plate and began filling it.

Antonio shrugged and resumed his seat. Dickce was appalled—though not much surprised—by Wade's rudeness, and the ensuing silence felt awkward to her. Even An'gel seemed at a loss for words.

Junior stood uncertainly in the doorway for a moment before he followed his uncle to the sideboard. He glanced at Antonio, then quickly away, as if embarrassed. Dickce wondered whether he agreed with his uncle's opinion of

Antonio. What if Maudine and Bernice felt the same way? Things could become increasingly uncomfortable if the others resented Antonio as much as Wade seemed to do.

Dickce tried to catch her sister's eye, but An'gel appeared focused on her plate for the moment. Dickce wondered where they would put Antonio as she ate her ham sandwich and potato salad. Would he want to share Rosabelle's room? It seemed only natural, since he was her husband. Juanita would have to move the trundle bed to the other guest room in that case. Of course, Rosabelle might not want him in her bedroom. Hard to predict how Rosabelle would react to her "dead" husband's sudden resurrection.

Wade and Junior left the room with their plates and canned soft drinks. Dickce felt the atmosphere lighten with their exit. An'gel must have felt it, too, because she raised her head from her plate and spoke.

"Everyone is a bit on edge, Antonio, because of what happened." An'gel patted her mouth with a linen napkin. "Our sheriff's department is working on the case, and an extremely capable deputy is in charge of the investigation. You will have a chance to meet her soon."

Antonio reached out to touch An'gel's hand lightly, and Dickce was amused to see her sister's face redden the tiniest bit.

"You have no need to make excuses for my stepson's behavior, An'gel. He does not like me, because he believes I am a man with no resources of his own. Therefore, I am the sponge." He shrugged. "It is true that when Rosabella and I first married, I was, how do you say, in reduced circumstances. All my income was tied up in the family business in Italy, but the circumstances, they have changed. Business has much improved, and now I am able to repay my darling Rosabella for her generous support."

That was certainly smooth, Dickce thought. The man oozed charm and sincerity the way a cat shed its hair. He was the most attractive specimen of maleness she had encountered in a long time. She couldn't help responding to his courtly manners earlier, and even now she felt the appeal of his gorgeous voice and charmingly accented English. That attraction aside, however, she didn't completely trust him. Watching him was going to be truly interesting, she decided.

"I'm sure Rosabelle will be delighted to hear it," An'gel said. "I do have a question for you, Antonio, if you don't mind my asking."

"But of course," Antonio said. "I could never refuse so charming a hostess."

Dickce almost snickered when An'gel turned red again. Neither of them was used to such flowery language.

"You are too kind," An'gel said. She took a sip of her water. "I was wondering how you knew where to find Rosabelle."

"Ah, I see." Antonio picked up his water glass and drained it. He rose from the table to refill it. "That is a strange thing. Three, no four, days ago, I received the text message from my wife that she would be visiting her friends here in Mississippi." His drink replenished, he came back to the table. "My Rosabella, you see, is not a person who is fond of the technology. She does not know how to send the text message. Or so she has told me before. In fact, she does not much use the cell phone I gave her, though I insist that she keeps it with her in case of emergencies." He shrugged. "Perhaps someone else send it for her, or she get someone to teach her. *Non importa*."

Dickce figured Rosabelle was simply playing the helpless

wife to the strong and loving husband. That was certainly her style. *I'll bet she knows pretty dang well how to send a text message.* She glanced at An'gel and could tell her sister was probably thinking the exact same thing.

"How interesting," Dickce said. "A member of the family must have sent it for her, then. Although Rosabelle told us when she first arrived that she ran away from home and they didn't know where she was going."

Antonio smiled and shook his head. "One cannot have the play without the audience, eh? My darling must always have the audience for her little productions."

"Truer words were never spoken." An'gel dropped her napkin beside her empty plate and leaned back in her chair. "How fortunate we are that Rosabelle chose to stage her *little production* here. Sadly it has turned out to be a mystifying tragedy."

"Rosabelle told us she thinks a member of the family is trying to kill her," Dickce said. "At first we were inclined to dismiss that as one of her ploys for attention, but we know the accident that killed your daughter-in-law was no accident. It was premeditated."

Antonio frowned. "Before I left California several weeks ago to return to Milano and my business there, Rosabella told me she was uneasy. She almost fell on the stairs in our home one afternoon while I was out. She insisted that it was an attempt by someone to harm her, but I did not believe her. I knew she was not happy, you see, because I had appointments that were of great importance. She wanted me to stay with her that day, but I could not."

Maybe someone should tell Rosabelle about the boy who cried wolf too often, Dickce thought. Her family must be really tired of her constant need for attention by now. *I wouldn't put up with it for very long, that's for sure.*

Dickce was reaching for her glass when a chilling idea struck her. Her hand faltered as she considered the implications. *What if a family member had simply been pushed too far by Rosabelle's behavior? What if one of them wanted her dead for that reason alone?* It might have nothing at all to do with money as Rosabelle claimed. Dickce had read of cases where long-term caregivers had finally snapped and killed the person in their care. They had been strained beyond endurance until the only solution, or so they thought, was to get rid of the source of their endless frustration.

That was possible, Dickce supposed after brief further thought. Money was a powerful motive as well, and if the two were combined—well, whoever killed Marla by mistake was sure to try again. Rosabelle wasn't going to stop being irritating anytime soon, not even to save her own life.

Would the killer make another attempt here at Riverhill? Or wait until Rosabelle and her family were back in California?

With those chilling possibilities swimming around in her head, Dickce realized that while she was lost in thought, An'gel and Antonio were still talking.

". . . not impose upon your so generous hospitality," Antonio said. "I am sure there is a fine hotel in your town nearby, and I will be quite content to take a suite there."

"That is of course up to you," An'gel said, "but we will be happy to accommodate you here. If Rosabelle isn't feeling up to sharing her room, then Dickce can move in with me. I know she would be delighted to let you have her room during your stay."

Oh, Dickce would, would she? She hadn't shared a room or a bed with An'gel since they were children, and she didn't relish the thought of doing it now. An'gel could be so fussy sometimes. Dickce knew her duty, however. "Certainly," she said with enthusiasm. "I know you will want to be close to dear Rosabelle as much as possible. It is not a problem at all."

"You two aren't going to let *him* remain in this house, are you?"

Startled, Dickce glanced toward the doorway. Maudine, hands on hips, glared at Antonio. Bernice, the ever-present shadow, hung back, her expression one of resignation, Dickce thought.

An'gel rose from her chair to face Maudine. "I remind you, Mrs. Pittman, you are a guest in my house. I decide who is welcome here. Are we clear on that point?"

"Well, don't expect me to eat in the same room with that man." Maudine whirled, pushed her sister out of the way, and stalked out of the room.

Bernice advanced toward them timidly. "Hello, Antonio. We didn't expect you here."

Antonio rose and went around the table to Bernice. He took one of her hands and bestowed a kiss on it. "Bernice, how charming to see you, as always. I am here because your mother summoned me to her side. Of course I could not refuse her. I am certain you understand."

Bernice simpered at him. Dickce had to look away to keep from giggling.

"Of course," Bernice said, a little breathless. "Mother has to have her way, no matter what the rest of us think. I'm sure she'll be glad to see you, even if Maudine and Wade aren't."

"I hope *you* are glad to see me, dear Bernice." Antonio smiled at her.

"S-s-sure I am." Bernice blushed. "I don't believe all those things Wade and Maudine say about you being a gigolo." She clapped a hand over her mouth, as if embarrassed by her own words.

Antonio smiled. "I appreciate your kindness to me. Won't you join us?" He moved to pull a chair out for her.

"No, I c-c-can't." She looked at An'gel. "If you don't m-m-mind, I'll take a plate up for Maudine. She'll have a headache soon if she doesn't eat something."

"Please do," An'gel replied.

Bernice nodded, then moved quickly around to the sideboard. She filled two plates almost haphazardly from what Dickce could see. *The poor woman can't wait to get out of here*, she thought. Was she frightened by Antonio? Or simply nervous at being in the presence of an attractive man?

Bernice scurried out of the room without a backward glance, and Dickce hoped she didn't trip and drop everything all over the floor.

Dickce was debating a second sandwich when she heard the doorbell ring. "I'll go," she said. She figured it was either Kanesha or one of her deputies. She hoped it was Kanesha herself, because the sooner Benjy talked to the deputy about the water pistol, the better.

An'gel nodded, and Antonio rose from his chair while she exited the room.

The doorbell rang again, and this time for several seconds. Whoever was at the door was certainly impatient, Dickce thought. She hurried down the hall to open the door before the caller could buzz again.

A scruffy-looking man in stained work clothes wearing a greasy cap stood there.

"Good afternoon," Dickce said. "Can I help you?"

"Howdy, ma'am," the stranger said. "I was wonderin' if by chance you seen a dog and a cat running loose anywhere around here."

CHAPTER 24

Dickce's heart sank. "A dog and a cat, you say?"

"Yes'm. Little bitty cat, kinda red-looking. Dog's about twenty-five pounds, blond-colored, I guess you'd call it." He stared hopefully at her.

"Why don't you step inside, where it's cooler." Dickce moved back and motioned for him to come inside.

"Naw, that's all right, ma'am." He glanced down at his feet. "I got mud all over my boots, and I sure don't want to mess up your floor. The heat ain't bothering me none."

"Very well, then." Dickce stepped outside and closed the door behind her. Outside was better anyway, she decided. She didn't want An'gel coming along and overhearing this conversation.

Upon closer inspection, she thought the man looked familiar. She had probably seen him in town somewhere or else driving a tractor on the highway. He looked like a farmer.

"I'm Dickce Ducote," she said. "I'm sorry, I don't remember if we've met."

"Oh, everyone around here knows you, ma'am." The man smiled shyly. "I'm Claud Thayer. My farm's not far from here, back the other way from Athena."

Dickce nodded. "You were saying, Mr. Thayer, you're looking for a dog and a cat? Are they yours?"

"Kinda," he said. "They was my mama's, and she passed away about a week ago. She didn't have them long, and I ain't got time to look after no animals in the house."

"I'm sorry about your mother," Dickce said. She vaguely recalled seeing an obituary for a Mrs. Thayer in the local paper recently. "Did the animals run away from the house?"

Thayer shook his head. "Naw, they was in the back of the truck. I was taking 'em to town to that animal shelter. I know they take animals and try to find 'em a good home." He looked troubled. "I hated not to keep 'em, seeing they was my mama's, and she sure did love 'em. But they're young, and they need attention, and I can't give it to them, the way I work."

Dickce felt better now. Mr. Thayer seemed like a good man who only wanted what was best for the animals. If he had been unpleasant, she was prepared to lie through her teeth to keep him away from the two pets.

"We did find your missing animals," she said. "A friend and I were driving to town this morning. We picked them up and took them to the veterinarian to be checked out."

"I'm glad you found 'em before they got hit by a car. I still don't know when they got out of the truck. I guess I wasn't paying enough attention, and they just jumped out. I looked up and down the road but I couldn't find 'em nowhere."

"Were they loose in the back of your pickup?" Dickce tried to keep the censure out of her tone. She didn't approve of animals riding in the beds of pickups like that, but it was standard practice with farmers and hunters around here.

"Yes'm," Claud Thayer said. "I reckon that wasn't the smartest thing I could'a done, but I was in a hurry to get to town and back. Got a lot of plowing to do, you see."

"They probably did jump out then," Dickce said. "They weren't hurt, as far as I could tell. As I said, the veterinarian in town is checking them over."

Thayer started to speak, but Dickce forestalled him, certain of what he was about to say. "Don't worry about the vet's bill. I took them, and I will pay whatever the charges are." She looked the farmer straight in the eye. "I would like to keep them here, if you have no objection, Mr. Thayer. They will have a good home with me and my sister." She tensed slightly, waiting for him to protest.

Thayer smiled. "That sounds mighty fine to me, Miss Ducote, ma'am. Mama would rise from the grave and haunt me the rest of my life if I didn't find a good home for her babies. You have relieved my burden, and I thank you."

Dickce was deeply touched by the man's heartfelt words, and she could feel the tears starting to form. "Your mama can rest easy. They'll have a good home." She sniffed. "What are their names? If they're already used to them, it might be better not to change them."

"Mama called the dog Peanut 'cause she said he was the color of a peanut hull right out of the ground." He smiled. "That's a good name for a dog, I reckon. She called the cat after somebody on her favorite TV show. Reckon it was because the cat's red. Ain't never seen a cat that color before."

"It is unusual," Dickce said. "What is the name?"

"Endora," Thayer replied. "Mama loved the *Bewitched*

program because she thought that Agnes Moorehead on there was such a pistol."

Dickce laughed. "She sure was. It sounds like a good name to me. Thank you, Mr. Thayer."

The farmer nodded. "And I thank you, ma'am. I can rest easy now knowing Mama's babies are going to be happy here." He ducked his head and headed for his truck.

Dickce watched for a moment. She uttered a brief prayer of thanks before she went back inside.

An'gel was coming down the hall toward her. "Who was that? It wasn't Kanesha, was it?"

Dickce shook her head. "No, only some farmer looking for missing animals." She hoped An'gel would leave it at that and not ask for details.

An'gel grimaced. "Farmers need to keep their fences up better. We don't need cows out on the highway. Someone could get killed."

"You're right," Dickce said, relieved. "We surely don't need cows loose out there." Before An'gel could pursue the subject any further, Dickce asked, "Were you serious about giving Antonio my room? Why don't we let him stay at the Farrington House if Rosabelle doesn't want him in her room?"

An'gel looked exasperated. "It's fine with me if he wants to go to a hotel. I felt I had to make the offer, though, because he *is* Rosabelle's husband. It will depend on what Rosabelle has to say. I wish she would come downstairs."

Dickce glanced up. "Here she comes now," she said in an undertone. "At least I *think* it's Rosabelle."

The vision of glamour moving slowly down the marble stars didn't look much like the Rosabelle who had arrived yesterday. Gone was the dowdy dress, replaced by a form-fitting silk sheath in a brilliant red. Rosabelle was indeed thinner than Dickce remembered from the last time she had visited, but certain parts of her anatomy were still shapely. Ropes of pearls lay across her bosom, framing a diamond pendant. More diamonds winked from her ears, and her hair was pulled back into a sleek bun at the nape of her neck. A diamond and pearl hair clip adorned the left side of her head, and Dickce saw more jewels on her hands. Red leather stilettos on her feet, Rosabelle moved with cat-like grace. She reached the bottom of the stairs and walked toward Dickce and An'gel.

"Juanita tells me that my wandering husband has returned," she said, her voice throatier and more languid than they had heard before. "Where is he?"

"In the dining room," An'gel said.

Dickce couldn't take her eyes off Rosabelle. She had never seen a transformation to match this one. Now she felt she could understand her old sorority sister's fascination for men like Antonio Mingione.

"Would you be a dear and tell him I would like to see him in the parlor?" Without waiting for a response, Rosabelle oozed forward into the parlor.

"I certainly will not," An'gel said, but too late for Rosabelle to hear. She turned to Dickce. "Have you ever seen anything like that in your life?"

"Sure beats television." Dickce grinned. "I'll be happy to inform the Conti di San Lorenzo that the Contessa is ready to receive him."

"You do that," An'gel said. "I'm going to the kitchen to talk to Clementine about dinner." She walked off in a huff.

Dickce headed for the dining room. She was trying to think of a way to include herself in Rosabelle's conversation with her husband. She was dying to hear what Rosabelle would say to him.

As she neared the dining room, she could hear Antonio talking. In Italian, she realized when she reached the doorway. He had a cell phone to his ear.

"*Sì, sì, carissimo. È necessario essere pazienti. Vorrei per il divorzio.*" He paused. "*Sì, prometto, mio caro. Non appena è saggio. Sì, sì. Prometto, prometto.*" He glanced toward the doorway and spotted Dickce. "*Ciao.*" He ended the call.

"Antonio," Dickce said, her expression bland. "I am so sorry to interrupt you, but Rosabelle is downstairs now and would like you to join her in the parlor."

Antonio gave her an odd look, but then he smiled. "How delightful. I am eager to see my lovely wife. I will go to her now."

Dickce stood aside to let him pass, then followed him down the hall. She was determined to witness his reunion with Rosabelle somehow.

Especially since he'd been talking to someone on the phone about a divorce.

CHAPTER 25

Dickce's Italian was rusty. The last time she and An'gel had traveled to Italy was seven years ago. She recalled enough of it, however, to get the gist of Antonio's conversation. He had promised someone that he would talk about a divorce. He had told the other person to be patient.

The really interesting thing was that the person on the other end of the conversation was a man. *Mio caro*, Antonio had said. *My beloved*, but the gender of the Italian phrase was clearly masculine. Not *mia cara*, as one would expect with a woman.

Perhaps Antonio had been speaking to his son. What was the name he had mentioned? Benedetto. The Italian for Benedict. Dickce supposed it wasn't all that strange for an Italian man to refer to his son in such a way. Italians were more emotionally expressive than Southern men—that was for sure.

It still sounded a bit odd, Dickce decided, as she followed

Antonio all the way to the door of the parlor. She stayed a couple of steps behind, and he didn't seem to realize she was right there with him.

He strode in, arms outstretched. "Rosabella, *cara mia*, I am so happy to see you. I told you I would return to you as soon as I could."

Dickce crept to the edge of the door and peered in. Rosabelle stood at the fireplace, from which vantage point she stared coolly at her husband. As Dickce watched, Rosabelle held out a hand and allowed Antonio to take it. He bowed and kissed it, then straightened.

Rosabelle still had not spoken. Antonio held out his hands. "This is how you greet your beloved husband after he returns to you? Do not be so cold, cara, for I bring you wonderful news that will make you so, so happy."

Rosabelle proffered a cheek, and Antonio stepped forward to bestow a kiss. "Your news had better be wonderful after the way you deserted me, you cad." She tossed her head. "I could have been murdered at any time without you here to protect me. I will have more to say about that in a moment." She moved away from the fireplace and sat on the sofa. She patted the cushion beside her. "Come tell me your news first."

Dickce wished she had her cell phone with her. She would love to have video to show An'gel later when she told her about this touching reunion à la Barbara Cartland.

"The lawyers have rescued me," Antonio said. "My inheritance is safe, and I no longer have need of your money. Is that not wonderful, my dear? Everything has been restored to me, and I am once again a wealthy man. A wealthy man with a wife who is bellissima."

He certainly loved that word, Dickce thought. *Most beautiful*, indeed. She almost snorted but caught herself in time.

"The *palazzo* in Venice, the country estate, the factory in Milan, and the buildings in Rome? All definitely yours now?"

Rosabelle sounded so mercenary.

"Yes, my dear, I can take you to Italy now and present you as the Contessa di San Lorenzo. You will love the *palazzo*, I assure you. It will be my delight to show you Venezia. And to show you to Venezia."

Oh, brother. The corn harvest bid fair to be substantial, if he kept this up. Dickce had to clap a hand over her mouth to contain her mirth.

"You will finally be able to fulfill your promises to me, then." Rosabelle touched his cheek briefly. Then she turned away. "It was almost too late."

"What do you mean, Rosabella?" Antonio sounded genuinely puzzled.

"Did An'gel not tell you about what happened in this very house yesterday?"

"She did tell me about the accident, yes, how the wife of your son fell down the stairs and died," he said. "She also said it was not really an accident, but I did not understand completely what she meant."

"It was an attempt to murder me," Rosabelle said in a flat tone. "One of my dear family put water on those stairs out there, waiting for me to slip and fall and break my neck." She laughed, a little wildly, Dickce thought. "Stupid Marla, however, saved my life. She went down before me and died instead."

"These stories you have been telling me then, about a person who wants to harm you, they are true?" Antonio shook his head. "I do not understand, my dear. Why would one of them want to do such a terrible thing?"

"They all *hate* me," Rosabelle said. "Except perhaps for dear Juanita, although she does pester me for money sometimes." Her voice rose as she continued. "That's all they care about. The money. They want me dead so they can have it all for themselves."

Antonio seized her hands and held them. "Calm yourself, cara. Now that I have returned, you will be safe. I will not let anyone harm you." He pulled a now-willing Rosabelle into his arms, and she rested her head on his shoulder. "Signorina An'gel tells me that a capable person is investigating and will soon know who did this terrible thing."

"So An'gel says," Rosabelle said as she lifted her head. "I have my doubts. But An'gel knows the woman, and An'gel is shrewd, if nothing else. You must stay by my side, Antonio. Now that you are here, I will be able to rest." She sighed. "I know I look haggard and careworn because I have lost so much sleep."

Rosabelle was even more shameless than Dickce remembered. Men could be such fools at times.

"You are as lovely as ever, cara mia," Antonio said. He kissed her cheek. "Do not tell me such silly things."

His mouth moved to hers, and Dickce looked away. Eavesdropping was one thing, but she drew the line at watching them necking.

After a moment, the embrace evidently ended. Rosabelle laughed in a way that Dickce figured was intended to be seductive. "Tell me more about your business with the lawyers. Did you talk to them about everything you promised me?"

Dickce peeked into the room again. Rosabelle had a stern expression, and Antonio was looking away from her.

"Yes, cara, I did talk to them, but it is not so easy, you understand, to change the will. I must think of Benedetto. He is my son."

"So you say." Rosabelle tossed her head.

A voice whispered somewhere near Dickce's ear. "What *are* you doing?"

Startled, Dickce drew back from the doorway to see An'gel, hands on hips, glaring at her. Dickce motioned for An'gel to follow her as she moved across the hall to stand in front of the library door. She could hear the murmur from the television set through the partially open door. She pulled it gently shut. No need to disturb Wade and Junior.

"What do you think I was doing?" she said crossly. "I was spying on Rosabelle and Antonio. You picked a fine time to interrupt me. They were talking about Antonio's will."

"I don't care what they were talking about, Dickce. Your behavior is outrageous," An'gel said. "What if they had caught you? Think how embarrassing that would be."

"Rosabelle loves an audience, you know that." Dickce snickered. "It was quite a performance, let me tell you." She did feel a tad guilty over her violation of the rules of hospitality, but she wasn't about to admit it to her sister.

"What goes on between Rosabelle and her husband is no business of ours," An'gel said.

"Even if it's pertinent to these attempts on Rosabelle's life?"

An'gel stared at her for a moment, and Dickce could tell she had hooked her fish. "Pertinent how?" An'gel said.

"If I understood everything correctly," Dickce said, "Rosabelle evidently gave Antonio a lot of money. His affairs were in a mess, and he had to have the lawyers in Italy get it all sorted out, which they did. He now has control of his inheritance, as he called it. A palazzo in Venice, a factory in Milan, buildings in Rome, and a country estate. I think he might even have tried to change his will to include Rosabelle—but that's where you interrupted me."

"I don't see how it's all that pertinent," An'gel said after a few moments' thought. "Let's say that Antonio is worth millions, and he includes Rosabelle in his will. He would have to die before her for her to inherit any of it. So why would someone try to kill her before she had a chance to inherit from him? Seems to me he would be the first target."

"You saw how Wade and Maudine reacted to him," Dickce said. "They apparently think he's a gold digger with no money of his own. Once they find out he really is rich, they will feel differently, you can bet on that."

"I wonder if Antonio is in Rosabelle's will," An'gel said. "Oh, what's the use of all this speculation? I don't think any of this is helpful."

"There's a bit more that you haven't heard yet," Dickce said. "I'm not sure if it's relevant, but you might as well hear it anyway." She gave her sister a summary of the phone conversation she had overheard.

"You're sure about the gender of the person on the other end?" An'gel asked.

"He was talking fast," Dickce said, "but I'm sure I heard it correctly."

"He was talking to his son, surely," An'gel said. "But the part about a divorce is certainly interesting. What do you want to bet he latched on to Rosabelle and her money so he could afford to pay the lawyers in Italy to get his inheritance back? Now that he has, he may be planning to divorce her."

Dickce shrugged. "That's what it sounds like to me."

"He's slick, I'll give him that." An'gel sniffed. "He didn't fool me for a minute, though."

"No, of course not," Dickce said, trying hard not to laugh. They had both been charmed by the man at first, no matter what An'gel was claiming now.

Footsteps on marble sounded above them, and Dickce

looked up to see Juanita descending the stairs, plates in hand. Dickce started forward to meet her.

"Let me take those," she said when Juanita reached the bottom.

"I don't mind taking them to the kitchen," Juanita said. "I'm going that way anyway. I thought I might have a bit more lunch."

"Please help yourself," An'gel said. "Thank you for taking care of all that."

Juanita smiled as she headed down the hall toward the kitchen.

"I think they've had enough time alone," An'gel said. "Come on, let's go talk to the happy couple."

Dickce wondered what her sister had in mind. She shrugged and followed An'gel.

They met Rosabelle and Antonio, arm in arm, coming out of the parlor. "There you are," Rosabelle said with a slight smile. "I was just coming to find you. Would you be a dear and tell everyone that Antonio and I have news we would like to share with them?"

Without waiting for a response, she turned and walked back into the parlor, taking Antonio with her.

CHAPTER 26

An'gel stared after Rosabelle. "The *nerve* of that woman."

"You mean the Contessa di San Lorenzo?" Dickce laughed. "She'll be worse than ever now. I'll pass the message to Wade and Junior"—she nodded toward the library—"and you can tell Juanita. Let *her* go upstairs and spread the news there."

"Good idea," An'gel said. She wasn't about to traipse up and down the stairs at some whim of Rosabelle's.

She found Juanita in the kitchen chatting with Clementine while the housekeeper supervised her granddaughter and Benjy. Antoinette was snapping green beans, and Benjy was peeling potatoes. They sat at opposite ends of the kitchen table, and Diesel went back and forth between them, chirping and tapping their legs with his paws. An'gel was glad to see that apparently neither one of them was giving in to his pleas for a taste of their efforts. She was sure he had already gained at least a pound from all the tidbits she and Dickce had given him over and above his regular diet. Charlie would probably fuss at them when he returned to find his large cat even larger.

"Juanita, sorry to bother you," An'gel said, "but your grandmother would like to see all of you in the parlor. Would you mind letting your mother and your aunt know?"

"Sure," Juanita said. "Did Grandmother say what this is all about?"

"No," An'gel replied. "She is with her husband, however."

Juanita looked thoughtful. "I wonder if they've made up." She laughed. "With my grandmother, you never can tell. I'll go fetch Mother and Aunt Maudine." She turned to Clementine. "Thank you for your advice on stains. Lipstick is such a pain to get out."

"You're surely welcome," Clementine said.

Benjy brought his bowl of peeled potatoes to the housekeeper. "Are you sure that will be enough? I don't mind peeling more."

Clementine took the bowl and set it in the sink. "No, honey, that's plenty. Thank you for your kind assistance."

"Glad to help." Benjy turned to An'gel. "Do you think she means for me to come? To the parlor, I mean, since I'm not really family."

An'gel frowned. "I'm not sure. Since I don't know what she plans to say, I have no idea whether it will affect you at all. You might as well be there, though."

"Okay, then," Benjy said. "I need to talk to Miss Dickce about something anyway."

An'gel wondered what that could be but she didn't pry. Her sister seemed to have established a rapport with the boy, and she saw no need to interfere. At least, not yet. She hoped Dickce wouldn't get too attached to him, because he would be on his way back to California soon. Along with the rest of them, An'gel hoped. She couldn't wait for the house to be empty of guests.

Benjy left for the parlor, and An'gel checked with Clementine to be sure that preparations for the evening meal were well in hand.

"Stop worrying," Clementine told her. "We're doing fine in here. You go on back to your guests."

An'gel would far rather have stayed in the kitchen, but duty called. Rosabelle hadn't said she and Dickce weren't included, so she might as well go herself. She and Dickce had a right to know what was going on in their own house.

When An'gel walked into the parlor, she saw that everyone was present, including her sister. Rosabelle and Antonio stood before the fireplace, with children and grandchildren occupying the sofas. Dickce and Benjy had claimed two of the nearby chairs, and An'gel took the third.

Rosabelle moved closer to Antonio and slipped her right hand into the crook of his arm. They smiled at each other.

"I have the most wonderful news to share with you," Rosabelle said. "My darling Antonio and I have reconciled."

"Carissima," Antonio murmured, his eyes fixed on his wife's face. "This is the happiest of days."

An'gel was surprised that neither Maudine nor Wade spoke up after this overly sweet display, given the loathing they had evinced toward Antonio. She wondered what kept them silent.

"Yes, it is, my darling," Rosabelle cooed back at him. She faced her family again. "With my generous financial support, Antonio has been in Italy, working with his lawyers to regain control of his inheritance and his business interests. I am so pleased to hear that he has been successful."

"I don't believe it," Maudine said.

"You mean he really *does* have money after all?" Wade sounded bemused.

"He certainly does, oodles and oodles," Rosabelle said. "You can no longer insult me or my husband with your vulgar displays. I cannot believe the word *gigolo* ever passed your lips."

"As I recall, you didn't believe him yourself," Maudine said. "In fact, you told us you were going to divorce him right after he left you. To go to Italy, apparently."

An'gel thought Maudine still sounded highly skeptical. An'gel had to admit that she was a bit skeptical herself, though she had no sound reason for doubting Antonio's claims to wealth.

"Is that it then? That's the big announcement? That Antonio is loaded after all?" Wade leaned forward. "If that's the case, then you can turn loose some of the money from my father's estate that should be coming to me. Right now I don't even have enough money to bury my wife properly."

"Yes," Maudine said. "Surely you can afford to be generous now, Mother."

"I have been far too generous already." Rosabelle tossed her head. "You've been living in my house, at my expense, for several years now. You could have gone out and gotten a job at any time if you weren't happy with your allowance under the terms of your fathers' wills. Nothing was stopping you." She paused to sneer. "Nothing except bone idleness."

"Rosabella, my dear, do not allow them to tarnish our

happiness in this way," Antonio said in a soothing tone. "You must not upset yourself."

"You are right, darling Antonio," Rosabelle said. "You will all soon have the house to yourselves anyway. You can do what you like. I am moving to Italy to live there with my husband. We plan to leave as soon as all the arrangements can be made."

"Are you out of your freakin' mind?" Wade jumped up from the sofa. "You can't do that."

An'gel was puzzled. Why would it matter to her children if Rosabelle wanted to live in Italy? From what Rosabelle had told her, the house would belong to Wade eventually, so surely they would all be able to stay in it, even if Rosabelle didn't live there.

"We can't afford the taxes and the upkeep on that house without you living there," Wade said. "You know perfectly well our incomes from the trusts aren't large enough."

"That's all *your* father's fault," Maudine said, pointing a finger at her half brother. "It was his stupid will that created this mess. He should have tied part of the trust income to the house itself."

An'gel figured out the situation. Rosabelle had been paying the taxes, upkeep, and general expenses for the house out of her income from the trust set up by her second husband, Wade's father. If Rosabelle wasn't living in the house, she no longer had to spend her income that way. It wasn't tied to her residence in the house.

Now she could understand why Wade and Maudine were so upset. When Rosabelle went to live in Italy, her income went with her. Wade and his half sisters would have to pay for everything themselves. An'gel had no idea as to the extent of their incomes from their trusts, but surely if they combined their money, they could afford to stay in the house.

Rosabelle was well within her rights to move to Italy with her husband. An'gel frankly had little sympathy for her children, because it sounded like they had been sponging off their mother for years.

"Don't blame Wade's father for this," Rosabelle said, eyes flashing. "It's not his fault that Wade throws away money at the racetrack like he was printing it in the basement. I've bailed him out for the last time. Maudine, you can sell that ridiculous collection of yours. Goodness knows you've spent an untold fortune on those stupid Barbie dolls. I get the creeps every time I go in your room. A woman your age still playing with dolls. It's obscene." She paused for a quick breath. "Bernice is the only one of you who has any sense where money is concerned. She at least managed to put her daughter through nursing school. I was the one who paid for your son to go to college, and it only took him seven years."

Rosabelle was panting by the time she finished her tirade. Her family appeared thoroughly cowed now, An'gel thought. *Good for Rosabelle.* It was way past time they all grew up and took responsibility for themselves. She realized Rosabelle herself had been at fault for letting them mooch off her for so long, but that was no excuse for their collective lack of backbone.

"Come, my darling," Antonio said, his expression the epitome of loving concern. "Let us retire so that you may rest. We have much to discuss in private, do we not?" He patted the hand still tucked in the crook of his arm.

Rosabelle nodded. Juanita got up from the sofa and approached her grandmother. "I think it's wonderful. I'm sure you'll love Italy. Will you allow me to visit once you're settled?"

"Of course," Rosabelle said. "But you'll have to buy the plane ticket yourself."

"Naturally, Grandmother, I wouldn't expect you to pay for it," Juanita said.

"Come along, Antonio," Rosabelle said, turning away from her granddaughter. "I would like to go to my room."

Her family remained silent until she left. Then a heated discussion broke out with talk of lawyers and injunctions and insanity hearings. Wade and Maudine talked over each other with their ideas, while Junior and Juanita sat and listened. Bernice wrung her hands and rocked back and forth.

An'gel motioned for Dickce and Benjy to follow her out of the room. In the hall she turned to them and said, "We might as well leave them to it. I have no desire to hear all of that nonsense."

"Me either," Benjy said. "They're disgusting, worse than a pack of hyenas."

An'gel couldn't help but notice that he looked miserable. Dickce must have noticed, too, because she put her arm around the boy. "Come along with me," Dickce said. "Let's go to the kitchen and get something to drink. I don't know about you, but I could use some caffeine right about now."

Benjy went willingly with Dickce. An'gel remained where she was and watched them until they disappeared into the kitchen. She wanted to talk to Dickce about the appalling idea that had occurred to her, but now obviously wasn't the time. Her sister was more concerned with Benjy.

An'gel walked into the library and sat at the desk. She pulled the phone over and punched in the number for the sheriff's department. Kanesha needed to know about this right away. For one thing, An'gel was sure the chief deputy wouldn't allow Rosabelle to swan off to Italy with her husband until the investigation was complete.

Far more worrisome was the realization that Rosabelle had now upped the ante for her own murder.

CHAPTER 27

Dickce suggested that they take their ice-cold cans of soda to the garage apartment, and Benjy agreed. She had watched him during Rosabelle's big announcement and its aftermath, and she could tell that he was worried. She suspected she knew the reason for some of his concerns, and she had an idea about how to resolve them. She hadn't consulted An'gel yet, but she didn't think her sister would have serious objections. Besides, Benjy might not like her idea at all.

She waited until they were upstairs and seated before she said, "I have good news about our two four-legged friends that will make you feel better."

"Did the vet call already? Can we go get them today?" Benjy sounded happy.

"No, the vet hasn't called."

Benjy's disappointment was obvious.

"I found out where they came from," Dickce said. She

told Benjy about her talk with the farmer and his willingness for Dickce to take the animals. "He told me their names, too. His mother named the cat Endora and the dog Peanut."

"Endora?" Benjy frowned. "Isn't that the name of that character from *Bewitched*? Oh, I get it, because of the red hair." He paused. "It's pretty cool, actually. Endora. I like it."

"I like it, too," Dickce said. "I also like Peanut. Mrs. Thayer thought Peanut's hair was like the color of peanut hulls, and that's why she chose that name for him."

"Peanut is a good name for a dog," Benjy said. "I'm glad he doesn't want them back. I just wish . . ."

"What do you wish, Benjy?" Dickce said, although she was sure she knew.

Benjy shrugged. "It doesn't matter. It would be stupid to even think I could."

"You mean take them to California with you?" Dickce said.

"Yes, ma'am," Benjy said. "I told you it was stupid. I don't have the money to take care of them, and I may not even have a place to live. I didn't have much to begin with, but now that the Wart's mother is going to live in Italy, he's sure not going to want me in the house. He already complains about how much I eat."

"You told me about your father," Dickce said. "You don't have any other relatives at all? Grandparents, cousins, aunts, uncles, anyone?"

Benjy shook his head. "My mom didn't have any brothers or sisters, and her parents died a long time ago. I don't know much about them and whether they had any other family. Even if they did, I have no idea who they are. Same thing with my father's side. I know even less about them."

If he did have relatives, they could be traced, but Dickce didn't see much point. Later on, Benjy might want to know more about them, but his most pressing need at the moment was a home. Dickce had the solution to that problem, but she didn't know whether Benjy would find it acceptable.

"Having Peanut and Endora living with An'gel and me will require some adjustments." Dickce decided to take a sideways approach to her idea. "We haven't had animals in the house since we were about your age. They're both young and are going to need a lot of attention. Not to mention a lot of energy, and I don't know if we're really going to be up to the task."

"You mean you think you shouldn't keep them after all?" Benjy looked distressed at the prospect.

"No, that's not what I meant at all." Dickce realized she needed to get to the point. "I think we need someone younger here who can help take care of them. Like making sure Peanut gets enough exercise, for example. An'gel and I are pretty fit, but a young, healthy dog has a tremendous amount of energy."

Benjy examined the top of his soda can. "Maybe someone young like me, you mean? To work for you and take care of the animals?"

"Exactly like you," Dickce said. "What do you think, Benjy?"

"I know how to do a lot of things." Benjy still wouldn't look directly at her. "Like laundry and cleaning and stuff like that. I did it all the time for me and my mom, even after we went to live with the Wart and his family. I could help Clementine a lot, and I think she likes me."

Dickce's plans didn't include turning Benjy into a full-time servant, but she knew it might be better for him, at least for a little while, to feel like he was earning his keep.

She would save her plans for him to go to college and on to veterinary school for a later time.

"I know you would work hard and be a lot of help," Dickce said. "The main thing would be to look after Endora and Peanut, of course. So what do you say? Would you like to give it a try?"

"Yes, please." Benjy finally looked at her, and she could see that his eyes were a bit wet. "I don't want to go back to that house and those people. I have a couple of friends out there, but nobody really special."

"Then it's settled," Dickce said. Her own eyes felt suspiciously wet now. "We can arrange for your things to be sent here, and you won't even have to go back for them, if you don't want."

"That's great," Benjy said, "except for Bert and Ernie. My tarantulas. I can't ship them, but one of my friends will take them."

Dickce was relieved to hear it. She wasn't that keen on sharing quarters with a couple of big spiders. An'gel most certainly wouldn't be keen either.

"That's a good idea," Dickce said. "Let's keep this to ourselves for now. Then at the appropriate moment we'll let everybody know you're going to stay here."

"Have you talked to your sister about this?" Benjy asked. "I'm not sure she likes me."

"She hasn't had the chance to get to know you yet," Dickce said. "Not like I have. You leave her to me. She won't have a problem with this." *Not after I get through with her*, she added to herself.

"You are going to tell her about Endora and Peanut tomorrow when you bring them home, aren't you?"

"As soon as there's a good time," Dickce said. "Before we go pick them up tomorrow, we'll have to do some shopping. Food, of course, and a litter box and so on for Endora. Toys and whatever else they'll need."

"I can make a list," Benjy said. "I found some paper and pencils in a drawer in the kitchen area here."

"That sounds like a good idea." Dickce reached over and patted his arm. "I'm so pleased, Benjy. I really do hope you'll be happy here." She rose from the sofa. "I'd better get back over to the house and see what's going on."

"I think I'll stay here for a while. It's too crazy over there for me." Benjy shook his head.

"I know exactly what you mean." Dickce laughed. "I'll see you later, then."

"Definitely," Benjy said. He got up and gave her a quick hug.

Dickce walked back to the house wearing a big smile. The moment she stepped into the kitchen, Clementine spotted her.

"Miss An'gel's looking for you. She's all worked up about something. You'd better go see. I think she's in the library."

Dickce sighed, her smile gone. "I will. I wonder what it is now." In her concern for Benjy, she hadn't given much thought to Rosabelle and her big announcement. On the way to the library, though, Dickce figured out what had probably gotten her sister riled up. Rosabelle was practically begging to be murdered.

She found An'gel in the library with Diesel. "Here I am."

An'gel, seated behind the desk, was stroking the cat's head. At the sight of Dickce, he meowed and padded over to her. She took a seat in a chair near the desk, and Diesel stood beside her. He tapped her leg with a paw to remind her that he needed attention. She laughed and patted his head.

"It's good to see you, too, you big handsome boy." Dickce wanted to tell him that, starting tomorrow, he would have a couple of playmates, but she couldn't, not while An'gel was present.

"Where were you?" An'gel asked.

"Talking with Benjy," Dickce replied. "I'm concerned about him. Did you know that he has no other relatives, now that his mother is dead?" She might as well plant a few seeds right away.

"No, I didn't," An'gel said. "I know you're taking an interest in him, and it's good that someone is. Wade Thurmond doesn't impress me much as the fatherly sort. That poor boy is in a difficult situation."

"What was it you wanted to see me about?" Dickce asked. She was pleased to know that her sister's interest was engaged. That would make things easier.

"After you and Benjy left, I came to a startling realization," An'gel said.

"You realized that Rosabelle had made herself an even bigger target by declaring her intention to move to Italy with Antonio."

"I thought you would probably see that, too." An'gel shook her head. "I am concerned over what could happen tonight. The killer may be even more desperate now."

"He or she might also target Antonio," Dickce said. "I hadn't thought of it before, but that would also be a way to stop Rosabelle from moving to Italy."

"Possibly," An'gel said. "But Rosabelle could inherit substantial property in Italy. I can't imagine that Antonio's son, Benedetto—wasn't that the name?—that Benedetto would be happy to have an American stepmother taking part of what he thinks of as rightfully his."

"True." Dickce felt a paw on her leg, and she resumed

rubbing Diesel's head. "I have to say, after hearing that conversation in Italian, I have an odd feeling about this Benedetto."

"What do you mean?"

"Remember I told you that he was talking to a man, whom he addressed as *mio caro*?"

An'gel nodded. "That may simply be a term of affection for his son. It's not something an American man might do, but he's Italian."

"Rosabelle said something a bit odd, too, in reference to Benedetto. It was right before you came up and startled me." Dickce paused for a moment. "Antonio said, 'I must think of Benedetto. He is my son.' Then Rosabelle said, 'So you say.' Don't you think that's a strange response?"

"In the context of changing his will, no, not necessarily. That could be all Rosabelle meant. 'So you say you have to consider your son.' "

"I suppose," Dickce replied. "Maybe I'm making too much out of it. There was something about the tone of his voice during that phone conversation."

"We're both letting our imaginations go into overdrive, I think, thanks to the stress of the situation." An'gel shook her head. "Back to what I originally wanted to tell you. I called Kanesha right away to tell her about Rosabelle's plans, and she's on her way here."

The doorbell rang, and Dickce started. "Perfect timing."

"Let's go." An'gel rose from the desk and headed out of the library. Dickce and Diesel followed.

An'gel opened the door to admit Kanesha, who greeted them both. Diesel started to dart out once the deputy was inside. He made it onto the verandah, but Dickce moved quickly enough to grab him. She got him back inside and waited for An'gel to shut the door.

An'gel wasn't moving. Instead she stood there staring out at the driveway and frowning.

Dickce released the cat and shut the door herself. She did take a peek at the driveway, but all she saw was Kanesha's patrol car. What was so strange about that?

CHAPTER 28

"There's no car," An'gel said. She stared at the door as if she could see through it.

"Yes, there is," Dickce replied, obviously puzzled. "Kanesha's squad car is right there on the driveway."

"Are you all right, Miss An'gel?" Kanesha asked. "Were you expecting another car?"

"There should be another car in the driveway," An'gel said. "All our other guests have put their cars behind the house, near the garage. I should have realized it earlier, when he arrived."

"What are you talking about, Sister?" Dickce said.

"Antonio," An'gel replied. "There's no car in the driveway, so how did he get here? He surely didn't walk."

"That's definitely strange," Kanesha said. "He could have taken a taxi from Athena."

"Then how did he get to Athena? Surely he didn't take a taxi all the way down from Memphis—assuming that he flew into Memphis, that is." An'gel couldn't make sense of it.

"We'll just have to ask him," Dickce said. "I'm sure there's a logical explanation." She chuckled. "Unless he got beamed down from the mother ship."

An'gel threw her a sour look. She turned to Kanesha. "Let's go into the library. Dickce and I have a few things to share with you before you talk to Rosabelle."

An'gel resumed her seat at the desk, and Kanesha and Dickce took chairs near it. Diesel sat in front of the deputy and chirped.

"Yes, cat, I see you," Kanesha said. Her hands remained on the arms of her chair. Diesel looked at her for a moment before turning and going to sit by An'gel's chair.

"Dickce, tell Kanesha about the phone conversation you overheard," An'gel said.

Dickce gave a quick summary of Antonio's side of the conversation.

"You're sure that he was talking to a man?" Kanesha asked when she finished.

"Yes," Dickce replied. "We think it could have been his son in Italy, but the tone of the words sounded a bit, well, intimate, for the lack of any other word."

"The main point is that he promised this person he was going to ask Rosabelle for a divorce," An'gel said. "There was no hint of it otherwise in his demeanor toward Rosabelle."

"That could be a side issue that has nothing to do with the murder," Kanesha said. "The main point, it seems to me, is the plan to move to Italy and the effect that could have." She frowned. "What should I call her? Sultan was her maiden name, wasn't it?"

An'gel nodded. "We still think of her that way. Keeping track of the three husbands and their names seemed like too much trouble. Antonio's surname is Mingione, but he also has a title, Conte di San Lorenzo."

"That makes her the contessa, then?" Kanesha asked.

"Yes," Dickce said. "Now that she wants to go live in Italy, you can bet she's going to make the most of it, too."

"Until we solve this case, I can't allow her to leave the country," Kanesha said. "She's a suspect along with most of her family."

"The only exceptions being Benjy and Junior, right?" Dickce said. "Because they had no opportunity to go upstairs and set the stage for the accident."

Kanesha nodded. "I've ruled them out. I need to talk to the contessa and her husband now. I need to make sure she understands the situation."

An'gel rose. "I'll go up and let them know you want to talk to them." She didn't relish the prospect of interrupting whatever little tête-à-tête Rosabelle and Antonio might be having. She couldn't put it off, however. When she arrived at Rosabelle's room, she tapped lightly on the door. She heard nothing from inside the room. Were they asleep? She rapped soundly three times, and after a moment, Rosabelle opened the door. She was in her dressing gown, and An'gel felt a bit awkward.

She looked at the doorknob as she spoke. "Sorry to bother you, but Chief Deputy Berry is here. She needs to speak to you and to Antonio right away."

"Now?" Rosabelle sounded peevish. "I suppose we might as well get it over with. Tell her we'll be down in about ten minutes."

The door shut in An'gel's face. Rosabelle hadn't even given her time to tell her where Kanesha was waiting for them. An'gel turned and went back downstairs.

"They'll be down in ten minutes," she reported to the deputy.

"Thank you, Miss An'gel," Kanesha said.

"Have you made any progress with this case?" An'gel asked.

"Not really," Kanesha replied. "I have gone over all the statements several times, and there isn't anything in them that is all that helpful. No one saw anything. There were no fingerprints on either the tube of Vaseline or the water pistol."

"So frustrating," An'gel said. "At some point, if you can't resolve this, you'll have to let all of them leave, won't you?"

"Yes," Kanesha said. "I can't keep them here indefinitely."

An'gel wasn't any happier about that prospect than Kanesha, but at the same time she was looking forward to the time when all the guests were out of the house.

They waited in silence for Rosabelle and Antonio. An'gel felt like she could use a nap. The unrelieved stress of the situation seemed to sap her energy more quickly than if she had been working hard at something all day long.

"Here we are, Deputy Berry," Rosabelle announced from the doorway. She advanced into the room with Antonio by her side. "You wanted to talk to us, I hear."

An'gel thought, a bit snidely, that Rosabelle entered like a contessa about to give audience to her peasants. An'gel took a bit of satisfaction from the knowledge that what Kanesha had to say would give her old friend a much-needed reacquaintance with reality.

"Dickce and I will leave you to it." An'gel rose from her chair. "Come along, Diesel, you, too."

Antonio stared at the cat. "What manner of creature is this? I have never seen a cat so big."

Dickce quickly explained about Diesel's breed and his

size. Antonio moved close to the cat and extended a hand. Diesel sniffed once, then moved away. He passed by Rosabelle and out into the hall. An'gel and Dickce exchanged wry glances. The cat was definitely not impressed by the conte or his contessa.

"Thank you for coming down," Kanesha said.

An'gel moved out of earshot, with Dickce ahead of her. When Dickce lingered in the hallway, An'gel grabbed her arm and pulled her along with her toward the parlor. "No more eavesdropping."

"Spoilsport." Dickce grinned and shook her arm loose from her sister's grasp. "I'm sure we'll find out soon enough, because la contessa will have something to say. She always does."

"No doubt about that." An'gel snorted. "Rosabelle has never met a silence she couldn't fill."

Diesel climbed onto the sofa beside An'gel and lay his head and front legs across her lap. She rubbed his head, and he rewarded her with his rumbling purr. Dickce sat at the end of the sofa, with the cat's tail in her lap.

"I could easily get used to this," An'gel said. "I'm going to miss you, big boy, when your family gets home and you go back to them."

She glanced at Dickce, who seemed to be considering something, to judge by her expression. She waited a moment, but Dickce didn't speak. She could ask whether her sister had something on her mind, but she knew all too well that Dickce wouldn't share whatever it was until she was ready. There was no point in prodding her.

Her mind returned to an unanswered question that still niggled at her. "When Kanesha is done with them, I want to ask Antonio how he got here. I still think it's strange that there was no car in the driveway."

"It is odd," Dickce said, "but I'm sure there's an innocent, logical explanation. You're making too much out of it."

Perhaps she was, An'gel thought. She simply didn't like not being able to account for each and every detail.

"Thank goodness the deputy will be in the house again tonight," Dickce said. "I don't know about you, but I feel pretty nervous over what could happen. I wonder if the killer is going to make another attempt."

"Surely if the killer has any brains at all, he or she won't try again. Not with a deputy in the house and all of us on alert." An'gel felt the tension increasing every hour. If only there were some way to bring the situation to a head, without anyone getting hurt or killed in the process. Could they possibly set a trap for the killer?

She considered that for a moment, then slowly an idea began to form in her mind.

A high-pitched scream interrupted her thoughts.

CHAPTER 29

An'gel winced as Diesel's front claws dug into her leg. The cat launched himself off her lap, over the arm of the sofa, and onto the floor on the second scream. He tried to wriggle himself under the sofa on the third.

By then An'gel was up off the sofa and heading for the door. She sensed that Dickce was right behind her.

In the hallway she saw Kanesha sprinting up the stairs. Rosabelle stood in the doorway of the library, her head on Antonio's shoulder with his arms around her. Her heart thudding painfully from the exertion, An'gel climbed the staircase as quickly as she could. Dickce passed her on the last three steps and hurried down the second-floor hallway ahead of her.

Bernice stood outside the door to the guest bathroom huddled against Wade. An'gel reckoned that Bernice was the screamer. As she neared them, Dickce still ahead of her, she could hear Bernice sobbing in Wade's arms.

"What's wrong?" Dickce asked when she reached them. An'gel caught up seconds later as Wade pointed, his expression grim, into the bathroom.

"Maudine," was all he said.

An'gel moved slowly to the bathroom doorway and peered in. The scene inside shocked her, and she thought for a moment she was going to faint. Then she felt an arm around her waist and realized Dickce was there to support her.

Kanesha knelt on the floor near the bathtub, where she was performing CPR on Maudine. Small black objects dotted the floor around them, and An'gel spotted a few on Maudine's body. Her eyes couldn't focus at first to allow her to determine what they were.

"I'll call 911," Dickce said and slipped away.

An'gel gripped the door frame for support. Her vision settled, and she figured out that the small black objects were spiders.

Spiders?

She felt nauseated. Where had so many spiders come from?

She noticed the spiders weren't moving. Were they all dead?

Or were they fakes?

She remembered suddenly that Maudine was terrified of spiders. Had someone come in the bathroom while Maudine was in the tub and dumped spiders all over her?

Maybe Maudine had fallen and hit her head while trying to get out of the tub and away from the spiders.

Kanesha continued to work on Maudine. An'gel's head began to clear. She turned to Wade and Bernice. "Mr. Thurmond, go find your niece. The deputy needs help."

She wondered where Juanita could be as Wade, after a quick nod, hurried down the hall.

Antoinette appeared at the head of the stairs and ran toward An'gel. "I can help," she said when she reached the bathroom. "I've had CPR training."

"Thank you." An'gel moved aside and leaned against the wall and closed her eyes. She couldn't bear to watch any longer. Then she heard crying and realized Bernice's distress was greater than her own.

An'gel pushed herself away from the wall and approached the distraught woman. "Why don't you come with me?" she said gently. "Kanesha and Antoinette will do everything they can to help your sister until the paramedics get here."

She led an unprotesting Bernice all the way down to the front parlor, where Rosabelle and Antonio sat together on the sofa. They had already helped themselves to the liquor cabinet.

"What's all the noise upstairs?" Rosabelle asked. "Bernice, what's going on?"

"It's Maudie," Bernice said. Her steps faltered, and An'gel feared she might collapse before they reached a chair. Antonio leapt up and came to assist.

"What's wrong with Maudine?" Rosabelle's tone was sharp.

"She apparently had a bad fall in the bathroom while taking a bath," An'gel said. She left Bernice to Antonio's ministrations and went to pour the shaky woman a glass of brandy. She brought it back and put the glass into Bernice's hands. "Sip this. It will help."

Bernice's hands trembled as they clasped the snifter and lifted it to her mouth. Her color began to return after a couple of sips, and her hands steadied. Antonio returned to his place beside his wife. An'gel pulled a chair close to Bernice's and sat to sip at her own brandy. She felt the familiar warmth begin to spread, and her tension eased slightly as her heartbeat slowed to normal.

"Maudine always was the clumsiest of my children," Rosabelle said. "Is she going to be all right?"

"I think you should prepare yourself for bad news," An'gel said. "I believe Maudine had a terrible scare, and it could have made her have a heart attack." She saw no reason to soften the blow, especially since she thought Rosabelle's attitude was far too casual. "Kanesha and Antoinette are performing CPR until the paramedics can get here."

"A scare? What do you mean?" Rosabelle finally sounded concerned. She started to rise from the sofa, but then her legs seemed to give way and she sat down hard.

Antonio put his arm around her to steady her. "Cara, you are too distressed. You must not try to go to her. You can do nothing to assist."

"There were spiders all over the floor, and all over her," Bernice said. Her expression revealed her horror at the memory of what she had seen. "I was in the bedroom, and I heard a noise like something falling next door. So I went to check on Maudie, and that's when I found her. There on the floor with spiders everywhere. So many spiders."

"Spiders? Why were there a lot of spiders in the bathroom? Doesn't anyone ever clean in there?" Rosabelle's voice rose on every word.

Antonio picked up a glass and put it in her hands. "Please, my darling, you must not excite yourself so. Drink this. Steady yourself." Rosabelle obeyed and drained the glass.

"Of course that room is cleaned. Regularly and thoroughly." An'gel glared at Rosabelle. "I don't believe the spiders are real, frankly. I think they're rubber."

"That means someone put them in there deliberately." Rosabelle shuddered. "Maudine was terrified of spiders beyond all reason. She got that from me. I can't stand the nasty things." She shook her head. "She has a weak heart, you know. A shock like that could kill her. Who is the monster in my family who would do such a thing?" She burst into tears and buried her face in Antonio's shoulder. He wrapped his arms around her and rocked her gently.

Rosabelle did have maternal feelings after all, An'gel thought. She had begun to wonder whether Rosabelle was so self-centered that nothing could shake her.

Dimly An'gel heard the wail of sirens, coming closer with every second. She glanced down and noticed a large plumed tail jutting out from beneath the empty sofa across from Rosabelle and Antonio.

Diesel.

She had forgotten all about the cat in the uproar. He was still obviously frightened by all the noise and the heightened emotion. Could she coax him out from under there? She did not want to be scratched, and she thought that might happen if she tried to drag him out.

"Miss An'gel, is there anything I can do?"

An'gel turned to see Benjy approaching. She wondered vaguely where Junior was and then realized he was most likely upstairs near his mother.

"If you could keep an eye on Diesel, I would appreciate it." She pointed to the twitching tail.

Benjy nodded. He moved quickly to kneel beside the sofa and put his head down at floor level. He spoke softly to the cat, and moments later Diesel crawled out. He let Benjy pick him up, and An'gel felt greatly relieved. The last thing they needed was a traumatized cat getting in the middle of everything.

"I'll take him out to the kitchen and keep him there," Benjy said.

"Excellent," An'gel replied. "Thank you."

Benjy hurried out with the cat still in his arms.

The sirens sounded loud, and An'gel knew they were coming up the driveway. Suddenly they stopped, and she got up and headed for the front door.

Dickce was already there, cell phone still held to her ear. As An'gel watched, Dickce swung the door open and stood back. The paramedics poured into the hall, and Dickce pointed them up the stairs. Three deputies followed.

Dickce crossed the hall toward her, and she and An'gel waited at the doorway, looking up.

A couple of minutes later, two of the deputies returned, escorting Wade, Juanita, Junior, and Antoinette down the stairs. Juanita had her arm around her cousin. His face contorted by grief, he cried quietly. Juanita led him into the parlor, Wade right behind them.

"I'll get them all some brandy," Dickce said.

Antoinette came over to An'gel, and the deputies returned to the second floor.

"Is there any hope?" An'gel said softly to the girl.

Antoinette shook her head. "No, ma'am. She never responded to me or to Kanesha, though we worked on her until the EMTs got there. I think she probably had a heart attack." She shuddered. "It sure was creepy, those stupid rubber spiders all over her and on the floor. There were some in the bathtub, too. She must have been pretty scared of them."

"Scared to death," An'gel said grimly.

"Whoever did that to her is sick," Antoinette replied. "Unless there's something else you need, I'm going to help Gran make some fresh coffee. They're all going to need it."

"Thank you," An'gel said. She stared after the girl as she moved down the hall. She kept thinking about the fake spiders. How was it done?

Did one of her family sneak into the bathroom while Maudine was in the tub and throw them on her? If that was the way it happened, she reasoned, then the perpetrator had to be either Bernice or Wade. They were the only two who were upstairs at the time, as far as she knew. Rosabelle and Antonio were downstairs with Kanesha. Where were Junior and Juanita when Bernice started screaming? Could they have been upstairs, too?

She simply couldn't see Bernice as a cold-blooded, heartless killer. Wade, well, she had little trouble seeing him that way.

Was this another attempt on Rosabelle's life that had gone wrong? Rosabelle said she was afraid of spiders, like her daughter had been.

Or was Maudine the intended target this time?

CHAPTER 30

"Miss An'gel."

Kanesha's voice brought An'gel out of her reverie. She looked up to see the deputy approaching her. She knew at once the news was not good by the set of Kanesha's tense jaw.

"She's dead," An'gel said.

Kanesha nodded. "Heart attack probably."

"She was terrified of spiders." An'gel felt sick to her stomach as the mental image of Maudine, lying on the bathroom floor, returned.

"They're rubber," Kanesha said. "Do you have any idea where they came from?"

"One of my guests must have brought them. Dickce and I wouldn't have such things in the house, not even for Halloween."

"That's what I figured, but I had to check. They must

have been in a bag or a container of some kind. My guys are upstairs searching now, trying to find it."

"How was it done?" An'gel asked. "Are there any indications? All I can think is that someone walked in and threw them on her while she was in the tub or when she was getting out."

"I'm pretty sure they were inside the towel she picked up to dry herself with," Kanesha said. "I found a couple on top of the table next to the tub and a couple in the towel itself. Looks like she picked up the towel, stepped out, opened the towel, and the spiders fell out and scared her so bad she had a heart attack."

"Sickening," An'gel said. "What kind of twisted mind comes up with a wicked trick like that?"

"It's diabolical," Kanesha said. "Whoever did it could have prepared the towel several hours in advance. When was the bathroom cleaned? There weren't any towels in the laundry basket."

An'gel's mind focused on the ordinary detail, pushing away the sad vision of Maudine. "Antoinette cleaned up there today. I'm sure she brought down any soiled linens and put out fresh ones."

Kanesha nodded. "I'll check with her, plus I'll have to find out when your guests took their baths."

"They probably spaced them out to make sure they each had enough hot water," An'gel said. "The guest bathroom has a separate tank from the one that serves my bathroom and my sister's. The guest bath on the third floor also has its own small tank."

"The only ones using the second-floor bathroom, then, would be Mrs. Sultan, her daughters, and her granddaughter, correct?"

An'gel nodded. "Yes, that's right."

"I'm going to talk to Antoinette first and find out about the towels," Kanesha said. "Then I want to come and talk to everyone. Will you ask them all to remain in the parlor? I won't be long."

"Certainly," An'gel said. "Benjy is probably also in the kitchen with Antoinette and Clementine, if you need him for anything. I asked him to keep an eye on Diesel."

"Thanks," Kanesha said. "I'll be back soon." She headed for the kitchen.

An'gel took a moment for a couple of deep, steadying breaths before she was ready to face Rosabelle and her family once again.

Bernice and Juanita occupied one sofa, with Junior between them. An'gel's heart went out to the young man, who was obviously distraught over his mother's death. He stared vacantly into space, but he held tightly to Juanita's hand.

Rosabelle didn't appear to have moved since An'gel left the room a few minutes ago. She still had her head buried in Antonio's shoulder, and he still had his arms around her. He rocked her slowly and murmured to her. An'gel could hear the soothing tone but not the words. Wade lounged near the liquor cabinet with a large glass of what looked like whiskey in his hand.

Dickce sat several feet away from the family, her chair in the front half of the large parlor. She glanced up when An'gel entered the room, her look one of inquiry. An'gel shook her head, and Dickce frowned.

An'gel faced the family. "Deputy Berry will be along in a few minutes to talk to all of us. She asked that we all remain here until she comes."

Wade and Juanita nodded. Junior and his grandmother

did not seem to have heard. Antonio inclined his head once, but his attention otherwise appeared totally focused on his wife.

An'gel sat near Dickce and regarded Antonio thoughtfully. He was the picture of devotion, but she couldn't forget the conversation Dickce had overheard. Was he really planning to divorce Rosabelle? Could his intention to divorce his wife or his winning back of his inheritance have anything to do with the two murders?

Perhaps there was no connection at all.

She surely didn't envy Kanesha the task of sorting out this twisted mess. Her head ached as she tried to make sense of it all.

An'gel sensed the tension in the room like a palpable force. There was also fear. She herself was afraid, not so much for herself or Dickce, but for the lives of her guests. One of them—minus Junior, who had an alibi for the first death—had murdered two people with heartless calculation, yet the obvious target for the cold-blooded campaign remained alive. Though not untouched, An'gel thought. The death of her daughter had truly shaken Rosabelle. An'gel couldn't imagine what it must be like to outlive one's own child, even if the relationship was stormy at best.

Kanesha returned a few minutes later. She walked to the fireplace, then turned to face everyone.

"I'm sorry for your loss, and I assure you my deputies and I will do everything in our power to resolve this situation." She paused for a moment to look at each person in turn. "Two women have been murdered in this house in the past twenty-four hours. One of you committed both these acts, and I'm not going to stop until I have you behind bars. I want you all to think clearly about what is going on here. I want you to think about everything you have heard and seen since you arrived yesterday. Everything you did. Even the smallest detail could help. I'm going to question each of you in turn like I did yesterday, and I want to hear about anything you think might have a bearing on these two murders."

While Kanesha had talked, An'gel's eyes had scanned each face in turn, over and over, in an attempt to discern any hint of emotion that could help identify the killer. Rosabelle had gently disengaged herself from her husband's arms to listen to the deputy. Her expression revealed little, An'gel thought, other than grief. Wade simply looked bored as he sipped away at his drink. Bernice, Juanita, and Junior appeared as sorrowful as Rosabelle. Antonio's blank expression revealed nothing to An'gel.

Rosabelle's trembling voice broke the uneasy silence that ensued after Kanesha's speech. "Deputy, could I say something?"

"Yes, ma'am," Kanesha said.

"I know that I am the target of all this hate," Rosabelle said. "I was the one who was supposed to fall down those stairs. But Marla happened to get there before me, so she was the one to die. I am almost as terrified of spiders as my poor Maudine was. I was the one who was supposed to find them and be frightened into a heart attack. But instead it was my oldest child." Her voice broke on the last three words. She took a moment to compose herself before she continued. "I don't know which of you is doing this, but I beg of you, confess and stop these acts of wickedness. I will do whatever you want, but just stop this." She burst into tears, and Antonio once again enfolded her in his arms.

An'gel realized she was gripping the arms of her chair tightly enough that her hands ached. She willed her body to relax, and her fingers eased their grip. She wondered whether Kanesha had deliberately tried to evoke a response like this. Rosabelle had risen to the bait, but would her impassioned plea have any effect whatsoever?

Wade moved away from the liquor cabinet and into his mother's line of sight. "Nicely done, Mother. You really missed your calling, you know. Dad really should have used his connections to get you in front of the camera. You'd have given Bette Davis and Joan Crawford a run for their money." He laughed, and An'gel wondered how much whiskey he'd had.

Rosabelle's face whitened as she pulled away from Antonio. "How dare you say such things to me? Have you no decency?"

"There's nothing decent about *you*," Wade said in a sneering tone. "Or about what's going on here. I think you're the one who needs to confess, Mother dearest. You hated Marla, so you figured out how to get rid of her and make it look like you were the intended victim. So convenient." He shook his head. "And poor Maudie, always asking you for money. That's a cardinal sin where you're concerned. You love money too much to want to share it with anyone, especially with your children, who deserve it every bit as much as you do."

An'gel marveled that none of the others had jumped to Rosabelle's defense, even her supposedly besotted husband.

"Deputy, I'm sure there's something you don't know about the terms of my mother's first husband's will. Did you know that, if Maudine and Bernice die before Mother does, their portions of the estate revert to Mother? They have to outlive her if they want to inherit anything to leave to their own children or a surviving spouse. My father's will is the same. That's why my wife and my sister had to die, and my mother killed them both."

CHAPTER 31

Dickce had never in her life heard such a vicious attack as the one Wade launched against Rosabelle. She had been watching him steadily work his way down to the bottom of a nearly full bottle of whiskey. She was amazed he was still upright, much less able to articulate his hatred of his mother so forcefully.

She could tell that An'gel was distressed by the nasty scene. She was, too, but part of her was curious to see how Rosabelle would react. Her own cynicism sometimes startled her, but with Rosabelle, she had decided over the past two days, every display of emotion was suspect.

Dickce had only seconds to wait. Rosabelle's expression changed from disbelief, to horror, and finally to outrage as Wade spoke. When he concluded, she rose from the sofa on unsteady legs, and Dickce thought Rosabelle was going to attack her son physically. Instead she stood in place and launched a verbal assault.

"Your father knew how weak his son was and always would be. He made me promise on his deathbed that I would do my best to keep you from sheer destitution. He knew you were completely incapable of managing money, and he arranged things so that you would always have something. You ought to be grateful to me that you weren't out on the streets foraging through garbage cans years ago. Instead you live in a beautiful home with plenty of food and a generous allowance. Right now if I could, I would throw every last cent of your inheritance in your face and tell you to go to the devil."

Wade shrank back from the furious onslaught of his mother's words. Dickce felt sorry for him, though he really had brought it on himself. Rosabelle was a vicious opponent, and surely he ought to have known that by now. She gave no quarter. Evisceration seemed to be a skill she had mastered long ago.

Dickce glanced at Kanesha. Would she put a stop to this? Or was she deliberately letting it go on in hopes of forcing the killer's hand? Dickce wasn't sure how that would work. If Rosabelle was the killer, as Wade had claimed, she seemed proof against this particular ploy.

Dickce glanced at Bernice, Junior, and Juanita. All three looked shell-shocked, as well they might.

"Excuse me, Deputy Berry. I need to speak with you."

Startled, Dickce turned to see one of the male deputies in the doorway. He took a couple of steps into the room. The chief deputy didn't appear to be all that happy about the interruption. Things had hit a boiling point, and now the heat dissipated.

Kanesha left her spot by the fireplace to confer in an undertone with her subordinate. "You'll have to excuse me for moment," she said to everyone before she followed him out of the room.

Rosabelle remained on her feet, her gaze locked upon her son. She seemed not to have heard Kanesha. Wade appeared thoroughly cowed now. He stared at the glass in his hands and shifted his weight back and forth from one leg to another. The air of tension in the room began to increase again, and Dickce wished suddenly that she could simply get up and walk out. She had had enough of the drama.

Kanesha carried a purse encased in a large plastic bag with her when she returned about two minutes later. Dickce stared at it. If she wasn't mistaken, it was the handbag Rosabelle had had with her when she arrived yesterday.

The chief deputy walked back to the area in front of the fireplace. She held the plastic bag up so that everyone could see its contents. "Can anyone identify this purse?"

"It's mine." Rosabelle stepped forward to claim it but faltered when Kanesha shook her head.

"Thank you for the identification," Kanesha said. "I'm sorry, but I need to hold on to it for a little while."

"That's outrageous," Rosabelle said. "What do you need with my handbag? You have no right to be going through my things without my permission. I demand that you show me your search warrant. Do you have one?"

Kanesha regarded her coolly. "No, ma'am, I do not. I don't need one in this situation. I am investigating a crime scene, and I'm within my rights to search wherever I think it's necessary. In this case, the crime scene involves the whole house."

Dickce thought Rosabelle might protest further. She

was so riled up now, she might do anything. To Dickce's surprise, however, Rosabelle stepped back and resumed her place on the sofa beside Antonio without another word. She continued to glare at Kanesha.

"In the course of the search for evidence," the chief deputy said, "one of the deputies came across this handbag. Inside it he discovered a plastic bag that contained one rubber spider. The spider in that bag matched those that we found in the bathroom with Mrs. Pittman."

Rosabelle gasped. "I don't believe this. Someone else put that in my handbag. I can't stand to be anywhere near a spider. There's no way I would ever carry even fake ones around with me."

"When was the last time you looked in this bag, ma'am?" Kanesha asked.

"I'm not sure." Rosabelle frowned. "Probably last night before I went to bed. I didn't need it for anything today. I left it sitting on the dressing table. Anyone could have come in the room while I was out and put that plastic bag inside."

Kanesha regarded her for a moment before she turned to Juanita. "Miss Cameron, you are sharing the room with your grandmother. Correct?"

"Yes," Juanita said. "And if you mean by that, did I have an opportunity to put the bag of spiders in Grandmother's purse? Well, I did. Have the opportunity, I mean." She grimaced. "I'm not fond of crawly things either. I don't even like to touch fake ones."

"There's one person who doesn't mind crawly things like spiders," Wade said. "My stepson Benjy has two tarantulas he keeps in his room at home. You ought to be questioning him. Somebody put him up to playing a prank with those spiders, I'll bet." He laughed, the sound harsh and disturbing.

Dickce wanted to leap out of her chair and slap the man. How dare he try to involve poor innocent Benjy in this horrible mess? She forced herself to take a deep breath before she spoke.

"I think you'll find, Deputy Berry, that Benjy had no opportunity to do that. He hasn't been up to the second floor of the house at all. He was with me most of the morning, and if you'll recall, we were out of the house. Since we returned, he has been with other people the entire time, I believe." That ought to put an end to that, Dickce thought with satisfaction. She wasn't going to sit idly by and let someone try to make Benjy out to be a malicious prankster.

She noticed An'gel looking at her rather oddly. She shook her head slightly to indicate that she would talk to her sister later. An'gel frowned but turned her gaze back to Kanesha as she responded to Dickce.

"Thank you. Your statement is helpful. However, from my discussion with Miss Buford, the housekeeper's granddaughter, I know that Mr. Stephens had an opportunity to be alone with the towels for at least a minute before she took them upstairs and put them in the guest bathroom."

Dickce knew Kanesha had to consider every angle, every possibility, but still it disconcerted her to hear the deputy speak so coolly about Benjy. She had to concede that he might have had the opportunity to put the rubber spiders in a towel, but she couldn't see that he had a probable motive. As soon as she had the opportunity to speak to Kanesha on her own, she would give the deputy the benefit of her opinion of Benjy's character.

"I have to consider the possibility that every one of you

had an opportunity to put the spiders in the towel and then put the plastic bag into this handbag." Kanesha held it up again. "I will be asking you all more about this during our one-on-one interviews. Mr. Pittman, I would like to start with you. Will you come with me now?"

At first Junior didn't seem to have heard Kanesha. Dickce thought he looked completely forlorn. She felt sorry for him, as she did for Benjy. Both of them had lost their mothers in the space of a day.

Juanita patted Junior's hand. "Sweetie, the deputy wants you to go with her now, okay?"

Dully Junior looked at his cousin, then nodded. With what looked like great effort, he pushed himself up from the sofa and stood, blinking, at Kanesha. Then he moved slowly toward the door into the hall.

"Please remain here until I call for you," Kanesha said. "One of my men will remain in the room with you, and as before, if you need anything, please speak to him. This may take some time."

Dickce rose. "Deputy, would it be okay for me to go to the kitchen and see that coffee is prepared for everyone?" She figured Antoinette and Clementine had already made it, but someone would have to fetch it. Besides, it would give her a chance to speak to Benjy.

"That's fine," Kanesha said. "Now if you'll excuse me." She departed the room.

"I'll be back in a few minutes," Dickce said to the room at large. She did not look at her sister before she made a beeline for the door.

She almost ran into Kanesha's deputy as he exited the room. He managed to sidestep her as she hurried past, and she flashed him an apologetic smile.

Calm down, she told herself, *there's nothing on fire*. She slowed her pace. She remembered something she had completely forgotten earlier—the water pistol. The killer had taken it from Benjy's room back in California and used it to cause a fatal fall in her home.

What if the rubber spiders belonged to Benjy as well?

CHAPTER 32

Dickce sped up again and hurried into the kitchen. She hoped like anything those spiders weren't Benjy's property. If they were, things could get ugly, because Benjy was the outsider in Rosabelle's family. He would make a convenient scapegoat, even though Dickce knew Kanesha was far too smart to accept such a pat answer. Or to force evidence to fit it.

In the kitchen Dickce found Antoinette at the table by herself, drinking a diet soft drink. There was no sign of Benjy, Diesel, or Clementine.

Antoinette stood. "Are you ready for the coffee yet, Miss Dickce? I made a couple of pots and put them in the big urn. I figured I'd better wait to bring it until you or Miss An'gel came and asked for it." She nodded to indicate the serving cart, laden with the urn and all necessary items for coffee service.

"Thank you, dear," Dickce said. "Would you mind

taking it to the parlor for me now? And can you tell me where Benjy is? I suspect your grandmother is out back smoking."

"I'd be happy to," Antoinette said. "Benjy took Diesel with him out to the garage apartment a while ago. And, yes, Gran is out smoking." She grimaced. "I have tried and tried to get her to quit, but nothing works. Mama says that when Gran passes on, they'll have to leave the casket open three days to let the smoke clear." She grasped the handle of the serving cart and pushed it toward the door into the hall.

"Thanks." Dickce smiled. She had heard that expression before, and in Clementine's case, she reckoned it was appropriate.

She found the housekeeper in her usual spot on the back porch. She paused to tell Clementine that she had asked Antoinette to take the coffee to the parlor, then hurried across the back lawn and driveway to the garage. She opened the apartment door, stepped inside, and called up the stairs, "Benjy, are you up there?"

"Yes, ma'am," he called back, and moments later he appeared at the top of the stairs, Diesel beside him. "Come on up. I won't be long. I was just calling my friend in California, the one I told you about? He said he would keep Bert and Ernie. He's been looking after them while I'm gone anyway."

"That's good," Dickce said as she climbed up toward him. "Kanesha has started to question people one-on-one, and I decided to slip out for a few minutes. I wanted to talk to you about something."

Benjy stepped back, frowning, as Diesel rubbed himself against Dickce's legs. "I'll bet it's about the rubber spiders, isn't it? Antoinette told me about them and how they were all over the bathroom."

"Yes, it is," Dickce said. She walked over to the battered sofa and sat. She patted the space next to her. "Please, come sit with me."

Benjy slowly complied with her request, and Diesel jumped up to occupy the space between them. He put his head in her lap and his back legs and tail across Benjy's. Dickce absentmindedly began to scratch his head, her thoughts focused on the questions she had for Benjy.

"Did the deputy ask you about them?"

"No, she didn't," Benjy said. "I haven't seen her. Right after Antoinette came back from upstairs and told me and her grandmother what happened, I brought Diesel out here. I had to get out of there."

"I don't blame you," Dickce said. She knew Kanesha might be angry with her for talking to Benjy about the rubber spiders before she had a chance to do so officially, but Dickce would deal with that later. Right now she wanted to know whether Benjy was connected to them in any way.

"I know what you're going to ask." Benjy looked at her, and she could read the plea in his eyes. "I'm pretty sure those rubber spiders are mine. I bought a bag of them two or three years ago for Halloween. I was going to put them around the house as a joke, but then my mom told me about how scared Mrs. Pittman and her mother are of them. So I stuck them in the closet and forgot about them, like I did the water pistol."

"Did anyone else know about the spiders?" Dickce asked.

Benjy frowned. "My mom told the Wart, and then he yelled at me in front of everybody about it. They all knew about them."

"Thank you," Dickce said. "Did you bring the spiders with you?"

"No," Benjy said. "I'll bet the Wart is telling everybody that I did it as a joke, but I didn't. I swear I didn't."

Diesel, perhaps sensing the boy's distress, shifted himself so that he could sit next to Benjy and rub his head against the boy's shoulder. Benjy smiled briefly.

Dickce reached across the length of feline between them and squeezed the boy's hand. "I know you didn't, but Deputy Berry will have to ask you about them. You just tell her what you told me. You still haven't told her about the water pistol?"

"No, ma'am," he replied. "I really haven't had a chance to, but I will as soon as I can."

"Good." Dickce rose. "Why don't you and Diesel come back to the house with me now? You can stay in the kitchen, if you like, but it's best to be close at hand when the deputy wants you."

Benjy agreed to come with her, and the three of them set off for the house.

"I feel bad for Junior," Benjy said. "He's lost his mom now, too, but he got along with her most of the time better than I did with mine. It really bites."

He sounded so forlorn, Dickce wanted to stop and hug him right then. Instead she said, "Losing your mother bites no matter how old you are and no matter how the two of you got along when she was with you. An'gel and I lost our mother quite a few years ago now, and there are very few days that go by that I don't think about her and miss her."

"How do you stand it, knowing you're not going to see her again?" Benjy said. "I guess at least you've got your sister."

"Yes, I'm lucky to have my sister," Dickce said. "Having

someone to share the memories of a loved one with means a lot, but even if you don't have brothers or sisters, you can count on friends to help you through the rough times."

Diesel warbled loudly as they climbed the steps to the back porch. Benjy paused to rub the cat's head. When he spoke, his voice sounded thick with emotion. "If it weren't for you, I wouldn't have anyone much to count on."

Dickce squeezed his shoulder gently. "I'm glad we can be friends."

Benjy nodded and opened the door for her. Inside they found Clementine back at the stove, and Antoinette was at the oven basting the roast.

"Sure smells good," Benjy said. Diesel chirped in agreement as he padded over to Antoinette. He sat at her feet and stared up at her. Antoinette grinned at him and shook her head to let him know he wasn't getting any roast.

"Miss An'gel's looking for you again, Miss Dickce," Clementine said.

"Seems like An'gel's always looking for me," Dickce said. "Y'all excuse me. I'd better go see what she wants."

When Dickce walked into the parlor, she noticed that Junior was still evidently with Kanesha, because everyone else was present. Wade was sitting in the outside corner of the room at the front of the house. Dickce wondered if that had been his own idea, or had Rosabelle suggested it? Either way it was probably just as well he stayed as far away from his mother as possible for the time being.

No one spoke upon her return, but An'gel motioned for her to take her former seat. As she did so, An'gel edged her own chair closer to Dickce's.

"I presume you talked to Benjy." An'gel spoke in a low tone.

"Yes," Dickce said. She really didn't want to discuss

what Benjy told her right now. An'gel might get annoyed with her, and the last thing they needed was to have an argument here in front of Rosabelle and her family. An'gel was a bit hotheaded, and her temper might get the better of her.

"I'll tell you all about it later," Dickce whispered. She could tell her reluctance to talk didn't sit well with her sister, but she refused to be drawn into conversation. It wouldn't do An'gel's temper any good, but she didn't always need to get her way over everything.

The afternoon wore on, and once a person left to talk to Kanesha, he or she did not return. Bernice was called next after Junior, then Wade and Juanita. Rosabelle followed, and that left Antonio with An'gel and Dickce.

An'gel suddenly got up and went over to the sofa and took the spot Rosabelle had vacated moments before. Dickce wondered what her sister was up to.

"Have you decided whether you will stay here with us tonight?" An'gel asked. "I suddenly realized that you had no bags with you when you arrived. Nor did you appear to have a vehicle."

Antonio smiled. "Ah, yes, I perhaps should have mentioned that I have a car and driver. We went first to the charming Farrington House when we arrived in Athena. I have reserved a room there because I was not certain, you understand, of my reception from my dear wife, even though she summoned me. She is a whimsical creature, but that is part of her charm." He laughed. "Now that I know she really needs me, I of course will call the driver and have him bring what is necessary. He will remain at the hotel because I realize you do not have room for my man."

"I'm afraid that's correct," An'gel said. "We would have to bed him down on the sofa in the library, but of course he would be welcome to do that if you prefer to have him near you."

"No, no, that is not necessary," Antonio said. "He will stay at the hotel."

Was it her imagination, Dickce wondered, or did Antonio seem a little uneasy over the idea of having his manservant in the house?

CHAPTER 33

An'gel wondered whether it was her imagination, or was Antonio protesting a bit too much about his manservant? What reason could he have for not wanting the man to stay here at Riverhill? True, it would be somewhat inconvenient in terms of sleeping arrangements, but on the other hand, having another able-bodied man in the house in case of trouble wouldn't be a bad thing. Kanesha might prefer not to add a new person to the mix, she realized, and she decided to let the matter drop. Her curiosity over the manner of Antonio's arrival was finally settled.

"Signor Mingione, would you come with me, please?"

An'gel turned to see a deputy standing nearby.

"If you will excuse me, ladies," Antonio said with the flash of a smile. "Yes, Officer, I will come."

"Miss Ducote," the deputy said to An'gel, "Chief Deputy Berry asked me to let you know she'll be ready to talk to you and your sister shortly."

"Thank you," An'gel replied. When he left the room, she noticed the deputy who had remained in the room all this time went with him. She motioned for Dickce to join her on the sofa.

"Now we can talk," An'gel said. "Tell me about Benjy."

"All right," Dickce replied. "Here's what he told me." She gave An'gel the details about the rubber spiders and repeated Benjy's denial that he had anything to do with frightening Maudine to death with them. "I believe him," she concluded.

"I reckon I do, too," An'gel said, "but it sure looks like someone is trying to implicate him in all this. He had no opportunity to squirt the water on the stairs, nor did Junior. Since neither of them could have set up the first accident, then I think we have to rule them out as being responsible for the second."

"I agree," Dickce said. "Who was the target, though? Rosabelle was insistent that she was the intended victim the first time, and then she said she is just as terrified of spiders as Maudine was."

"I don't know," An'gel replied. "I keep going round and round with it, but I never come out with a clear answer. I found Wade's accusation that Rosabelle is the murderer interesting. I have to confess I wondered myself if she wasn't responsible."

"Me, too," Dickce said. "I wouldn't put anything past her now, not after the displays we've seen. Wade might be right. What he said about his father's will could be important."

"Rosabelle told me that the trusts set up by her first and second husbands would dissolve with her death, and her three children would receive their shares to use as they see fit." An'gel paused. "According to Wade, if one of the children dies before Rosabelle, that portion doesn't pass to the grandchild and instead reverts to the estate."

"And to Rosabelle," Dickce said. "She does love money, but do you think she would really murder her own children to get it?"

"Let's say she would. Why then would she want to murder Marla, her daughter-in-law? Marla would have no claim on the estate, even if she outlived Wade."

"Out of spite?" Dickce said. "Or a trial run maybe?"

"Possibly," An'gel replied. "But if Rosabelle died first, Wade would inherit his father's money. Marla would benefit that way. And possibly Benjy as well, if he is in either Wade's or Marla's will."

"That's really pushing it," Dickce said. "Think instead about Bernice and Juanita. With Maudine gone before Rosabelle, Bernice's share doubles because Junior gets nothing. What about that?"

"If Bernice outlives her mother, then she inherits a considerable amount," An'gel said. "Then Juanita inherits from her mother."

"I wonder what Rosabelle could do with the money if all three of her children predeceased her?" Dickce said. "Would she be able to will it to anyone she chose, since the beneficiaries of the trust were dead?"

"It's like a maze," An'gel said. "So many potential routes to the answer. But which one is the right one?"

"If there's another murder, that would give us a clearer picture," Dickce said.

"Don't say that, even in jest," An'gel said sharply. "I can't stand the thought of another murder in the house."

"I know," Dickce said contritely. "It is horrible, isn't it?"

"I hope Kanesha figures this out soon. I want all these people out of our house, and I never want to see any of them again," An'gel said. She glanced at her sister, expecting total agreement. Instead Dickce looked uneasy. "What is it?"

"Oh, nothing, really," Dickce said. "I hope it's over soon, too."

An'gel wasn't satisfied with that answer, but she knew that pressing Dickce about it wouldn't get her anywhere. Dickce could be stubborn to the point of madness, and right now she didn't have the energy to force the issue. She had a sneaking suspicion Dickce was hiding something from her, but whatever it was would have to wait.

She checked her watch. Nearly six o'clock. She'd told Clementine earlier they would eat at seven. The food would be ready, but would everyone want to sit down to dinner together after what happened this afternoon?

If they didn't, she decided after brief reflection, they could fill their plates and take them to their rooms. She really didn't care. It might even be less stressful for all of them. She didn't relish another scene like the ones they had witnessed last night or today.

"Ladies, would you come with me now?"

Startled, An'gel realized the deputy had come to take them to Kanesha. "Of course." She was more than ready.

She and Dickce followed the deputy across the hall to the library and took their seats in front of the desk. An'gel thought Kanesha looked frustrated and tired, much as she herself probably looked to the chief deputy.

"Have you made any progress?" An'gel asked.

"Hard to tell," Kanesha replied. "Not a single one of them saw anything that is useful. From what they've told me, they all might as well be invisible once they get up on the second floor." She shook her head. "I thought surely, if I took them through their movements, one of them at least might have seen one of the others coming out of a room, going into one. Anything that could give me a break in this case. But not a single thing."

"Have you talked to Benjy Stephens yet?" Dickce asked, rather abruptly, An'gel thought.

Kanesha nodded. "Yes, ma'am, before I talked to Signor Mingione. He told me about the water pistol and the rubber spiders."

"You're not seriously considering him a suspect because they belonged to him, are you?"

An'gel thought her sister sounded militant all of a sudden, almost as if Benjy were her son instead of someone else's. What was going on in Dickce's head? And more important, in her heart?

"They do link him to both murders," Kanesha said. She held up a hand as if to forestall another protest from Dickce. "I know it's only circumstantial. According to Mr. Stephens, everyone knew about the water pistol and the rubber spiders. Everyone also had access to his room in California, and I see no reason to doubt that. I am sure he didn't have the opportunity to go upstairs and set up the accident that killed his mother. I also strongly doubt that he had anything to do with putting those spiders in a towel for someone to find."

"That's good," Dickce said. "He's a nice boy, and I'm sure he has nothing to do with all this. He simply has the misfortune to be connected to an ill-fated family."

An'gel thought that made Benjy sound like a Tybalt or a Mercutio, both of whom paid dearly for their membership in two feuding houses. She resisted the urge to snort at her sister's hyperbole.

"So what's next?" An'gel asked.

"My first concern is to stop another murder from happening," Kanesha said.

"Do you really think there will be another attempt on Rosabelle?" An'gel said.

"It's entirely possible," Kanesha said. "I don't think the murderer has achieved his complete purpose yet."

"Does that mean you think Rosabelle is the intended victim?" Dickce asked.

"Eventually, yes," Kanesha replied.

"What do you mean by that?" An'gel asked, startled.

Kanesha smiled grimly. "I'm almost certain that Mrs. Pittman was the intended victim today, and not her mother."

CHAPTER 34

"How can you know that?" An'gel asked.

"I asked them all when they took their baths," Kanesha said. "I found out that they didn't know about the water heaters, and none of them likes cold baths. So they discussed it and came up with their own schedule. Mr. Thurmond always showers at night, as does Miss Cameron. They set times an hour apart, although it wasn't necessary from what you told me."

"I forgot to tell them about the hot water," An'gel said. "Did you say anything, Sister?"

"No, I didn't think of it," Dickce said.

Kanesha continued with her list. "Mrs. Cameron likes to bathe first thing in the morning, and Mrs. Sultan, or rather, Mrs. Mingione, likes to sleep in. She had her bath shortly before her husband arrived, as it turns out. That left Mrs. Pittman, who decided to have hers after lunch."

"Antoinette cleaned up in that bathroom while they

were all eating lunch," An'gel said. "She put fresh towels in there."

"It wasn't until after Antoinette put in those fresh towels," Kanesha said, "that the killer hid the spiders inside the one on the top. Antoinette removed three towels from that bathroom and replaced them with four more."

An'gel considered what Kanesha shared with them and realized the chief deputy was right. Maudine Pittman was the target, not her mother. The evidence seemed clear.

An'gel recalled her conversation with Dickce before they were asked to join Kanesha a few minutes ago. "Maudine was the target for the second murder, then. What about the first one? Do you think Rosabelle was the target, as she claims? Or was Marla the intended victim all along?"

"That depends on the overall motive," Kanesha said. "What would be the motive if Signora Mingione died before anyone else? The most obvious answer is money. But how much? I think the amount depends on the order in which they die. If the signora dies first, her three children get their money from their fathers' wills, and then they can do whatever they want with it. Spend it all or leave it to their heirs. If she dies after any of the children, she benefits until her death. I've got a call in to her lawyer in California to discuss the situation with him. I don't know whether I can get him to talk without getting the client involved, but I have to try."

"Dickce and I were discussing all the possibilities while we were waiting to talk to you," An'gel said. "The variables make it so difficult to figure anything out."

"Yes, they do," Kanesha said. "Ladies, I think I need to remind you that figuring this out is my job. I appreciate everything you've done to help, but I want you to be extremely careful. I have no reason to believe that the killer would go after either of you—unless you somehow stand in the way. Please do not do anything that would make the killer think that you are a significant obstacle."

An'gel appreciated the chief deputy's concern for their welfare. She did not want to attract the murderer's attention, nor did Dickce. Of that she was certain. The fact remained, however, that there was a killer in her house. One who had killed twice and, she was convinced, intended to kill again. She wanted it to stop.

She realized Kanesha was waiting for a response. "We both understand."

"Yes, we do," Dickce said tartly, with a slight stress on the pronoun.

"I'm going to ask both of you the same thing I asked everyone else," Kanesha said. "I want you to consider everything you've seen, every interaction you've had with your guests, and if the slightest thing seems odd, I want you to tell me. It doesn't matter how trivial it might be. I want to know about it."

"I'll do my best," An'gel said, this time careful not to answer for her sibling. Dickce could be so touchy sometimes about being the younger sister.

"I will, too," Dickce said.

"One more thing," Kanesha said, "and then I think we're done for the moment. I want to post two of my men in the house overnight, along with the off-duty man you've hired. I want to monitor everyone's movements as much as possible. Once everyone has gone to bed, I'll have my two men remain in the upstairs hall. Your man can patrol the first floor. Is that all right with you?"

"I'm frankly relieved," An'gel said. "Very pleased as well. Thank you."

"What about the garage apartment?" Dickce asked.

"What if someone manages to slip out of the house and attacks Junior and Benjy?"

"I don't have another man to spare for that," Kanesha said. "I'm liable to be shorthanded as it is, especially if there's some kind of emergency. Perhaps it would be best if Mr. Pittman and Mr. Stephens spent the night here in the house."

"Is there possibly another off-duty deputy who could keep an eye on the area between the house and the garage?" An'gel asked. She thought Junior and Benjy would be safer if they weren't in the house overnight, but she didn't want to say that to Kanesha.

"I'll check for you," Kanesha said. "I appreciate your willingness to keep them all here in your house, despite the reservations I have about the potential danger. If it weren't for the fact that moving them to a hotel could make it more difficult for us to keep an eye on them, I would have moved them out tonight."

"I understand, but I don't think anything will happen tonight with your men on duty in the house," An'gel said. "I'll simply have to hope that this will be the last night and that tomorrow you'll have the killer in custody, and I can send them to a hotel if they have to remain in town for a while."

"Amen to that," Dickce said.

"I suggested they all go to their rooms and stay there until it's time for dinner," Kanesha said. "I have a deputy already on duty upstairs, and the other man will join him around eight P.M." She rose from behind the desk. "If you need anything at all, call me. Use my personal cell number, not the sheriff's department line."

An'gel walked Kanesha to the front door. "I'm going to pray we have a quiet night."

The chief deputy flashed a smile. "Like Miss Dickce said, amen to that. I'll be back in the morning."

An'gel closed the door and leaned against it for a moment, her eyes shut. What she wouldn't give for a short nap right about now. The stress of the situation continued to sap her energy.

"I'm going to see if anything else needs to be done in the dining room," Dickce said from the doorway of the library. "Poor Antoinette and Clementine are probably exhausted by now. We'd better give them both overtime for all this."

An'gel nodded. "I'll be along in a moment." For a few seconds more she wanted to stay right where she was and enjoy the silence.

There was still much to do, however, before they could go to bed. She would insist that Clementine go home soon. She was sure Antoinette had kept an eye on her grandmother and insisted she rest during the day. Clementine was a hardy soul for the most part, but she couldn't put in many sixteen-hour days. This was the second, and unless there was significant progress, An'gel realized, tomorrow would be another long, long day for all of them.

The doorbell rang, and An'gel was so startled she almost jumped away from it. She took a moment to catch her breath before she opened the door. She figured it was probably Kanesha coming back to tell her something she had forgotten to earlier.

The person standing before the door was definitely not Kanesha. An'gel had to stifle a gasp when she caught a glimpse of the young man's face. She had never in her life been so close to a man this beautiful. Dark curly hair, liquid brown eyes, a strong nose, sensual lips, tanned skin, and chiseled features made her think of film idols of her youth. He was tall, with broad shoulders and a thin waist. His dark jacket and trousers accentuated his coloring perfectly. He could have stepped right off the cover of a romance novel.

An'gel realized she was staring rudely at the young man. She blinked and tried to focus her thoughts. "Good afternoon, what can I do for you?"

He smiled, and dimples appeared in both cheeks. "*Scusi,* signora, I will speak to Signor il Conte, *per favore.* I have come with his *valigia*, how you say, luggage." He nodded, evidently pleased that he had remembered the English word.

"You are the manservant of Signor Mingione," An'gel said. She should have figured that out right away. She might have, had she not been so stunned by his appearance. He was exotic for Athena, to say the least. "Please, do come in, and I will let the signor know you are here."

"*Grazie, signora,*" he said. He picked up two large suitcases with apparent ease and brought them inside, where he set them gingerly on the floor.

An'gel closed the door. "Why don't you wait in the parlor?" She gestured toward the open door.

He frowned but then nodded. She thought he might not understand the word *parlor.* She should have used the Italian word, but her mind blanked when she tried to recall it.

The young man walked into the parlor and stood there. An'gel decided she had better get herself up the stairs to let Antonio know about this arrival. She couldn't continue to stand here and gawk at the handsome gentleman.

She walked quickly, but with care, up the staircase and knocked on Rosabelle's door. This time Antonio answered right away. He smiled as he stepped out of the room and closed the door behind him.

"You have come to tell me that my *valletto* has arrived with my luggage. I called him and asked him to do so. I will come down at once to retrieve it."

"Yes, your valet is waiting downstairs for you," An'gel said. "He told me he wanted to speak with you. He's waiting for you in the parlor."

That did not appear to be welcome news, An'gel thought. Antonio's mouth tightened as if he was clenching his teeth, but then he suddenly relaxed.

"I will see what he wants and send him on his way." Antonio brushed past her toward the stairs.

"That's up to you," An'gel said, following more slowly. "He was perfectly polite, in fact, a charming young man, I thought."

Antonio did not reply, although An'gel was sure he had heard her. What was it about this valet of his that seemed to make him tense? She couldn't figure it out.

She hurried to catch up to Antonio once she reached the bottom of the stairs. She was curious to hear what he would say to the young man. She knew it was none of her business, but her curiosity was aroused. Exactly what happened to Dickce earlier, she realized, when her sister eavesdropped on the meeting between Rosabelle and Antonio. An'gel would think about that later.

As she neared the door, she heard her sister's voice. What was Dickce doing in the parlor? She was supposed to be in the kitchen helping out.

An'gel strode forward into the parlor. Dickce stood smiling at the gorgeous young man while Antonio glowered at him. The young man smiled, too.

"An'gel, I invited Luca to stay and have dinner with us, and he said yes. Isn't that delightful?"

CHAPTER 35

What was Dickce playing at? An'gel wondered. She didn't mind if Luca stayed for dinner, but from what she could tell, Antonio wasn't pleased.

Perhaps he objected to sharing a table with his servant. These Old World types could be stuffy about such things, but An'gel and Dickce were the hostesses here. If he couldn't stand having Luca at the table with him, Antonio was welcome to take his plate elsewhere.

"You are very kind, signorina." Luca flashed beautifully white teeth in a disarming smile.

Antonio rattled off something in Italian so quickly that An'gel couldn't make sense of it. Her recollection of the language was too rusty.

Luca's face darkened, and he stepped away from Dickce and toward his employer. Luca replied, and the men gestured and talked until Antonio threw up his hands. "*Basta!* All right, you may stay."

Luca smirked. "*Grazie, signore.*"

"What time is dinner?" Antonio asked.

"Seven," An'gel replied.

"Thank you." Antonio inclined his head toward her. "I will return at seven with my wife." He hurried from the room.

"It's close to seven now," Dickce said. "Luca, would you like to wash up before dinner?"

"*Scusi, signorina?*" Luca looked puzzled.

Dickce mimed washing her hands, and Luca smiled. It really was a rather dazzling sight, An'gel decided.

"Yes, please," Luca said.

Dickce took his arm and led him out of the room. An'gel followed, determined to keep an eye on her sister and the handsome manservant. The minute she could get her sister to herself, she intended to ask Dickce what she was up to.

Dickce showed Luca to the downstairs half bath and indicated she would wait for him. He nodded and then shut himself in. Moments later An'gel heard the sound of the faucet running.

"What's going on here?" An'gel said, keeping her voice low.

"What do you mean?" Dickce asked. "I simply invited a young man to dine with us. He'll enjoy Clementine's food much more than he would room service, even at the Farrington House."

"It really is sweet of you to be so concerned about his meals," An'gel said. "I know you, though. There's more to it than that."

Dickce shrugged. "Has it occurred to you that Rosabelle might not have met Luca before? I thought it would be interesting to bring them face-to-face in the same room with Antonio."

Suddenly the implications of Dickce's words hit An'gel.

Dickce thought Luca was the *caro mio* to whom Antonio had spoken earlier. Dickce obviously also thought there was more to the relationship between the two men than that of employer and employee.

That would explain Antonio's seeming discomfort over having Luca remain in the house for dinner, An'gel reasoned. He would be uncomfortable having his wife and his lover—his male lover—share the same dinner table.

"I don't think this is such a good idea," An'gel said, her patience with her sister at its breaking point, "but it's too late to do anything about it now." Shaking her head, she walked past Dickce to the kitchen.

~

Dickce felt only a smidgen of guilt as she watched An'gel stalk off, obviously in a snit with her. Dickce knew she could be playing with fire, but she couldn't stand not knowing whether Luca was really Antonio's lover. She figured Rosabelle deserved to know if he was, since Antonio intended to divorce her. Because of Luca, she was convinced.

She couldn't blame Antonio, she decided. Luca was the most beautiful thing she'd ever seen. No matter how she gussied herself up, Rosabelle couldn't compete with his youth and sheer gorgeousness. Dickce felt a little vindictive toward Rosabelle, and she would have to pray for forgiveness about it later. Right now, however, she wanted to shake her old friend up.

If Rosabelle was the killer—and Dickce was willing to bet she was—introducing Luca into the mix might rile Rosabelle up so much she would reveal herself. Dickce wasn't clear on how she might do it, but she knew that rattling Rosabelle's cage ought to produce interesting results.

Luca stepped out of the half bath and smiled at her

again. Oh, my, she could look at that face for an hour without wanting to move. She sighed.

"Let me show you the dining room," she said, once again taking Luca's arm. *His strong, well-muscled arm*, she thought.

"Why don't you sit here?" Dickce gestured to a chair across from where she thought Antonio and Rosabelle would probably sit. She intended to sit next to Luca. She wanted to be able to observe every gesture, every nuance, every glance, during the meal.

"What would you like to drink?" she asked as Luca pulled out his chair.

"*Vino rosso*?" he said. "Red wine?"

"What an excellent idea," Dickce said. Liquor to loosen the tongues and lower the inhibitions—she should have thought of that herself. They had several bottles of a Bordeaux that would be perfect with roast beef as the main course. "I'll be back in a minute."

Luca smiled and nodded, and Dickce had to tear her gaze away. *Really, this is getting ridiculous*, she scolded herself as she hurried to the kitchen to fetch the wine. *You can't keep staring at him like a besotted schoolgirl.*

An'gel looked up from the stove when Dickce came into the kitchen. "Good, you're just in time," she said. "We're ready to take everything into the dining room."

"I'm going to open a couple of bottles of wine," Dickce said. "I thought it would be pleasant to have it with Clementine's roast."

"You'll have to get out the wineglasses yourself," An'gel said. "Antoinette and I will carry in the food. I sent Benjy and Diesel to remind Junior about dinner."

An'gel still had her snit on, Dickce decided. Probably anxiety over the coming meal. There would be fireworks of some sort. Dickce was counting on it. An'gel could chew her out later if she wanted.

Dickce took two bottles of the Bordeaux from the wine cabinet and opened them. She bore them to the dining room on a tray with the wineglasses. An'gel and Antoinette were arranging the food on the sideboard. Dickce set the wine on the table and put a glass at every plate. Luca watched all the activity with his pleasant smile, and Dickce noticed Antoinette stealing peeks at the handsome young Italian. He did not appear to notice the beautiful young woman in the room, and that cemented Dickce's belief that he was gay.

Dickce poured wine for herself and Luca. He picked up his glass, swirled the wine, then sniffed. He tasted, then nodded approvingly. "*Squisito. Salute.*"

Dickce raised her glass to him and smiled. She tasted the wine. It was as delicious as she remembered.

In the next few minutes An'gel and Antoinette had the sideboard loaded with roast beef, mashed potatoes, green beans, homemade rolls, and whipped sweet potatoes. Their guests began to appear, Wade first, followed shortly by Bernice and Juanita. Benjy and Junior came next. Dickce introduced them all to Luca, who smiled and repeated their names. They all had trouble taking their eyes off Luca as they arranged themselves around the table, Dickce was amused to see. Even An'gel kept glancing his way. She thought Juanita and Benjy, in particular, seemed fascinated by the new guest.

Soon after, Rosabelle made her entrance with Antonio escorting her.

Dickce thought Rosabelle looked peevish, and she wondered how much Antonio had told her in advance about the unexpected addition to their dinner party. Luca rose as his employer and Rosabelle neared the table.

Dickce watched Rosabelle's face as she beheld Luca for the first time.

Rosabelle's eyes widened, and then she smiled. Dickce had to stifle a giggle. Rosabelle couldn't resist the allure of an attractive man, and Dickce knew Rosabelle was getting ready to be at her charming best with Luca. *Is* she *in for a surprise*, Dickce thought.

Antonio glowered at Luca as he spoke. "Rosabella, dearest, allow me to introduce to you my *valletto*, Luca Cavalcante. Luca, my wife, the Contessa di San Lorenzo."

Rosabelle held out her hand, and Luca bent over it, his face impassive. "*Piacere, Signora la Contessa*."

"*Piacere*, Luca. I'm delighted to meet you. Antonio, the naughty man, has told me so little about you." Rosabelle fluttered her eyelashes at Luca, who merely nodded. Rosabelle frowned, obviously disconcerted at the lack of further response.

"Please help yourselves, everyone," An'gel said. "There is red wine for those who would like it; otherwise there is iced tea and water."

There was no conversation as the guests lined up to fill their plates at the sideboard. Wade went first. His consumption of whiskey earlier in the day didn't seem to have affected his appetite, Dickce mused as he piled his plate high with roast and mashed potatoes. Within a few minutes everyone was seated again at the table, and Wade grabbed a bottle and filled his glass. More bottles were passed up and down the table, and Dickce noted that everyone except Benjy and An'gel partook of the wine. She would probably need to fetch another bottle or two. She didn't think Wade would be content with a single glass nor, she suspected, would Antonio.

The latter focused on his food, with frequent sips of wine. Probably trying his best to ignore Luca's presence, Dickce figured.

Rosabelle, however, picked at her food while casting furtive glances at the manservant. *Trying to figure him out*, Dickce thought with amusement. *She's not used to men who aren't immediately dazzled by her.*

"Luca, my husband has told me so little about you," Rosabelle said. "How long have you worked for him?"

Luca, wineglass to his lips, drained the contents and set the glass down before he replied. "Three years we have been together, but I remain in Italy when he comes to the United States." He scowled as he picked up the nearest bottle and emptied it into his glass.

Rosabelle smiled. "Then you have worked for him a year longer than I've been married to him."

"*Si, è vero.*" Luca lifted his wine and drank half the glass.

Rosabelle's eyes narrowed. "Sorry, I don't speak Italian. What does that mean?"

Luca curled his lip. "It means, yes, it is true." His tone sounded insolent to Dickce, and she could see that Rosabelle was bothered by it.

"There's no need to be rude, young man, because I don't speak your language." Rosabelle poked her fork hard into a piece of roast and stuck it in her mouth.

Luca shrugged, and Dickce thought the gesture even more insolent than his tone. *This is getting good.* How much more would it take before the fireworks started?

Antonio spoke rapidly in Italian, and Dickce found it almost impossible to follow. He was chastising Luca for his behavior, she knew that.

Luca muttered under his breath for a moment, then

spoke clearly. "*Sì, Signor il Conte.*" He inclined his head toward Antonio.

Rosabelle turned to her husband. "Does he behave like this frequently? I would not put up with this from any servant of mine, not for a minute."

"It is no matter, my dear," Antonio said in a soothing tone. "We Italians are a passionate race, and sometimes we sound angry or insolent to others when we are simply talking in a normal fashion. Do not be upset."

Rosabelle didn't look convinced, and Dickce could sense the tension building in Luca. He fired off a comment in Italian, and Dickce had to stifle a gasp of surprise. She understood just enough of it to know that the young man had basically asked Antonio if he made love to his wife as often as he made love to Luca.

She stole a glance at An'gel. From what she could tell, her sister hadn't understood any of it, which was just as well. She would have had a fit on the spot.

Antonio's face turned purple with rage. Rosabelle stared back and forth at him and Luca, aware that something had gone wrong but not sure what. Antonio stood suddenly, pushing his chair back with a jerk. He threw his napkin down on the table and started yelling at Luca.

Luca rose from his place and yelled back.

An'gel got to her feet. "Stop this at once," she roared.

Antonio stopped in mid-yell and stared at her, as did Luca.

"This is ridiculous," An'gel said in a more normal tone. "I will not have this outrageous behavior at my dinner table."

"I am appalled, Antonio, that you would behave like this with your servant in front of everyone." Rosabelle shook her head. "You are a gentleman, a nobleman, and this is surely beneath you."

Wade laughed, surprising them all. "Mother, how stupid can you be?" He laughed again. "Don't you get it? Haven't you ever heard a lovers' quarrel before?"

CHAPTER 36

An'gel could happily have wrung her sister's neck at that moment. Dickce had deliberately stirred this up, and it was even worse than An'gel feared. Rosabelle might have a stroke at any second if any of this were true.

"Wade, that's utterly ridiculous. You're simply trying to drive Antonio and me apart with this nonsense." Rosabelle directed a furious glare at her son, but he laughed at her.

"Oh, I think Luca over there has already done that." Wade lifted his glass and toasted the young man.

Luca grinned. "Grazie." He mimed a kiss at Antonio.

Rosabelle shrieked at the sight of that gesture, "Is it true, then? He really is your lover?" She clutched at her heart with both hands. "Antonio, you're having an affair with another man?"

Antonio reached for Rosabelle, but she batted his hands away. "Don't you dare touch me."

"Rosabella, cara, it is not how you think," Antonio said.

An'gel heard the desperation in his voice, but she wondered why he would want to placate Rosabelle at this point. She didn't believe Rosabelle could ever forgive him for betraying her with a man. A woman she might have forgiven, thinking she could easily win him back. But not with Luca standing there and smirking.

"It is *exactly* how I think." Rosabelle picked up her wineglass and threw the contents in her husband's face. There was only a dribble, and Antonio wiped it away with one hand.

Rosabelle's chest heaved. "I only wish that was acid instead."

"Miss Ducote, what's going on here? Do you need assistance?"

An'gel, startled, looked up to see one of the deputies in the doorway. She walked over to him while Rosabelle continued to scream at Antonio.

"A domestic quarrel," she told the deputy. "I doubt it will get much worse than this, but please stay here in case."

"Yes, ma'am," the deputy said. He moved to stand near the head of the table, where no one could fail to see him.

Rosabelle paused mid-tirade and crooked her finger at the deputy. "Officer, I want you to escort this man out of the house immediately. I never want to see his face again."

"Perhaps that would be best," Antonio said as he backed away. He turned to An'gel. "My sincere apologies for this most unfortunate incident. It is a poor way to repay you for your generous hospitality."

An'gel was at a loss to know how to respond to him, given the bizarre nature of the circumstances. She finally settled on a simple "Thank you, Antonio." She couldn't state with any honesty that having him as a guest was a pleasure, not with what just happened.

He nodded. "Good-bye to you all." He stared at Luca for a moment, then jerked his head. "Come." He stomped out.

Luca turned toward Rosabelle and executed an exaggerated bow. "Farewell, signora. It has been a great pleasure."

Rosabelle shrieked again. She picked up a dinner roll from her plate and threw it at Luca. The roll struck his broad chest and bounced onto the table. Smiling, Luca picked it up and took a large bite out of it. "Grazie." He turned and sauntered out, eating the rest of the roll as he went.

An'gel watched him go, thankful that at least part of the drama was at an end. She knew the second act would begin right away, however. She glowered at Dickce and was not surprised to receive a smug smile in response. An'gel hoped Dickce was satisfied with the fireworks she had brought about.

"Well, Mother, think you'll get your money back now?" Wade laughed. "I told you he was a gigolo, but you wouldn't listen."

"I hope you have all enjoyed seeing me be humiliated so publicly." Rosabelle regarded her family with fire in her eyes. An'gel tensed, nervous over what Rosabelle might do next. She had better not throw anything else, or An'gel would kick her out, no matter what.

"We did," Wade assured her. "I haven't been this entertained in years."

An'gel feared her son's mocking tone would enrage Rosabelle further. Instead, Rosabelle seemed to ignore him.

"I am going to my room now," she said. "I do not want to see any of you, so you will please leave me the hell alone tonight." She walked slowly out of the room.

An'gel wondered uneasily whether she or Dickce ought

not to go with her. Then she remembered that the second deputy was upstairs. He could keep an eye on Rosabelle, she decided gratefully.

Should she call Kanesha and let her know that Antonio was no longer in the house? No, the deputy would probably do that. One less thing for An'gel to worry about.

Her appetite was gone, but she could see that Wade's was unaffected by the contretemps. If anything, she thought, he was eating with even more gusto than before.

Bernice, on the other hand, was obviously distraught. She was crying, and Juanita was patting her hand.

"Now, Mother," she said, "it's no use you getting upset like this. Grandmother is, well, always going to be Grandmother. She's not going to change at her age."

"I know that," Bernice said. "Mother has been an embarrassment to me all my life. Fifty-seven years of one humiliating thing after another." She sobbed for a moment. "Mother has never cared for anyone other than herself. You don't know how I've struggled over the years because of her utter selfishness."

"I know, Mother." Juanita shot An'gel an apologetic glance. "Here, have a sip of wine. It will help calm you down."

"No, I don't want any." Bernice pushed the glass away so violently she forced Juanita to spill some of the wine on the tablecloth. "I'm going upstairs to my room." She shoved back from the table and almost tripped over her chair as she scurried out of the room.

Juanita mopped at the tablecloth with her napkin. "I'm so sorry, Miss Ducote. Mother doesn't usually get this upset, but I guess tonight was too much for her."

"I understand," An'gel said. "Please, there is no need for you to try to clean the stain. Clementine will deal with it first thing in the morning." She hated to let the stain remain overnight, but she was simply too tired to worry about it. Besides, Clementine was far better at stain removal than she.

"Clementine is a genius with stains." Juanita stopped trying to blot the wine with her napkin. She stood abruptly. "If you'll excuse me, I think I'd better go up to check on my mother now." She hurried out.

"I think I'll be going, too," Junior said. "See you tomorrow, I guess."

Wade continued to eat. An'gel marveled again at his appetite. Benjy, she noticed, had eaten little from his plate. He stared at his stepfather and shook his head.

An'gel felt truly sorry for the boy. Wade had made it clear enough that he cared little for Benjy's welfare. What would become of him, she wondered, when he returned to California? She did not like to think of his being at the mercy of Wade and the rest of Rosabelle's family. Perhaps she and Dickce could think of a way to help him.

She was ready to start clearing the table. The sooner that was done and things put away in the kitchen, the sooner she could retreat to her bedroom and try to rest. While Wade was still eating, however, it would be rude to begin cleaning up. That was ironic, she thought, worrying about rudeness after all that had happened in the house in the last day or so. Even so, she couldn't bring herself to interrupt the man.

Dickce apparently had no such compunction. She stood and started gathering plates and stacking them.

"Let me help," Benjy said.

An'gel started to protest but decided against it. If Wade hadn't had enough by now, he could fix himself a snack in the kitchen later. There was plenty of food left over. Clementine had actually prepared two roasts, and about two thirds of the second one remained.

"I guess I'm finished." Wade dropped his napkin by his plate. "Miss An'gel, I have to say that's one of the finest meals I've had in a long time. Your cook is talented woman."

"Thank you," An'gel said. "I will be happy to convey your kind words to her." She nodded in the direction of the sideboard. "As you can see, there is plenty left over. If you get hungry in the night, you're welcome to help yourself."

"Thank you," Wade said. "I might just do that." He glanced at Benjy. "Be careful with those dishes. You can't afford to break one."

For a moment An'gel thought Dickce was going to crawl across the table and slap Wade Thurmond. She had seldom seen her sister so angry. Benjy simply looked resigned, evidently used to such treatment from his stepfather. No wonder the boy referred to him as "the Wart," An'gel thought indignantly.

Wade seemed to catch on that he had upset Dickce. He mumbled "sorry" and walked out of the room.

"I cannot stand the sight of that poisonous man," Dickce said. "The minute he's out of the house, I'm going up there and sterilize everything in his room."

"Don't pay him any attention, Miss Dickce," Benjy said quietly. "That's the way he is, and nothing will change it. Just like his mother. I'm used to it."

"You shouldn't have to be," Dickce said. "You deserve far better than that."

"I agree," An'gel said. An idea had been forming in the back of her mind, and after Wade's latest display of boorishness, she made a firm decision. That poor boy could not be left to the mercy of Wade and the rest of the family. She had a solution to propose, but she had no idea whether Benjy would find it acceptable.

"Benjy," she said, "how would you feel about staying here with Dickce and me and going to college in Athena?"

To her great surprise, Dickce and Benjy looked at each other and started laughing.

CHAPTER 37

Dickce couldn't help laughing. An'gel's expression was priceless. Dickce was delighted, however, that An'gel had come to the idea on her own without any prompting.

"What's so funny?" An'gel asked.

Dickce knew she'd better answer before her sister got really annoyed. "Benjy and I have already been talking about that idea." She patted the boy's arm. "He has no family that he knows of, and he isn't eager to depend on Wade for anything. I don't think Wade will care one way or the other."

"He won't," Benjy said. "Miss An'gel, I promise I'll work really hard and do anything you want me to do to help out. I know how to clean and do laundry."

"Benjy, I'm sure you would work hard," An'gel said. "I think this is an idea we should all discuss further, but I am in favor of it. Let's wait until things are calmer around here before we talk any more about it. All right?"

"Yes, ma'am," Benjy said with a big smile. "Thank you."

Dickce nodded approvingly at her sister. "Why don't you leave this to Benjy and me? I can see how tired you are, and it won't take us long to get this all put away. Go on upstairs and get ready for bed."

An'gel nodded. "I'm too tired to argue. It's still early, I suppose, but I'll be happy to get some rest. Thank the Lord that Kanesha's deputies are on watch tonight. We should have a quiet evening."

"Have you checked with Kanesha about that other deputy?" Dickce didn't want to be more specific than that because she didn't want to alarm Benjy. Surely An'gel would catch on to the fact that she was talking about a deputy to keep an eye on things outside the house.

An'gel looked puzzled for a moment, then her face cleared. "Thanks for reminding me. I haven't heard, so I'll call when I get upstairs. I'm sure everything will be fine, though. Good night."

Dickce and Benjy wished her good night as they continued to clear the table. After three trips to the kitchen, they had removed everything from the dining room except the tablecloth and napkins.

"I'll go get it," Benjy said.

"Thanks." Dickce started putting food away in containers to be stored in the refrigerator. Right after Benjy left, she suddenly heard a scratching noise.

Where was it coming from? She stopped scraping potatoes into a plastic container and listened intently.

There it was again. Coming from the back porch, she decided. What could it be?

She picked up one of the sharp carving knives and walked slowly to the back door. The scratching continued, becoming louder and more frantic.

Then she heard sounds she recognized as those of a frustrated cat trying to get in the door.

Laughing, she unlatched the door and opened it to allow Diesel to enter. He meowed at her and padded past her. He meowed several times more, and Dickce thought he was complaining about how slow she was to answer the door.

"I'm sorry, Diesel." She walked past him to restore the knife to its place in the rack. "I had forgotten all about you, poor kitty." Hands now free, she rubbed his head, and he began to purr.

"We have company," she said when Benjy returned moments later, his arms full of tablecloth and napkins. "You can put those over there for now."

"Hi, there, boy." Benjy piled the linens on the table as directed. "I guess Junior didn't close the door completely." He glanced at Dickce. "When we left to come over for dinner, I made certain the door was latched so he couldn't get out. Junior didn't think about it when he went back, I'm sure."

"The automatic latch was on the back door, too," Dickce said. "Clementine always sets it when she leaves for the day. Even Diesel isn't clever enough to open that."

"Can I give him a few bites of roast beef?" Benjy asked.

"Sure," Dickce said. "But only a few."

The cat munched happily on his tidbits while Dickce and Benjy finished their work in the kitchen. Diesel padded off to the pantry, and Dickce could hear him lapping up water.

When the cat came back, they were done. "Time for bed for all of us," Dickce said. "Would you like to take something with you in case you get hungry during the night? You didn't seem to eat much at dinner."

Benjy shook his head. "No, I'll be fine. I had enough."

"All right then. You two had better scoot off to bed. I'll see you in the morning." Dickce stood in the back door and watched until they were safely inside the garage apartment. She made sure the automatic lock was still on, then she dimmed the lights and headed up to her room. She nodded at the deputy on duty downstairs and bade him good night. She did the same for the two on duty upstairs as well, one at either end of the hall.

She was happy to reach the tranquility of her room. She was feeling pretty tired now herself, and she did not take long to get ready for bed. She turned off the light, adjusted her covers, and fell asleep not long after.

An'gel took her time undressing and getting ready for bed. She contemplated having a nice warm soak in her tub but decided against it. Too much effort, even for that. Instead she climbed into bed as soon as she had her nightgown on. She turned out her light and got comfortable. Yawning, she closed her eyes.

Then she opened them again. Her body was tired but her brain refused to rest. Overstimulation, she decided. What a day this had been. Dramatic, emotional scenes, another murder, enough tension to float an ocean liner—she hoped never to have such a day again for the rest of her life, however long that might be. Any more days like this, she thought with black humor, and the rest of her life wouldn't be very long at all.

She was annoyed with herself for not being able to figure out who had killed Marla and Maudine. She was used to solving problems. In fact, she prided herself on her ability to sort out any situation she encountered. Why, then, was this so difficult to resolve?

She had two chief suspects in mind, Rosabelle and Juanita. Whatever illusions she might have had about her old sorority sister before the past day or so, they were shattered beyond repair. She had no trouble believing that Rosabelle, the single most self-absorbed person she had ever met in her long life, could have killed both Marla and Maudine. Yes, she acknowledged, Rosabelle *had* seemed appropriately grief-stricken at the news of Maudine's death. Rosabelle was a superb actress, however, and the grieving mother was a role she could probably play as easily as breathing.

While she leaned heavily toward Rosabelle as the culprit, An'gel also thought that Juanita could be the killer. Juanita had behaved politely and sweetly, she had to admit, but that was what bothered her. Juanita seemed a little *too* sweet and polite. An'gel suspected that Juanita might be just as good an actress as her grandmother. Juanita had a compelling motive to murder her grandmother and her aunt—money. With Maudine out of the picture, Bernice's share of their father's trust doubled. As long as Bernice outlived Rosabelle, Juanita probably stood to inherit a fortune.

If Juanita was the killer, An'gel reckoned, Rosabelle had better watch her back. Even Bernice could be in danger, once Rosabelle was out of the way.

Was Juanita truly that ruthless?

An'gel wasn't sure, but the girl reminded her in some ways a little too much of Rosabelle at that age. Rosabelle had been able to play the demure self-effacing type when she thought it would get her what she wanted. Was Juanita's niceness a façade, as her grandmother's had always been?

Money was a compelling motive for Rosabelle, too. Particularly now that her wealthy Italian husband had been revealed to be an adulterer. Rosabelle could kiss her dreams of living the rich life in Italy good-bye. She might be able to salvage something out of the divorce settlement, but An'gel doubted that Antonio would grant Rosabelle any concessions. The lawyers would have to settle it all.

If Rosabelle was the killer, then Bernice and Wade could be her next targets. Juanita and Junior should be safe. Killing them wouldn't benefit Rosabelle monetarily.

An'gel groaned. Her head ached from all the speculation. She pushed aside the covers and went into her bathroom. She had a prescription for a mild tranquilizer that would help her get to sleep. She didn't like taking it because she had a horror of becoming dependent on it, but tonight she felt desperate for sleep.

Back in bed, she made an effort to relax and clear her mind until the pill could take effect. Eventually she began to feel sleepy and finally dozed off.

Sometime later a light rapping at her door roused her. Groggily she glanced at her clock—a few minutes past one. She stumbled a little getting out of bed as the rapping continued. She put on her robe and switched on the light before she opened the door. She blinked at Bernice. "What's wrong?"

Bernice said, "I'm so sorry to bother you at this time of night, but my blood sugar is low, and I don't have anything in my room to eat. Would you mind going down to the kitchen with me so I can find something? I'm a little afraid of going down by myself, and you know where everything is." She smiled weakly.

"Of course," An'gel said, her hospitable instincts kicking in. She yawned. "Pardon me." She stepped past Bernice and started down the hall. She shook her head to clear it a little. Ah, that helped.

"Ma'am, is something wrong?"

An'gel stared at the man in uniform. What was he doing here? She started to ask, then she remembered. He was a deputy watching the house.

"Nothing," she said. "I'm taking my guest downstairs for something to eat. Low blood sugar."

The deputy nodded and resumed his post. An'gel wandered on, dimly aware that Bernice was shuffling along behind her. Lights on the first floor provided enough illumination that An'gel and her guest could navigate down the stairs and into the kitchen.

An'gel flipped the switch, and then she blinked at the sudden brightness. She headed for the refrigerator. "I'm not sure what you'd prefer," she said over her shoulder to Bernice. She pulled open the refrigerator door and peered inside. "Maybe it would be better if you just ate some sugar."

She started to straighten and close the door. She felt a blow to the back of her head and blacked out. Her body slid slowly to the floor.

CHAPTER 38

Why was someone shaking her so hard?

Dickce surfaced from a deep sleep confused and alarmed.

"What do you want?" she asked crossly. "Stop that."

"Miss Dickce, you have to get up," Juanita said urgently. "There's a fire, can't you smell it?"

Fire.

That word woke Dickce immediately. She tossed off her covers and climbed out of bed. She stuck her feet in her slippers and grabbed her robe.

"We have to get out of the house," Juanita said. "Come on." She took hold of Dickce's arm and started pulling her toward the door.

Once they hit the hallway, Dickce could smell the smoke.

"We have to wake up An'gel." Pulling herself loose from the younger woman's grasp, Dickce darted over toward her sister's door.

"She's not there." Juanita grabbed her arm again. "I already looked. I can't find her or my mother. I'm praying they're already outside. Come on."

Dickce ran for all she was worth to the head of the stairs, then moved more carefully down until her feet hit the floor again. The front door was open, and she and Juanita dashed out. Wade was already out there, but there was no sign of Rosabelle, An'gel, or Bernice.

"Where are they?" Dickce asked. "Wade, where is my sister? Have you seen her?"

"No," Wade said. "One of the deputies knocked on my door and told me to get out of the house. I pulled on some shoes and got out as fast as I could. I haven't seen the deputies or anyone else since I got out here."

"I'm going back in there," Dickce said. "I have to find An'gel." She pushed Juanita away when the girl grabbed at her. "No, let me go."

"The deputies will find her," Juanita said as she took a firm hold of Dickce's arm. "You'll only put yourself and them in danger if you go back in the house. You need to stay here. I don't know where my mother is either, but we can't go back in there."

"What if they don't know she's not out of the house?" Dickce tried as hard as she could to get loose from Juanita but the young woman was stronger than she was.

"They'll know," Juanita said.

"Where is the fire?" Dickce asked. "Maybe that's where An'gel is, helping them put it out."

"At the back of the house," Wade said. "In the kitchen, I think."

"Let me go," Dickce said. "I've got to go see if An'gel is all right."

"I'll go with you," Juanita said. "Maybe my mother and

grandmother are there, too." She turned to her uncle. "You wait here in case they come out. The fire truck ought to be here soon."

"There it is," Dickce said. She could hear a siren in the distance, quickly coming closer. "Come on." She started for the rear of the house, pulling Juanita with her.

The outside lights were on, and that made it easier for Dickce to see her way around to the back. Juanita kept pace with her, even caught her once when she stepped in a slight depression in the ground and stumbled.

Even before they reached the corner of the house, Dickce could see light from the fire. Her heart felt like it stopped for a moment. She worried that An'gel was trapped somewhere inside. *Lord, let her be safe. I don't care if the whole house burns down as long as my sister is safe.*

Juanita guided Dickce toward the driveway in front of the garage, and Dickce did not protest. Her gaze was riveted on the house and the fire inside the kitchen. She prayed over and over that An'gel would be all right. As she watched, one of the deputies came out of the house with a woman in his arms, her arms around his neck.

Dickce darted forward, too quickly for Juanita to grab her and hold her back.

A few steps closer, and Dickce could see that the woman in the deputy's arms was her sister. At that moment a fire engine swept around the house and stopped. Another was right behind it.

Dickce stopped and watched as the men from the Athena Fire Department went into action. Two of them ran up to the deputy with a gurney. They placed An'gel on it and then carried her across the driveway toward Dickce and Juanita.

"An'gel, thank the Lord you're alive," Dickce said. She

wanted to cry with relief. The sounds and the activity around them were loud and disorienting. There was a light wind blowing the smoke away from them. Dickce was thankful for that small mercy. She thought the noise might drive her mad if it didn't end soon. This was like a living nightmare.

An'gel looked at her strangely as the EMTs set the gurney down near the garage. "My head hurts," she said. "What happened?"

"Let me have a look at you, ma'am." One of the EMTs claimed An'gel's attention, and Dickce moved back out of the way. She noticed that Juanita was gone, then she saw her speaking to the deputy who had brought An'gel out of the house.

"What's going on?"

Dickce turned to see Junior and Benjy, the latter with Diesel in his arms, coming out of the garage apartment.

"Miss Dickce, are you and Miss An'gel all right?" Benjy asked.

"I am," Dickce said. "They're checking An'gel right now."

"Where are all the others?" Junior asked. "I see Juanita, but I don't see Uncle Wade, Aunt Bernice, or Grandmother."

"They're out front by now, I hope," Dickce said. "I know Wade is, but I'm not sure about Rosabelle and your aunt. Juanita didn't know where they were either. We hoped they would be back here, but I haven't seen them."

For the first time Dickce realized how odd it was that neither Bernice nor Rosabelle had made an appearance. Had something happened to them?

She looked at her sister. The EMT was still checking her out. An'gel said her head hurt. Had someone struck her?

What if Rosabelle and Bernice were still in the house

somewhere? Rosabelle might use the confusion as an opportunity to kill Bernice. Maybe she had even set a fire for that very purpose.

Dickce had to talk to that deputy. He was still with Juanita. She darted forward.

Juanita turned at that moment and came forward. "It's all right, Miss Dickce," she said. "I've told him about Mother and Grandmother. They'll find them." She took Dickce's arm. "Let's stay over here out of the way."

Dickce thought Juanita seemed strangely calm. Why wasn't she more upset over her relatives' failure to appear? "Would you like to go back around to the front and check on them? They are probably there by now with your uncle."

Juanita shook her head. "No, we don't need to do that. Everything will be fine. I hope the firemen will be able to stop the fire from spreading. I would hate to see you lose your lovely house."

Thoroughly bemused, Dickce allowed Juanita to lead her back to where the EMTs were still examining An'gel. She and Juanita stood beside Junior, Benjy, and Diesel and watched the firemen. Dickce figured she and the others were far enough away from the house, plus the wind was blowing away from them, that they should be able to remain here safely.

She wanted to talk to her sister, but she knew it was best to let the EMTs take care of her. The minute they were done, however, she would be right over there, demanding to know what had happened and whether An'gel was all right.

From what Dickce could tell, the fire crew appeared to be making headway against the fire. She could no longer see anything burning, though there was a lot of smoke. She prayed that the fire was out and had been contained in the kitchen. They would have to have the house thoroughly cleaned, of course. Not to mention the repairs to the kitchen and wherever else the fire might have spread. She let her mind roam back and forth over these mundane details. As long as she and her sister were alive and relatively unharmed, nothing else mattered.

One of the EMTs approached her and drew her a few steps away from the others. Dickce recognized him after a moment. He was the grandson of one of her school friends, Norma Faye Allenbury. She couldn't recall his name, though.

"Miss Dickce," he said, "I don't know if you remember me. I'm Grant Tisdale. My grandmother is a friend of yours."

Dickce nodded. "I recognized you," she said. "I'm sorry I couldn't remember your name."

Tisdale smiled. "No worries. I wanted to let you know that we are going to take Miss An'gel to the hospital. She's going to be fine, but she did have a bump on the head and was unconscious for at least ten minutes or more. She's stable, heart rate and everything are fine, but it's a good idea to have the doc in the ER check her out."

Greatly relieved, Dickce nodded. "Yes, I think that's a very good idea. Has An'gel objected?"

Tisdale smiled again. "Only a little bitty bit. Would you like to come with us in the ambulance?"

"Yes," Dickce said. She saw a dark form coming toward them. When the person walked into a less dim area, she could see it was Kanesha Berry. "Let me speak to the deputy for a moment, and then I'll be ready to go."

"That's fine," Tisdale said. "We'll be over there."

Dickce scurried over to Kanesha, conscious that she was in only her nightgown, slippers, and robe. "Thank the Lord you're here."

"Are you and Miss An'gel all right?" Kanesha asked. "I got here as soon as I could."

"They want to take An'gel to the ER and have her checked by a doctor," Dickce said. "The EMTs think she's okay but it's better to be sure. I'm going with her."

"You do that, and don't worry about anything here," Kanesha said. "I'll make sure everything that needs to be done will be."

"Thank you," Dickce said. "I'll be at the hospital with An'gel."

Kanesha nodded. "I'll catch up with you there as soon as I can."

Confident that Kanesha was in charge, Dickce walked over to where the EMTs waited with An'gel. "We're going to the ER," she said in her best no-nonsense tone.

"All right," An'gel said. "I don't have the energy to argue." She held out a hand, and Dickce grasped it. "As long as we're both here, that's all that matters."

Dickce felt the tears forming, but she was determined not to let An'gel see her cry. She simply nodded.

On the way to the hospital in Athena, Dickce thought briefly about the fate of Rosabelle and Bernice. She had the oddest feeling that something bad had happened, but all she could concentrate on right now was her sister.

CHAPTER 39

"So it was *Bernice* who attacked you?" Dickce, still fuzzy from lack of sleep, stared at An'gel.

Her sister nodded, then winced. "Remind me not to nod for a few days." She lay her head back against the pillow.

Dickce rose stiffly from the hospital recliner to adjust the blinds. The sun was too bright for her tired eyes. "There, that's better."

"Thank you," An'gel said. "The light was bothering me, too." She shifted in the bed. "I cannot get comfortable in this bed."

"You'll have to figure out how," Dickce said, though not without sympathy. "The earliest Dr. Kenyon said you could be released is tomorrow morning. He wants to keep you here for at least twenty-four hours, remember?"

"Yes, though I don't see why. I told him I felt fine except for a little stiffness in my neck and a sore head. A few aspirin and a day's rest at home, and I'll be right as rain."

"We don't know yet if we'll be able to rest at home," Dickce reminded her. "Until we hear from Kanesha about the extent of the damage, we don't know whether we can stay in the house. The smell of smoke might be too strong, or there could be structural damage. Your room is right over the kitchen."

"Yes, yes, I know all that," An'gel said.

"Why did Bernice attack you like that?" Dickce asked. They were both so tired, they couldn't stick to the subject. "I was sure Rosabelle was the murderer."

"I was, too," An'gel said. "But why would Bernice attack me if she isn't the killer?"

"I don't know," Dickce said. "What do you think happened to her?"

"How do I know?" An'gel said. "When did Kanesha say she'd be here? I hope she'll have some answers for us."

Dickce glanced at the clock on the wall of An'gel's room. "It's eight twenty-five now. She said she'd be here by nine."

"Well, she should hurry up."

"Stop being so fretful," Dickce said. "You sound like a four-year-old. She'll get here when she gets here."

"That's certainly profound," An'gel snapped at her. Then she frowned. "Don't mind me. I feel bad, and I want to take it out on someone."

"Lucky me," Dickce murmured.

"What was that?" An'gel's eyes narrowed.

"Never mind," Dickce said. "I hope they're all okay. I thought about them a little during the night. As angry as I am over what happened to you and to our house, I still don't want anyone else to be dead."

"Surely they've got Bernice locked up somewhere by now," An'gel said. "I guess she snapped."

"How so?" Dickce asked. "Are you talking about what she said at dinner last night after the big scene?"

"That, and other things as well," An'gel said. "Think back over how Maudine treated her. She was the oldest, and Bernice was the middle child. She seemed to be under Maudine's thumb, and we know Bernice felt humiliated by Rosabelle."

Dickce knew what it felt like to have the thumb print of an older sister on her back. She forbore to mention it at the moment, however. "So you think Bernice set out to kill her mother and got Marla by mistake?"

"Yes, I think so," An'gel said. "Then she got rid of Maudine for the money. I'm sure Rosabelle was her next target."

"For all we know, she did manage to kill Rosabelle," Dickce said. "I wish Kanesha would get here. The curiosity's driving me mad."

An'gel did not reply, and they sat in silence. Dickce watched the minute hand of the clock creep slowly toward the hour. An'gel dozed off, and Dickce wished she could.

At five minutes after nine, An'gel's door opened, and Kanesha stood in the doorway. Dickce waved her in.

"How is she?" Kanesha said softly as she nodded toward An'gel.

"I'm fine," An'gel said as her eyes popped open. "You look exhausted."

Dickce agreed. She had never seen the deputy with such dark circles under her eyes. Kanesha looked like she was ready to drop in her tracks.

"I am." Kanesha smiled faintly and pulled the other chair close to Dickce. She sat heavily and leaned back a moment, her eyes closed. Then they popped open. "The damage to the kitchen wasn't too bad, and it didn't get any farther than that," she said. "My deputies got to it pretty quickly with the fire extinguishers. Most of the damage is from smoke."

"Where did the fire start?" Dickce asked.

"In the sink," Kanesha said. "She set fire to some paper."

"Clementine always keeps a stack of newspaper on hand to wrap things," An'gel said. "It's right there on a shelf near the refrigerator."

"Will we be able to live in the house while the repairs are done?" Dickce asked. She knew she ought to ask about Bernice and Rosabelle, but now that Kanesha was here, she felt curiously reluctant. She wasn't sure she could take any more bad news.

"Yes, ma'am," Kanesha said. "Cooking will be a challenge for a while, but that's about the worst of it."

"Good," An'gel said. She looked at Dickce. Dickce looked back at her, willing An'gel to be the one to ask the question.

An'gel sighed. "What happened? The last thing I remember—vaguely—is going down to the kitchen with Bernice." She frowned. "I believe she said something about blood sugar. I had taken a mild tranquilizer to help me sleep, and I was groggy."

"We don't know for sure," Kanesha said. "But here's the way I think it happened. She knocked you out, then she dragged you out of the kitchen and onto the back porch near the steps. I don't think she was trying to kill you."

"Thank heaven for small mercies," An'gel said.

Kanesha smiled. "Then she set the fire in the sink. She took a knife from the rack and went back upstairs. She hid the knife in her robe, because my deputy on duty near the head of the stairs didn't see any sign of it. He said she stopped to tell him you would be up soon after you had a bite to eat, then went into her room and closed the door."

"Was she waiting for the fire to be noticed?" An'gel asked.

"Yes. I think she was counting on the fact that the deputies would both run downstairs when they smelled smoke. That's what they did, and I'm going to have a talk with them about that. One of them should have remained on duty while the other one went downstairs to check out the situation. That was not acceptable." She looked grim, Dickce thought. She pitied the poor deputies. Kanesha would not spare their feelings.

"By the time one of them ran back upstairs to start alerting everyone to get out of the house, it was too late." She paused. "I'm sorry to have to tell you this, but Signora Mingione is dead. Mrs. Cameron must have gone to her room as soon as the deputies went downstairs, then she stabbed her."

Dickce could see her own feelings of horror mirrored in An'gel's expression. "Poor Rosabelle," she whispered. She uttered a silent prayer for her friend.

"What about Bernice?" An'gel asked after a long moment.

"When one of my men went back upstairs to warn everyone to get out of the house, he found only Miss Cameron in the bedroom they shared. She appeared to be asleep. She said she had no idea where her mother was, but she wasn't in their room. She was positive of that. The deputy left her and checked in the bathroom while I believe Miss Cameron came and roused you. That's what she told us."

"Yes," Dickce said. "She's the one who woke me up. I asked her about her mother, but she said she was sure her mother and grandmother were already out of the house. I was so worried about An'gel, I didn't really stop to think about it." She paused as the remembered terror came back to her. "Juanita insisted An'gel wasn't there and we needed to get out of the house, and that's what we did. We found Wade already outside when we got there, but he was alone."

"The three of you were out of the house by the time one of my men discovered the signora's body," Kanesha said. "He realized nothing could be done for her, so he searched quickly for Mrs. Cameron. He found her body in the closet in her room. She had been smothered to death by her daughter."

"Why?" Dickce said. "Why would Juanita do such a thing?"

"Are you sure Juanita didn't murder her grandmother and then her mother?" An'gel asked before Kanesha could answer Dickce's question.

"We're sure," Kanesha said. "Mrs. Cameron had blood on her hands and robe, and Miss Cameron's hands and robe were clean. Miss Cameron discovered what her mother had done. She confronted her mother who then lunged at her with a knife. Mrs. Cameron stumbled as she tried to attack her daughter and hit her head when she fell. That's when Miss Cameron grabbed a pillow and smothered her. She said she couldn't bear to see her mother go to jail or to a mental hospital." She shrugged. "It could have happened that way. She might get a reduced sentence. It's hard to say."

"Four women dead and the other in serious trouble." An'gel sounded dazed.

Dickce felt dazed herself. She found it all hard to take in.

"Did Juanita believe her mother killed Mrs. Stephens and Mrs. Pittman also?" An'gel asked.

"Yes, she told me she found an odd stain in the pocket of her mother's dress," Kanesha said. "She couldn't figure out what it was at first, but when she learned about the Vaseline on the banister, she realized that had to be it. She tried to get it out of her mother's dress, but I imagine there's still some residue."

"That's what she meant," An'gel said. "I should have picked up on it."

"What did who mean?" Dickce asked. "Juanita?"

"Yes," An'gel replied. "I walked into the kitchen once when she was talking to Clementine. She said Clementine told her how to get lipstick out of clothing. Then at dinner last night, remember she said that Clementine is a wizard with stains. She must have tried to find out how to get the Vaseline out of her mother's dress."

"There was a clue right in front of you," Dickce said.

"And I didn't pick up on it," An'gel said, obviously irritated with herself.

"Don't blame yourself, Miss An'gel," Kanesha said. "If I had known about it, it might have helped, but who's to say? Miss Cameron is clever enough, I'd be willing to bet she had a lipstick stain on a piece of her own clothing in case anyone got curious about her chat with Clementine."

"I presume you have Juanita in custody," An'gel said.

"Yes, and I have moved Mr. Pittman and Mr. Thurmond to the Farrington House. They seemed eager to leave."

"Can't say as I blame them," Dickce said. "What about Benjy and Diesel?"

"If anything has happened to that cat," An'gel said, sounding stricken, "I'll never be able to face Charlie Harris again."

Kanesha smiled. "Benjy and Diesel are fine. Benjy insisted on staying there. Clementine and Antoinette are there, too. If I know Clementine, she already has a contractor lined up to come in and take care of getting your kitchen back into shape."

Dickce felt the tears forming, and this time she let them

flow. They were tears of relief and gratitude. Benjy and Diesel were fine, and Clementine—always their rock—would make sure everything was okay with the house.

Dickce glanced at An'gel. The Good Lord willing, An'gel would be fine, too.

She just hoped An'gel wouldn't have a relapse when Dickce told her about Peanut and Endora.

Time enough for that tomorrow, she decided. She had always liked tomorrow.

Turn the page for a preview of Miranda James's next Cat in the Stacks Mystery . . .

ARSENIC AND OLD BOOKS

Available in paperback
from Berkley Prime Crime!

I checked my watch, then glanced at the clock on my computer. They both told me that it was seven minutes after one P.M. I resisted the urge to get up and pace around the archive office. Instead I turned my chair and looked at the large feline dozing on the wide windowsill behind my desk.

Diesel, apparently sensing my gaze, yawned and stretched. He meowed and rolled onto his side, head twisted so that he was staring at me almost upside down. He warbled a couple of times, as if to ask, "Why are you so restless, Charlie?"

"The mayor said she'd be here at one, and she's late. You know how that bugs me," I told the cat. "I'm curious to find out about these family documents she wants to talk to me about. The Longs have already given so many collections of papers to the archive I have to wonder what they've been holding on to."

The cat calmly began washing his right front paw.

"You may not be curious, but I am," I told him. "It's not every day that I get consulted by such an august person as Lucinda Beckwith Long."

I heard a cough, and it didn't come from Diesel.

"I beg your pardon. Are you Mr. Harris?"

I swiveled my chair to face the office door, and I could feel the blush starting. The mayor stood in the doorway, her expression puzzled.

I rose from my desk and walked around to greet Mrs. Long. "Yes, I'm Charlie Harris, Your Honor. Please come in. I was, well, I was chatting with my cat. It's a habit I have, you see."

Mrs. Long nodded as she extended her hand. "I quite understand. My husband and I have three poodles, and we talk to them all the time."

"Won't you be seated?" I indicated the chair in front of my desk, and Mrs. Long moved forward along with her black leather handbag. She set the latter on the floor beside her when she took her seat. Clad in a chic crimson suit with a white silk blouse and colorful scarf knotted loosely around her neck, she looked cool and crisp and ready to get down to business.

I had seen the mayor on several public occasions, but never this close. She was shorter than I expected, probably no more than five-three, when she wasn't standing on the spike heels I had seen her wear. Though I knew her to be in her mid-sixties, she exuded an air of youthful energy, as if she could barely contain herself. Even now I could hear her toe tapping on the hardwood floor of my office. I figured a mayor's life must be hectic, even that of the mayor of a small city like Athena, Mississippi.

Mrs. Long appeared to be assessing me as I waited for her to speak. Diesel hopped down from his perch and padded around my desk to approach the mayor. He sniffed at her bags and then attempted to stick his head in the opening of the tote. Mrs. Long touched his head lightly to discourage him. "No, no, kitty, what's in there is too old for you to play with."

The cat stared up at her and warbled as if to say, "Are you sure?"

Mrs. Long smiled. "He seems to understand what I said, like our dogs do."

"He's a smart cat," I said. "He's also extremely curious." As I spoke, Diesel batted a paw at the tote bag. "No, Diesel, stop that."

The cat threw a baleful glance my way. He stood, made a circle around Mrs. Long's chair, and then came back to his perch in the windowsill behind my desk.

"Apparently he understands a firm *no* when he hears one." Mrs. Long laughed. "Our dogs aren't always so compliant."

"He isn't either," I had to admit. "Depends on his mood." I waited a moment for the mayor to speak again. When she didn't, I decided it was time to move the conversation to the reason for her visit. "I believe you wanted to consult with me about some family documents."

Mrs. Long picked up the tote and settled it in her lap. She delved inside and pulled out a large manila envelope. She leaned forward and placed it on my desk. A faint mustiness, overlaid with a whiff of mothballs, wafted out of the open end.

"Inside that you will find a volume of a diary written by Rachel Afton Long. I forget at the moment how many times a great-grandmother she is, but she was born in the late 1820s and died in the mid-1890s, if I am remembering correctly."

I stared at the envelope before me, my excitement growing over the thought of handling an old document. "How many volumes of her diaries survive?" I pulled open a side drawer of my desk and extracted a pair of cotton gloves. If I was going to be handling a book that was over a hundred years old, I had to be careful with it.

"Four," Mrs. Long replied. "I have glanced at them, but I find the writing hard to read. From what I could glean, however, I believe she started the diaries a few years before she married my husband's ancestor. The last diary is dated around 1875." She shrugged. "I'm not entirely certain. The handwriting is small and cramped, and I got a headache trying to decipher just one page of it."

"I'll have a look at it," I said. I held up my hands to show that I was wearing gloves before I extracted the volume, sliding it carefully out of the envelope. I let it lie on the desk as I put the envelope aside and examined its outward appearance. The cover binding of brown leather was cracked in spots and rubbed thin in others, and the spine was in similar condition. My nose twitched at the strong musty odor. I hoped the diaries hadn't suffered water damage.

"Where have they been stored?" I asked.

"My son, Beck, discovered them recently in a trunk in the attic while hunting for something else entirely. I'd never seen them before, and I don't believe my husband was aware of their existence either."

Andrew Beckwith Long Jr., known as Beck to most, was an aspiring politician. His father, Andrew Sr., had so far served four terms in the state senate. Recently, however, rumors had begun to circulate that Andy intended to retire when his current term expired. Everyone assumed that Beck would easily win his father's seat, but there appeared to be strong opposition, in the form of Jasper

Singletary, a young firebrand who served on the city council. Singletary was openly ambitious, and he had been publicly less than complimentary about the Longs and their political legacy.

"Are you and Mr. Long planning to add these to the collection of Long papers and memorabilia that we already have?"

"Yes," Mrs. Long said. "They need to be better preserved than they have been. We have no idea how long they've been up in that attic, and there could be damage. None of us looked through them much because we were afraid to cause further problems. That's why I wanted to bring them to you." She paused. "I'm sure you're aware of the terrible times that Athena faced during the Civil War and the brief occupation by Union troops. If Rachel Long recorded any of that, her information might be useful to historians."

I nodded. My knowledge of Athena during the Civil War was sketchy, but in elementary school we had heard tales of the depredations of the Union army in the winter of 1863. Our teacher, Mrs. Bondurant, had seemed so old to us at the time, we figured she was speaking from personal experience. I discovered later, when I was older and possessed a better sense of a person's age, that Mrs. Bondurant was only thirty-eight and her grandmother, a Confederate widow, was the source of her stories.

"I'm sure there will be graduate students in the history department eager to examine them," I said. "The Southern history students are always looking for local primary sources for their theses and dissertations."

"Excellent," Mrs. Long said. "My husband and son will be delighted to hear it. They're both avid readers of history, particularly of Southern history."

"Do you have a few minutes, while I make a quick

examination of the volumes?" I asked. "I can give you a rough idea whether we will need to do any conservation work with them."

Mrs. Long consulted her watch. "I have about ten minutes before I need to be back in my office."

"Good." I opened the cover of the volume on my desk with a gentle touch. The inch-thick binding was loose enough so that the cover lay open on the desk without strain. I wrinkled my nose at the smell, but I knew I would soon become accustomed to it. The more the volumes were allowed to air out, the more the odor would dissipate.

The first page of the diary had only a few words in a small, but elegant, hand. I recognized the slightly tilted lettering as Copperplate, a style of handwriting popular in the nineteenth century. The words proclaimed this as the diary of Rachel Adeline Afton, aged sixteen, with the date July 4, 1854. The paper was yellowed but still in good condition. I suspected that it was the more expensive rag paper rather than the cheaper wood pulp. The latter would have turned brown and brittle years ago and begun to disintegrate.

I turned pages carefully and skimmed the contents as I went. There were no blemishes I could see, no water stains, mold, or mildew. Overall, the diary appeared to be in remarkably good condition, other than the state of the binding and the worn cover. "If the other volumes are in similar condition," I said, "then everything should be fine. Conservation work will be minimal, though we will store them in archival folders. The paper is acid-free and won't affect the contents."

"That sounds fine." Mrs. Long smiled briefly. "We are placing no restrictions on these diaries, Mr. Harris. We want scholars to be able to use the contents for their work." She stood and passed the tote with the other volumes to me.

I took the bag and pulled out the three remaining manila envelopes, each with a diary inside. "That's excellent news. As soon as I've had the time to check each one more thoroughly, I'll let the history department know about them."

"They are already aware of the gift," Mrs. Long said. "One of my husband's good friends—and mine as well—is Professor Howell Newkirk. He was dining with us last night, and I happened to mention it to him."

"I see." That was unexpected news. I was acquainted with Dr. Newkirk. He was elderly, irascible, and pushy. He was also the most eminent historian on the Athena faculty, and he knew it. He demanded, and was usually given, what he wanted. I was surprised he wasn't already in my office asking to see the diaries.

Mrs. Long smiled. "I know Howell can be, well, rather insistent on things, but I suggested that he give you a few days with the diaries before he assigned a student to work on them."

"Thank you," I said. "Then I will make sure they are ready sooner rather than later."

"Excellent," Mrs. Long said. She hesitated a moment before she continued. Her eyes focused like lasers on me. "You might be aware that my son, Beck, plans to run for office in the near future. Also that he is facing a challenge. Rachel Afton Long was an extraordinary woman, and the more the voters know about the history of the Long family and its achievements and triumphs, the more they will want to see a member of the family in office."

With that, she nodded, gathered up her purse, and departed.

I stared at the pile of diaries on my desk. Why would the mayor think that Rachel Long's writings could affect the outcome of a twenty-first century political race?